THE
a B Y S S
SURROUNDS US

THE

∂ B-Y-S-S

SURROUNDS US

EMILY SKRUTSKIE

flux®
Woodbury, Minnesota

First Edition
First Printing, 2016

Book design by Bob Gaul
Cover design by Kevin R. Brown
Cover illustration by Chris Nurse/Debut Art
Map by Llewellyn art department

Flux, an imprint of Llewellyn Worldwide Ltd.

Library of Congress Cataloging-in-Publication Data
Names: Skrutskie, Emily.
Title: The abyss surrounds us / Emily Skrutskie.
Description: First edition. | Woodbury, Minnesota: Flux, [2016] |
    Summary: Cassandra Leung—a seventeen-year-old trainer of Reckoners,
    sea beasts bred to defend ships—is kidnapped by the pirate queen Santa
    Elena and ordered to train a Reckoner pup to defend Santa Elena's ship.
Identifiers: LCCN 2015032027 (print) | LCCN 2015033064 (ebook) |
    ISBN 9780738746913 | ISBN 9780738747613
Subjects: | CYAC: Science fiction. | Sea monsters—Fiction. |
    Pirates—Fiction. | Youths' writings.
Classification: LCC PZ7.1.S584 Ab 2016 (print) | LCC PZ7.1.S584 (ebook)
    | DDC [Fic]—dc23
LC record available at http://lccn.loc.gov/2015032027

Flux
Llewellyn Worldwide Ltd.
2143 Wooddale Drive
Woodbury, MN 55125-2989
www.fluxnow.com

To Fritz, Tim, and the other guys in the
Schwartz scene shop—because they asked.

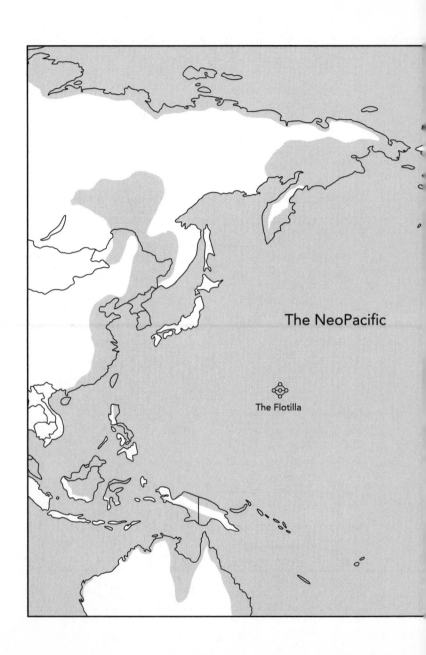

The NeoPacific

The Flotilla

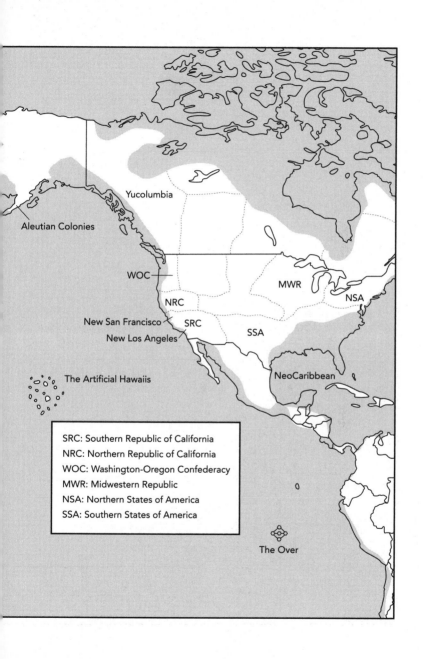

Yucolumbia

Aleutian Colonies

WOC

NRC

New San Francisco

New Los Angeles

SRC

MWR

NSA

SSA

The Artificial Hawaiis

NeoCaribbean

SRC: Southern Republic of California
NRC: Northern Republic of California
WOC: Washington-Oregon Confederacy
MWR: Midwestern Republic
NSA: Northern States of America
SSA: Southern States of America

0

The Over

1

Any other morning, I'd dive into Durga's observation bay without hesitation, but this is the day before my life begins. I hang back on the concrete meridian and raise the Tanto strapped to my wrist, jabbing the button that ignites the miniature LED beacon.

As the blue lights glow and a low tone rings out over the water, she rises. Durga's head is the first thing to emerge from the waves, the brutal lines of her reptilian beak fading into the soft wrinkles that wreathe her huge, round eyes. She lets out a snort that blasts seawater from all three blowholes lined along the ridge of her skull.

The smell of salt, sea, and carrion washes over me, and I drink it in, letting the familiar aroma drain the nervousness from my body. Everything starts tomorrow, but I have nothing to fear with Durga by my side.

She raises one massive, clawed foreleg out of the water and

slams it down, sending up a spray that plows over the meridian, leaving me drenched and sputtering and regretting hanging back on the barrier. Reckoners may be ruthless killing machines, but they're downright cheeky when they know they can get away with it.

When I finish blinking away the brine, I swear I can see a twinkle in her eyes. I snap off the Tanto and pull my respirator up from around my neck, slipping the rubbery mouthpiece between my teeth as I fasten the straps behind my head. My mask comes next, slightly fogged from the warm August air.

Once I'm sure I'll be able to breathe and see, I take a running leap off the meridian and dive headfirst into the water.

The ocean swallows me in a rush. The morning light dances through the waves, shrouding Durga's bulk in glittering beams. With a few short strokes, I draw up to the tip of her beak and grab the edge of her keratin plating.

Durga blinks once, then lifts her head.

I crimp my fingers tighter as she raises me up out of the water. She's horrendously gentle for a beast the size of a football field. Her eyes never leave me.

"Good old girl," I murmur against her plating, then let go. The water engulfs me again, and I immediately lunge forward to grab the keratin covering her chest. I rap my knuckles against it twice. As long as I remind her where I am, Durga will be careful not to crush me.

I dive deeper, running my hands along the knobby, leathery skin between her plates. Most of the other trainers hate getting stuck with morning once-over duty, but it's always been relaxing for me. Checking over Durga is like exploring an alien planet. As I glide along beneath her belly, I map out her ridges and crevices, the tectonics of muscles working beneath her skin, the subtle shifts of coloring that patch her hide. Her primary genes come from snapping turtles, giving her the wide, bulky body and spiny plated shell, but the length of her limbs and the muddled regions of red and green that swath her skin are reminders of the marine iguana DNA woven into her makeup.

She's a big dumb turtle four times the weight of a blue whale, but there's no denying the elegance of her construction.

I'm halfway down her left foreleg when it happens. Something pulses through the water, and it takes me a second to realize that Durga just *shivered*.

Reckoners don't shiver.

I press my palms flat against her leg, the respirator whining in my mouth as it waits for a breath I've yet to release. Five seconds pass, and then another tremor shakes the water around me as the muscle shudders beneath my hands.

I kick for the surface, rapping my knuckles against one of her keratin plates when my head clears the water. Her reptilian eyes fix on me as I roll over and swim for the edge of the bay. My heart flutters, worry creeping up my spine. I need to calm down. I need to breathe.

It's probably nothing, I chide myself. I've been around Durga since the day she hatched, and I sometimes forget that she can still surprise me. I spit out the respirator and rip off my mask, tossing them to the side as I haul myself out of the observation bay and onto the divide.

Squinting against the early morning sun, I glance down

the row of observation bays to the outcropping where the research facility stands. The building's glass exterior glitters like a jewel on the edge of the NeoPacific, harshly framed against the rocky coastline. Just below it lies the dock where we start bonding training with Reckoner pups and their companion vessels. Eight bays lie between me and the buildings, but only four of them are occupied. The two closest to the facility host two pups, still training to bond with their companion ships.

As I flash the Tanto to let Durga know she's free to submerge, the third resident bares her teeth and splashes her fluke at me from the pen on the other side of the divide. Fae is a younger cetoid, a plated whale with a bit of a mean streak. I clamber to my feet and stick my tongue out at her.

Fae's in for medical observation. The *Irvine*, her companion, ran afoul of a pirate raiding party, and though the Reckoner did her duty, she took some heavy hits in the fight and came back to the Southern Republic of California in serious condition. Her hide still stinks of smoke where the pirates' rockets hit her, and her keratin plates bear the singe marks to match. She's gotten cranky after an entire week away from the *Irvine*, and I know for certain she'd try to rip off my arm if I got in the water with her now.

Just in case, I switch the Tanto to her signal set and flash a quick burst of light and noise that tells her to leave me alone. She huffs and clicks loud enough that I have to cover my ears. A rumble from below the water on the other side of the divide marks Durga's reply. A mewl rises from the pups' pens, and I start off toward the research facility, letting the noises of my monsters put me at ease.

My mother's lab is on the second floor of the building, fortified by cement walls and a scanner that reads my palm before unbolting the massive steel doors. A blast of warm air hits me as I step inside.

"Mom, something's up with Durga," I call, peeling out of the top half of my wetsuit.

Artificial wombs line the walls of the lab, nearly all of them occupied with incubating Reckoner pups. They float in the canisters, tethered by an umbilical line that supplies them with nutrients. At this stage, they're nothing but little nuggets of flesh and nerve, each ready to develop into a beast capable of ripping a pirate ship to shreds. Some of them are brand new, barely the size of my thumb, with no distinguishing features. Others have already gestated to the point that their type is obvious. My gaze lands on a terrapoid embryo whose forelegs are twitching as if the little turtle-type is already dreaming of the day he sees battle. In the womb next to it, a cephalopoid slumbers with its stumpy tentacles wrapped around itself. Farther down, I spot the familiar knot of a serpentoid embryo's twisting coils. We've developed so many breeds, each uniquely crafted to serve the companies that commission them for their ships.

The gel in the womb gives off a soft glow. It keeps them at a suspended stage of development, curbing them until the day we transfer them to a big, leathery purse and let them grow until they're ready to hatch. Ready to train. Ready to destroy.

Until then, they're all just waiting.

I'm so stuck on the eerie sight of baby Reckoners that it takes me a few seconds to realize my mom's not alone in here.

She stands with her back to me, her arms folded as she stares down at a cryo-crate, and Fabian Murphy is at her side. He glances my way and motions for an extra minute.

I nod back to him, a flush building in my cheeks. Murphy is our International Genetically Engineered Organisms Council liaison. One of the biggest figures in the Reckoner business. A man who controls the entire industry. And I definitely shouldn't have traipsed into the lab in nothing but my wetsuit.

"I'm sorry, Mrs. Leung," he tells my mother, giving her a consoling pat on the shoulder. He looks worlds out of place in his tailored suit. "I know it reflects poorly to lose so much of your stock, but you've got to remember that by catching unviable embryos early, we minimize the risk of disappointing our investors. Between that and the recent … security concerns, we need to be taking extra steps for the good of the business. There have been reports of theft, of break-ins at some of our top stables. The new crop of pups has to be stronger than ever."

Mom shakes her head, and I don't need to see her face to know that she's got her lips pursed the way she always does when she's calculating something. Finally she turns to Murphy and offers a hand. "Thank you. Your business is appreciated, as ever."

He grasps her hand and gives it one firm shake, his gray eyes sparkling in the lab's bright lights. "Until next time," he says, wearing the grin of a man who's gotten exactly what he wants. The IGEOC agent grabs the handle of the cryo-crate and begins to drag it toward the massive doors. "Cassandra," he says, nodding to me.

I nod back, folding my arms over my chest.

"Good luck out there tomorrow," he offers, but there's something strange caught in his throat as he says it, and for a moment he looks profoundly uncomfortable.

As if I needed another reason to be nervous about what tomorrow holds.

Mom waits to speak until the door's bolted behind him. "How many times do I have to tell you to *change* before coming up here? You're dripping everywhere—did you even towel off?"

"Sorry, it's just—"

"Cas, I've said it before. Think things *through* before charging in."

"Mom, something's wrong with Durga."

That gets her. I see the shift happen in her eyes, her parent-brain batted to the side as scientist-brain takes over. "Symptoms?" she asks, gliding over to the computer and dragging up Durga's records with one elegant swipe of her finger.

"She seemed unsteady when I was checking over. Tremors in her legs."

"That's it?"

I nod.

"No discoloration? No signs that she hasn't been eating?"

I shake my head.

Mom peers closer at the charts. "I've never known her to be unsteady, but there's a first time for everything. Do you think she's fit for duty?"

Mom's asking for my judgment. Durga's in *my* charge. Tomorrow afternoon, she'll ship out with her companion, the *Nereid*, and for the first time in my life I'll be working as her sole trainer. Her life in my hands, and my life in hers. It's my call, and mine alone.

"I'll keep an eye on her, but I think she should be fine. No need to worry the *Nereid*."

Mom smiles, and I feel like I've just passed a test. Like I can be trusted with the monsters she creates. Granted, Durga's probably the easiest charge she can give me. The *Nereid* is a cruise ship, not an important cargo boat like the one Fae escorts. Durga's been with the ship for twelve years, and in that time she's sunk only ten pirate vessels, most of them in her first years on duty. She's an old titan now, and none of the NeoPacific's worst want to tangle with her.

And this is my big opportunity. My chance to show Mom and Dad that I'm ready, that I can be a Reckoner trainer full-time. After seventeen and a half years of waiting for the day I finally become the person I'm meant to be, it's almost here.

Tomorrow, my life begins.

2

When it comes time to say goodbye, I hug my brother first.

Tom tugs the end of my ponytail, and I thump him on the back in return. "If you never come back, I get your room, right?" he asks when he lets me go.

"If I never come back, you get my morning shift," I tell him. He flashes me an impish grin and tries to ruffle my hair. Tom's two years younger than me, but he's six inches taller and he never lets me forget it.

The dock around us is choked with tourists, some waving to people already on the *Nereid*, others fiddling with their luggage. They're decked out in the season's brightest colors, all of them determined to make the last month of summer count. Apparently two weeks on a boat is the best way to do that.

I turn to Mom and Dad, who sweep me into a hug before I can get a word in. "Be safe out there," Mom mutters in my ear.

"Of course I'll be safe," I tell them. "I have Durga."

She releases me, but Dad holds on tighter. Over his shoulder, I watch Mom shepherd Tom back toward the parking lot, and the anticipation pooled in my stomach swells.

Dad takes a step back, one hand still on my shoulder, and reaches into his pocket. He draws out a little blue capsule, and I feel every molecule in my body screaming at me to run. Dad must catch the panic in my eyes—he squeezes my shoulder and holds out the capsule. "Cas, it's fine. It's going to be fine. This is *just in case.*"

Just in case. Just in case the worst happens. The ship falls. Durga fails, I fail, and the knowledge I carry as a Reckoner trainer must be disposed of. That information can't fall into the wrong hands, into the hands of people who will do anything to take down our beasts.

So this little capsule holds the pill that will kill me if it comes to that.

"It's waterproof," Dad continues, pressing it into my hand. "The pocket on the collar of your wetsuit—keep it there. It has to stay with you at all times."

It won't happen on this voyage. It's such a basic mission, gift-wrapped to be easy enough for me to handle on my own. But even holding the pill fills me with revulsion. On all of my training voyages, I've never had to carry one of these capsules. That burden only goes to the full-time trainers.

"Cas." Dad tilts my chin up, ripping my gaze from the pill. "You were born to do this. I promise you, you'll forget you even have it." I suppose he ought to know—he's been carrying one for two decades.

It's just a rite of passage, I tell myself, and throw my arms around his neck once more.

———————

I board the *Nereid* with a suitcase full of trainer gear trundling behind me, a travel bag slung over my shoulder, and a growing sense of optimism as I spot Durga's shadow lurking beneath the ship. A trail of bubbles against the hull marks where she rests her snout against the metal, her body pressed up against the keel.

I don't think it's possible to love someone as much as a Reckoner loves her companion ship.

Once I reach the main deck, I lean against the rail and watch my family make their way back down the dock. As I look on, Tom turns, shielding his eyes against the afternoon sun as he tries to spot me. I wave my hand once, then tip him a little salute. Tom salutes back, and I can feel the jealousy radiating off him from here. Like me, he's been waiting his whole life for the day he gets to do this on his own.

A firm hand taps my shoulder, and I turn to find a mountain of a man towering over me. He's dressed in a smart uniform, but his gut tugs at the waist in a way the jacket clearly wasn't tailored to handle.

"Miss Leung," he says, extending a hand as large as my head. "Welcome aboard the *Nereid*. We're very pleased to have you. I'm Captain Carriel."

I take his hand and give it the firmest shake that I can manage. "Glad to be of service, sir." I'm not sure if you're supposed to call the captain of a cruise ship "sir," but I figure it can't hurt since the guy's paying my salary.

"I have a key for your bunk." He hands me a card on a lanyard, which I loop around my neck as I gather all my gear back up. "I'm guessing you've got it all handled from here though, huh?"

I can't figure out if he's joking or if he actually has this much trust in me. It's difficult to tell when you've never seen a person do anything but smile.

The *Nereid* thrums to life as I drag my gear down to the lower decks and find my assigned bunk. It's cramped, and the dull rumble from the ship's engines is constant down here, but there's a tiny window in my room that looks out on the sea. As we undock and turn for the open waters of the Neo Pacific, Durga swims at our side. She lifts from the waves, water sloughing off her back, her forelegs carving through the sea as she keeps the *Nereid*'s pace. She seems much more cheerful now that she's reunited with her companion vessel, and as I unpack, I feel even more of the worry lift off my shoulders.

Once my phone connects to the ship's uplink, I post a quick status update to put my parents at ease. Then I gather my gear and make my way through the narrow service hallways to the trainer deck at the ship's aft. Up above, I can hear the thunder of feet, the shouts and shrieks of the passengers celebrating the start of their vacation. For me, the work is just beginning.

———

Life at sea moves in a strange rhythm. I wake early in the morning to check on Durga, drawing her up to the trainer deck at the rear of the ship with an LED homing beacon the size of a suitcase. The deck is right above the engines, low enough that she can tap the beacon with the tip of her beak.

Each Reckoner gets trained on a signal set assigned by the IGEOC, a unique collection of lights and sounds that ensure we alone control our beasts. Some are grating, but Durga's is one of my favorites: a pulse of blue lights and a low humming noise. During the day, Durga tends to wander away from the ship, hunting neocetes and whatever else she can scarf down. I carry a tracker on my belt that lets me know if she strays too far, but of course she never does.

While she's away, I wander the upper decks and mix with the tourists. They don't pay much attention to me—my trainer uniform makes me as invisible as the waitstaff. But on the third night of the voyage, that changes.

The old man finds me on the main deck, reclining on one of the pool chairs and staring out at the ridge of Durga's shell, highlighted by the moonlight. At first I don't realize he's there—I've gotten so used to being ignored—but then he clears his throat and says, "You're quite young."

I bristle at that, and not just because he's quite old, his face cracked with lines, his hair barely a wisp. "First time," I tell him as he settles on the chair next to me.

"Big responsibility," he says, nodding toward the Reckoner, then remembers to introduce himself. "Hiro Kagawa. I was a Senator in the Southern States of America back in the day—I was actually on one of the subcommittees that authorized Reckoner justice in our waters."

It takes me a second to connect the dots. The Southern States began the Reckoner trade long before the Southern Republic of California did, their hand forced by the swollen Gulf that was already choked with pirate strongholds. They had started raising monsters within years of the Schism. Which means...

"You lived in the United States, huh?" I ask.

"I was elected right after the Schism," Mr. Kagawa says, his eyes sparkling in the low light. "But I lived through the worst of it, right before the world started to split."

I figure it's only fair to let him do what old men do best. "What do you remember?"

He sighs, rolling his head back toward the stars. "Oh, mostly rhetoric. 'Smaller Governments, Bigger Hearts,' all those catchy phrases being tossed around. Names too. Midwestern Republic. Southern States of America. Things with heft that people could get behind and trust to look after them. The seas were swelling, the floodwalls—" His voice cracks, and he blinks. "Well, you know the rest."

I know enough. I know that one by one, the world governments started divvying up their lands, running algorithms, optimizing the care they could provide for their citizens, until the lines had been redrawn. No more United States, no more China, no more India, no more accounting for thousands of miles and billions of people under the rule of a single power.

It was so long ago that the world had already gotten used to it by the time I was born.

Mr. Kagawa blinks again, his gaze dropping to Durga's distant form. "The floodwalls. That's my story, that's the best one I can tell." He bows his head. "I lived in ... well, you know them as the drowned cities. New Orleans was one of them. The floodwalls had stood for years, but that didn't matter in the end. I was eight years old the night it happened, and I've never forgotten a moment of it. The screaming, the roar of the skiffs as they rushed up the canal streets and under the supports of the apartments. My mother grabbed me and my sisters and threw us into our boat. But my father wouldn't budge. He'd lived his whole life in the shadows of those floodwalls, and I guess in the end he decided to die with them."

He runs one hand absently over what's left of his hair. "My mother knew him well enough to let him. We were three miles out when the walls came down."

The sea is still tonight, and the decks are silent. "I'm sorry," I tell Mr. Kagawa, meaning it wholeheartedly. He came on this ship to relax, not to relive the memories that haunt him.

But he waves off my apology, a tense smile cracking over his face. "It's one of the greatest gifts you can give someone, knowing their stories."

Off in the black, Durga's blowholes release a long-held blast of air, sending up a spray of saltwater cut by moonlight.

———

Durga's tremors are getting worse. On the first days of the voyage, I barely noticed them, but now her legs shudder like the engines beneath my feet. She's begun to lag behind the ship, forcing the *Nereid* to slow. I spend an entire afternoon sitting on her back, scouring her plating for any sign of an infected wound that would explain her worsening condition. There's nothing but old scars. Reckoners don't get sick—they get injured, but it's been months since the last time she fought off a pirate attack.

The stench of carrion hangs heavily in the air around her, and it lingers on my clothes as I make my way to the *Nereid*'s navigation tower.

Captain Carriel's face goes taut when I step through the door. "Miss Leung," he says, turning away from the ship's instrumentation panel.

"I'm sorry—" I start, but he raises his hand to cut me off. He already knows exactly what I've come for.

"We need to make it to our first island by tomorrow evening. If we slow the ship any more, we'll be putting this whole voyage drastically behind schedule."

My face flushes, and I find myself stammering for my next words. No Reckoner should be a burden to her companion ship. "Sir, I'm sorry," I manage. "But something's wrong. I don't know what's happening, and I'm severely concerned for Durga's health."

He raises an eyebrow. "You've never seen anything like this?"

I shake my head. "I've been talking to my pa—the other trainers on the uplink, and they don't have any theories. As far as we know, nothing like this has happened to a Reckoner before." The last time I spoke to my mother, we'd both been crying. Me from concern for Durga and her from the frustration of being unable to figure out why one of her monsters has suddenly fallen ill.

From somewhere behind us, a keening groan rings out. Durga rarely vocalizes, but today she's been making all sorts of noises.

Captain Carriel runs a hand over his beard, his eyes darkening. "Give it one more night. We'll drop anchor for her scheduled rest, and in the morning we'll make a judgment call."

I don't know what that kind of call would entail, but I nod along. The captain claps me on the shoulder, steers me out the door, and leaves me in the hall, stewing in the ever-present smell of rotted flesh.

That night, I can't sleep.

The next morning, the entire ship awakens before dawn to Durga's unearthly screams.

3

I spring out of bed and struggle into my wetsuit as fast as I can. My heart aches inside my chest as I sprint for the trainer deck. I've been hearing Reckoner noises all my life, but never like this. This isn't a groan of discomfort, a roar of fury. No, this is a shriek of pure agony.

I burst onto the trainer deck and snap on the LED beacon. It flashes her homing signal into the dark, and immediately she surfaces, her shadow looming against the glow on the horizon. I grab a spotlight and shine it on her as she approaches.

A wave of nausea threatens to overtake me, and I have to fight to keep the spotlight pointed at her as she draws near.

Durga is bleeding all over. The sickening stench of her blood washes over me as if it clots the air. Sores dot her back, some of them burst and ragged-looking, and I realize with a jolt that several of her keratin plates have fallen off. She groans again, the noise causing the deck underneath me to shudder, and I watch, horrified, as the plate protecting the top of her head slides forward, pulling free with a meaty *snap*. It plunges into the NeoPacific, sending up a spray of salty, gory water in its wake.

I know I should call Mom and Dad immediately, but I can't leave her side when she's like this. "It's gonna be okay, girl," I call out to her. It's a lie.

"Miss Leung!" A deckhand stumbles out onto the trainer deck, his uniform askew. "Carriel wants to know what's going on."

My lips struggle to find words that aren't there. Nothing in my training has prepared me for this. This voyage was supposed to be effortless. Easy. And now Durga is dying, and I can't do anything to stop it. "I . . ." I start, but can't finish. She's hurting so much. The water that surrounds her is clouded with blood, and I don't have the tools to put her out of her misery.

The ship's all-call crackles on. "Ladies and gentlemen," Captain Carriel says, a slight tremor in his gravely voice.

No.

"Our radar has picked up a pirate vessel heading our way."

Not now.

"We ask that you please stay calm and remain inside your cabins until an all-clear is given. Locks will be engaging on the doors in five minutes."

Any time but now.

"In the meantime, the ship's companion will see to the threat."

A chill starts at the base of my spine and works its way

up until I feel like my brain's been plunged into ice water. Durga can't fight. Not like this. I spin, running my hands through my hair as I scan the trainer deck for something, *anything* to end her suffering. But Reckoners were made to be nigh impossible to kill, and there's no humane way of ending the life of a beast this size.

I'm suddenly acutely aware of the pill in the collar of my wetsuit.

When I turn back to Durga, they're on the horizon.

The boat comes screaming in from the East, the rising sun at its back as it swings wide around the *Nereid*. It carves the water like a butcher's knife and looks like it's been cobbled together from bits of yachts and warships, the unholy bastard of some pirate colony junkyard. Its upper decks bristle with weaponry.

I've let everyone on this boat down. Without Durga, we're dead in the water against this sort of artillery. We'll be boarded, looted, and killed, and it's all my fault.

Which is what I'm still stuck on when Durga wheels, swinging her snout toward the pirate ship. Her blowholes flare, her tail thrashes, and she launches herself toward the boat, the sea churning around her.

Shit.

She's not strong enough to do this, but she also can't suppress the instinct ingrained in her. Durga is bonded to the *Nereid*. Reckoner imprinting behavior ties them to their companion ships, and she'll fight to the death to protect hers. But in her condition, there's no way she'll succeed. She's already dying. It'll only be more painful if the pirates have a say in it.

And she's only going to piss them off more. She's going to give them a reason to kill every soul aboard this ship if she goes after them.

I've got to stop her. I've got to do something.

I hoist the homing beacon onto my back and take off, back down the ship's tunnels, just as the gunfire starts. The deckhand runs after me, but I tune out the words he's yelling—I can't afford to think about anything but drawing Durga back to the ship. An explosion rocks the back of the *Nereid* and the floor lurches beneath my feet as the engines stop. We're dead in the water.

I round a corner and haul open a hatch, stumbling out onto the lowest deck on the ship where a foldout platform lies waiting. I yank the lever that extends it and leap on as the platform unfurls, landing on the ocean's surface with a wet slap. It rolls out in front of me, nearly fifty feet in length, and I sprint for the end of it, my fingers fumbling on the homing beacon as I go.

The LEDs snap on, nearly blinding me, and I slip, falling flat on my ass. I hold the beacon up, point it at Durga, and scream as loud as my lungs will allow, my voice harmonizing with the hum of her signal.

The pirate ship has already outmaneuvered her and docked with us, the crew swarming the *Nereid* like flies on a corpse. Durga's attention flickers to me, and she draws up short. The Reckoner shakes her head, letting out a deafening roar as she wavers between heeding my call and doing the very thing she was bred to do.

Maybe it's my familiarity, maybe it's just a merit of her

training, but Durga turns again and surges for the platform, her beak pointed squarely at the homing beacon.

"That's right," I rasp, dropping to my knees. "Good girl. Come here. It's okay. It's all going to be over soon."

Then the pirate ship opens fire.

They aim for her eyes. The bullets riddle Durga, and blood sprays from her already-ragged flesh. She roars again, the sound rippling the ocean's surface, and turns on the ship. Smoke from the artillery pours out over the waves until all I can see is her looming shadow and the outline of the *Nereid*. Somewhere in the haze, her beak snaps shut, the sound rolling over the ocean like a thunderclap. I stumble back down the platform, still holding the beacon high, my eyes running. I can't tell if it's the smoke burning my eyes, or if I'm just crying.

A wave lifts the platform, knocking my feet out from under me, and I plunge into the water. My hold on the homing beacon slips, and it sinks away into the vast dark of the ocean below. Lungs burning, I kick for the surface and come up clinging to the platform. I choke in a breath as I feel the water around me thicken.

A shadow crosses me. Someone has strode out onto the platform, a wide-brimmed hat shading her features and a rocket launcher hoisted over her shoulder. She takes aim at Durga, braces herself, and squeezes the trigger. The whole platform vibrates from the recoil and I almost lose my grip.

The rocket explodes into Durga's side. She screams, her leathery skin rippling as she wheels to face the pirate, who only frowns, takes aim, and shoots again.

I haul myself out of the water and lunge for her, but a pair of arms grabs me from behind and holds me back. The second rocket strikes Durga's shoulder, taking out a chunk of flesh so large that her foreleg goes limp instantly. I struggle against my captor, but it's no use. I'm not a fighter.

Durga's the fighter, and she lunges for the woman with the rocket launcher even as a third shell barrels into her chest, right where her keratin plates should be. The sickening stench of Reckoner blood and decaying flesh fills the air with an increasing inevitability, overpowering the smoke of the guns.

The fourth rocket hits her head.

And…

I'm five years old and sharing a kiddie pool with a newly hatched Reckoner pup. I'm eight, standing on her back for the first time. I'm thirteen, and the only refuge from my first breakup is in floating alongside her, holding onto the ridge above her eye where my hand fits perfectly.

I'm seventeen years old, and I can do nothing but watch as Durga's thick blood paints the sea.

Now I'm sure it's not just the smoke. Tears roll down my cheeks, and I go limp in the grip of whoever's restrained me. They can kill me now. They can do whatever they like. Everything's gone still, and even though I can hear the chaos of the pirates taking the *Nereid* behind me, it sounds like it's on the other side of a glass wall.

I've failed.

The grip on me loosens, and I can finally twist around and look my captor in the face. She's about my age. Her blonde hair is desperately trying to recover from a sideshave, and she's got a feral grin on her lips. "Boss," she says, and the woman with the rocket launcher turns. "I think we're going to want to bring this one along."

4

The girl keeps my hands twisted behind my back as she hustles me toward the pirate ship, forcing me to step over the bodies that litter the hallways. Their uniforms mark them as the *Nereid*'s crew, and the guns in their hands mark them as the ones who put up a fight.

Her captain leads the way, the rocket launcher stowed in favor of a submachine gun that she cradles like a newborn child. In the early August heat, her brown skin is dappled with sweat, and she has her wildly curly hair bound back underneath her hat.

I don't know what's going on. All I know is that yesterday I'd never seen death up close and now I'm surrounded by it.

"Lock her in one of the closets. We'll deal with her later," the captain says. Gunfire rings out from somewhere down the hall, and she rolls her eyes. "Sounds like this bucket's putting up more of a fight than anticipated. I'll go see what needs shooting." She pivots and strides back into the depths of the ship, her coat flapping behind her.

The girl shrugs, then pushes me forward again, gentler than when the captain was watching. We come to a ladder hooked onto one of the lower decks and she nudges me onto it ahead of her. Her hand drops to the pistol in her waistband, just in case I'm thinking of making a break through the gap between the two ships' hulls.

I'm not. I descend onto the pirate ship, my hands shaking on the cold metal rungs, and the girl follows me.

"Why?" I ask as my captor jumps from the ladder, landing slightly off-balance on the ship's deck. She just grabs me by the wrist again and tugs me toward another hatch, another ladder. Once again, I go first.

The ship's interior is more well-lit than I expected. I'd call it homey if it weren't for the bullet holes in the walls and the pirate girl marching me through it. Probably has something to do with the strips of wood plastered to the walls in a halfhearted attempt at paneling.

We come to a heavy steel door at the end of the narrow corridor, which she twists open and shoves me through without another word. My head cracks against a low shelf and I yelp loud enough that she pauses. We make eye contact—her in her sleek body armor with a gun tucked in her pants, and me in my soaking wetsuit.

"You're going to be useful," she says, and no more than that. She slams the door behind her, leaving me with a throbbing head in what I'm just now realizing is a janitorial closet.

And the pill is still in my collar.

She didn't bind my hands. I reach up with shaking fingers and tug the zipper, flaying open the hidden pocket. The little blue capsule tumbles into my palm, and I sink to my knees in the tangle of mops and cleaning solvents.

My heart is thundering, and I feel as if every inch of my being is rearing away from the promise of death that sits nestled in my hand.

Do it now. Do it fast.

My whole arm is shaking.

How can I know for sure that this pill is the only solution? What if I could escape? What if the pirates aren't after trade secrets? My mind runs wild with possibilities, with options so much better than a quick death.

I tug at the ends of my limp, damp hair, trying to rein in my thoughts. The things I know for sure form such a short list. The *Nereid* is taken. Durga is dead. I've been captured by pirates. My name is Cas Leung. I smell like Reckoner blood.

And there's so much I'm not sure of. They might be sinking the ship right now, killing all of the people onboard. They might be stripping it and leaving it disabled in the middle of the NeoPacific. I wonder if Mr. Kagawa is still alive. I wonder what usefulness the pirate captain has planned for me.

I wonder if I'll ever see my family again.

I should have grabbed my phone instead of the beacon. There was never any hope of beating these guys, not with our Reckoner bleeding out. I used my last seconds of freedom in a futile attempt to spare Durga from an agonizing death and buy the pirates' mercy, and I couldn't even do that. I could have called home, could have told my family that I love them.

If I take this pill, the last they'll ever hear from me—the real me, not some missing persons report—is a call from last night when I was too preoccupied with Durga to ask about anything going on in their lives.

Footsteps sound in the hall outside, but no one opens the door. They must be finishing up now. The boat's engines start to hum and the floor underneath me feels less steady. I shudder, clutching the pill in my fist. The ridges of the raised lettering on the capsule dig into my skin. Six characters in total. *Epi-Tas*. Half of a Spartan phrase. *E tan e epi tas. With your shield or on it.*

Come back alive and victorious, or don't come back at all.

That's our way. That's our principle. That's how we protect our industry, which in turn protects the clients that commission us. If we can't defend them, we're worthless. If we can't defend ourselves, we're worthless.

Other Reckoners have fallen. Uli, off the coast of the Philippines, killed by heavy shelling. Kou, near the Dominion of South Africa, strafed by harpoons. And now Durga, by the Southern Republic of California, slaughtered with nothing but a shoulder-mounted rocket launcher.

Their trainers all did the right thing. Their trainers all took the pill.

Durga is dead. Dear, sweet Durga, the big, dumb, playful turtle who loved her ship more than anything, died falling apart from the inside, unable to protect herself from the pirate captain's rockets. Her body has probably settled on the floor of the NeoPacific. A whole ecosystem of bacteria and scavengers will gather to break down what's left.

It's only natural that I'm supposed to follow her there.

Hours must pass. My muscles ache, but I stay frozen on the floor, staring at my clenched fist and trying to conjure the thought that will bring it to my lips.

Every fight I've ever assisted in ended with a sinking pirate vessel, with my dad clapping me on the shoulder as I changed the beacons over to bring our Reckoner down from her seething, righteous frenzy. He would have known what to do today. The pirates wouldn't have won.

I wouldn't be sitting here with the capsule in my hand.

Nausea churns at my stomach, and for a moment the stench of Durga's blood almost overwhelms me. I dig my fingernails into the flesh of my arms, fighting to keep my last meal down. If I don't do this now, the pirates will use me. Whatever that means. They could force me to cough up information on every Reckoner my mother has ever engineered, every beast my father has ever trained. They could get me to confess weaknesses in our monsters, weaknesses in our facilities, anything that could give them an upper hand.

It's clear enough. I'm worth more to the industry dead than alive at this point.

The ships that can afford to commission a Reckoner are safe to carry the most valuable goods and people across the NeoPacific. Kill the monster, and the boat's practically gift-wrapped for you. If the pirates make me help them, I'll be compromising the safety of every single one of those ships and all of the trainers aboard them.

Including my father. Including Tom.

For them, I think as my fingers curl open. *For them*, I think as I raise the capsule to my lips.

For them.

The closet door slams open, light floods in, and the girl who dragged me in here lunges forward, slaps my hand away from my mouth, and sends the pill flying.

5

Her hands are around my wrists before I have a chance to scrabble for the capsule. "Don't you dare," she growls, twisting my arms behind my back. "Captain wants you."

I glance up to find a tall, slim boy in the doorway who's holding a pistol, horror written over his features. His eyes flick to where the pill landed, then back to my face. There's a tattoo etched across his cheekbone, but in the dim light of the closet, I can't figure out what it is.

"Varma, give me a hand here," the girl says as she attempts to wrestle me to my feet.

I keep my legs limp. I've blown my chance at ending my life—the least I can do is make it as hard as possible for the pirates to get what they want from me.

Varma loops one lanky arm around my waist and lifts. "C'mon, shoregirl. On your feet," he urges.

I twist my head to face the girl holding my wrists, a

snarl rising in the back of my throat. She winches her grip tighter, as if daring me to say something. "Have some dignity," she hisses.

"What's the deal with your hair?" I spit back.

It's the last thing she expected. I savor the look of utter confusion that flickers across her face. "What do you mean, *what's the deal with my hair?*"

"Watch it, Swift," the guy warns.

I hang my head, speaking through my teeth. "Did you get bored one day and hack half of it off? You look like you've had a close call with a weed whacker."

Swift releases one of my wrists and grabs me by the hair. Guess I've hit a sore spot. She tugs viciously upward and I cave, bringing my feet underneath me at last as I try to keep her from yanking my hair right out of my scalp.

I glance at Varma just in time to catch him mouthing, "The fuck's a weedwhacker?"

Maybe it was stupid to goad her, but there's only so much she can do to me if the captain wants me. She'll push me around and rough me up, but it's all posturing, like Reckoners do sometimes when they're starved for attention. And the easiest way to put a beast in its place is to snap back.

They wrestle me out of the closet and down the ship's narrow passageways to a pair of elegant wooden doors at the aft. I can hear voices on the other side, voices that stop when Varma knocks.

"Come in," someone calls.

Varma pushes the door open, and Swift shoves me in before her. She twists her fingers viciously around my wrist and gives my hair one last yank before she releases me, and my skin burns. I wince, but do my best to brush it off. Another rule of Reckoner training: you can't let them see if they hurt you.

The room is vast, probably once a bar or a lounge before it was torn out of whatever yacht it came from and repurposed. Now it's a throne room, choked with the pirate crew. They throng around a dais in the back of the room, where the captain lounges in an ornately carved chair.

So not only have I been captured by pirates—I've had the misfortune of being taken in by theatrical ones.

And their queen seems to have fully embraced her flair for the dramatic. She's wearing a crimson evening gown; I almost fail to recognize her as the woman who killed Durga. Gone is the wide-brimmed hat and long coat that cut her intimidating silhouette, but she's intimidating now in the same way that bonfires are. When her eyes meet mine, I can't help but shrink back a little. Looking at her is like looking into hell itself.

"Welcome aboard the *Minnow*, Cassandra," she says. She must have searched the *Nereid*'s file system, must have pulled data to find out exactly who she's taken prisoner. "I'm Santa Elena. You can call me that, or Captain. Swift here is a big fan of 'boss,' but I don't think we're quite on those terms yet."

Everyone in this room could kill me, and most of them look like they want to. Swift and Varma have joined their captain on the dais. They stand next to three others at Santa Elena's right, and I start to understand the hierarchy on this ship a little more. The pirates that crowd the room are the regulars, the muscle. On Santa Elena's left sits a child. He can't possibly be more than ten years old, and I'm stumped about his role until she ruffles his hair, a soft smile breaking over her cruel features. He has to be her son—by blood, it looks like, given the golden brown skin and wide nose they share.

But the five to the captain's right are different. They're all kind of young-looking compared to most of the crew, and unlike some of the crowd, their eyes never leave Santa Elena. Something sets them apart—some favor of the captain has elevated them to this position.

It seems like they're her protégées. It'd explain why Swift is such a showoff.

"You're quiet," Santa Elena purrs. She hauls herself upright and stands, the dress falling elegantly around her ankles as she steps from the dais and approaches me. "I'd imagine you're bursting with questions. Can't hurt to ask them."

I'm not going to give her the satisfaction of my curiosity. I wonder why I'm here, why the Reckoner trainer was the only one worth kidnapping on a ship that carried so many wealthy tourists, but the first words that leave my mouth are "What happened to the *Nereid*?"

"Depends. If someone responded to the distress call, there's a very large chance that the passengers will be rescued before the ship sinks. If not..." She doesn't need to finish the sentence. The devilish smile that spreads across her face tells me everything I need to know. "And we killed the crew that resisted, of course. We have to be efficient about these things."

"What did you take?"

I catch the slight twitch of her upper lip, see her resist the urge to sneer at me. "You. Cash, and a few finer goods. Food, to replenish our stock. No electronics—we don't want anything that could be sending out a signal. The dress is new. Do you like it?"

I draw my lips tight. My wetsuit is drying out and starting to itch, and I have to fight to keep myself standing as still as possible.

"When I ask a question, I'd like you to answer, Cassandra." She lashes out and grabs the collar of my wetsuit, dragging me toward her until I'm staring up into her deep brown eyes.

I can't blink. Not now. "It's beautiful," I tell her flatly, and it isn't a lie.

Her fingers go slack, and as she draws back, I notice a tattoo of a small fish over her heart. Santa Elena doesn't miss the way my eyes travel. This time she really does smirk. "Like it? Every loyal member of my crew has the ship's namesake inked on their body somewhere important. See, for me this ship is my life, my beating heart. So my Minnow is right here." She folds a hand over her breast. Her smile turns goading. "Maybe you'll earn yours someday."

I don't have the words nor the courage to tell her that's never going to happen. I grit my teeth and stand a little straighter, fighting to keep down the question that's burning inside me. She wants me to say it, wants me to cave to her will, and I can't let her have her way. I've got to show her that no matter how long she keeps me on this ship, she's never going to get me to bend to her.

One of her lackeys on the dais, a skinny white boy with jet-black hair, relieves me of my burden. "You gonna keep playing with her or let her know why she's here, Captain?" he asks, and several people in the crowd hiss with surprise.

Santa Elena grins wickedly, and for a second I worry that she'll pull out a gun and shoot the boy right here to make an example out of him. "Points for bravery, Code," she says, stepping back up on the dais and settling primly on her throne. "Johan, Yue, bring it on out. Let's shed some light for our guest."

Two of the pirates push through the crowd into a back room and return moments later, hauling a cylindrical object the size of a refrigerator. It's mounted on wheels and covered with a black cloth that sways ominously as it trundles forward. They push it in front of the dais, and Santa Elena leans forward, grabbing the hem of its cover.

She yanks it off with a flourish, and I want to sink to the bottom of the ocean in that instant.

Floating in the tank, lit by warming lamps that cast a brilliant red glow around the room, is a leathery purse, and inside that purse is an unborn Reckoner pup.

6

"We have a proposition," Santa Elena starts. "Wait, not necessarily a proposition—strike that. 'Proposition' implies that you can either accept or decline, and I'm really not giving you a choice here. We have … an arrangement."

I can't focus on anything but the pup, the happy, warm baby Reckoner curled in its sac. It's nearly ready to hatch, the swell of its body pressing against the membranes that hold it. Its head is nearly tucked into itself, the droll reptilian beak flush against the sac walls. It's a terrapoid.

Just like Durga.

I can't think straight, can't even begin to piece together what's happening. Reckoner production is highly regulated. It needs to happen in a controlled environment like Mom's lab, where every stage of growth can be monitored and any embryos with defects can quickly be eliminated. It shouldn't be possible for pirates to create a Reckoner without that kind of equipment. It shouldn't even be possible for them to obtain one.

But here lies proof to the contrary.

"We're a little tired of going up against beasts like your Reckoners," Santa Elena continues. "We think it's time to even up the playing field, and thanks to a fortuitous set of circumstances and some careful planning, we've finally got our chance. You have a very particular set of skills and the convenience of being presumed dead, and we've got a long winter ahead of us. While the ocean traffic slows and thins in the cold months, you're going to hatch our little monster, raise it up right, and put it to work for us come next summer's hunting season."

I've been so good about not crying up until now. My eyes sting, and I shift my gaze to the ground. The implications are sweeping over me like a tidal wave. The Reckoner trade is founded on principles of balance. Ecological balance that keeps them from devouring the oceans' biospheres and destroying oceanic life as we know it. Economic balance that ensures the Reckoner industry is profitable and competitive. Political balance that allows for Reckoner justice to be unquestionable on the open seas. It took decades to establish those balances, but a single pup on the side of the pirates could unravel all of that. And I'd be responsible.

"If it wasn't clear already, your life is tied to the beast. If it dies, you follow. I don't feed useless mouths on this ship. If your training fails, I'll slit your throat and dump you into the sea."

It takes everything I have left not to laugh. Five minutes ago, I was ready to die for my industry and my family. But now the balance of the NeoPacific is in my hands, and the last thing I can do is die. Somehow, impossibly, these pirates have gotten hold of a Reckoner pup.

And even if it means surviving when I shouldn't, I have to find out how.

It's the last smidgen of value my life has. I may have failed as a trainer, but the universe has a twisted way of providing second chances. Even if the last Reckoner I train is a pirate-born perversion, I can do some good by figuring out the pirates' source and getting the information back to shore.

So I nod, keeping my eyes fixed on the wooden floorboards, on the tassels of a carpet that once lay on the floor of a lounge in the *Nereid*.

Santa Elena stands again, her heels squeaking as she pivots to face her protégées, and I glance up to see what she's about to do. "Swift, you did an excellent job identifying her and bringing her aboard."

"Thanks, boss," she says, returning her captain's sharp-toothed grin.

"Since you seem so dedicated to making sure this endeavor goes just as planned, I'm putting Cassandra in your charge."

The word "no" leaves both our mouths simultaneously—mine whispered, hers groaned. For a second, our eyes meet. We glare. I can't be stuck with this girl. Give me any other person on this ship, give me *Santa Elena* for god's sake. Anyone but her.

Santa Elena grins wider. "I don't want you to misunderstand this, Swift. This is a *big* opportunity. You could really impress me here. But I don't want to be unfair to the rest of you, so naturally there's a bit of risk involved."

Swift blinks.

"If Cassandra here fails me, you'll be punished equally. Make sure she succeeds."

And for the first time since they dragged me onboard this boat, I smile. Swift can't do shit to me with Santa Elena watching, with her fate entwined with mine. It's like the captain's just given me my own personal guard dog.

But before I can let the feeling get to my head, I spot the looks curdling across the other four protégées' faces. The resentment. The ambition. Whatever this opportunity means for Swift, it's setting them back in some way.

And suddenly I feel as if I'm in the crosshairs of all four of them. From the looks of it, Swift can fend for herself. But I need a monster to stand between me and these people, and all I've got right now is a half-baked pup and a pirate girl who's looking at me like I'm a cloud of Reckoner shit.

There's far too much at stake for me to let that shake me. So I'll weather it.

I straighten my spine and meet the captain's gaze as she stalks back to her throne. Santa Elena flops into her seat, kicking her heels off and picking at something stuck between her teeth. "That'll be all," she says with a dismissive wave. "Swift, make sure your new pet gets fed."

The pirates filter out of the room in groups, some chatting, others slapping each other on the back. The lackeys all move in a knot, save for Swift, who ducks to the captain's side and mutters something quick in her ear. Santa Elena shoots back, her voice low. I wait until the other four lack-eys make their exits and then approach the throne, my arms folded over my chest.

Swift steps down and grabs me by my elbow before I can get a word out. She tugs me out through the wooden doors and I feel like I should be looking for steam rising from her half-shaved head.

"I'm supposed to give you a tour of the ship," she says. "Captain says to treat you like new blood."

"I—"

"Captain's wrong," she hisses, her eyes flicking down the corridor to make sure no one heard her. "You don't belong here."

"There's something we can agree on," I reply, trying to wrest my arm free. It doesn't work.

Swift narrows her eyes. "Look, I don't know if you're keen to how things work around here, so I'll lay it out simply. Santa Elena picks the best from the ranks to be her trainees. She teaches us the ins and outs of leading this ship and pays us a cut above the rest. And one of us is going to take her place someday. I fought tooth and nail to get where I am on this ship, and I wouldn't give two shits about you if my own neck didn't depend on it. But the captain's gone and made this one of the perverted hoops I have to jump through if she's ever going to name me as her successor. So if you could just shut your mouth, work with me, and not try to off your-self again, that'd be great. That'd really do me a favor."

We're alone in this empty hall, with the captain locked

away in her throne room and the other crew members dispersed. I'm starting to pick up Swift's patterns. She's a squall, a tantrum of hatred and stubbornness when someone's around to watch. But when it's just her—just her and someone she considers so far beneath her that their presence isn't worth acting for—Swift's just a survivalist.

I can almost respect that.

Almost.

I feel skewed, as if someone's taken my values and tugged them so far away from me that it seems ludicrous to reach out and try to grab them again. I can't be empathizing with these people. *Survive*, I remind myself. Everything is secondary to keeping myself alive. If I play my cards right, I can escape this boat, and no one will ever know what I had to do to get there.

So I'll play Swift's game until the time is right.

"I don't exactly have a choice," I tell her, making another attempt to break her grip. She lets me go this time, but her hand immediately drifts down to the gun on her belt. The imprint of her fingers lingers on my flesh, and I cringe.

"Right. Fine. Basics of the *Minnow*. Follow me."

I wait for her to grab me again, but it doesn't happen. Swift stalks away, and I realize this is the first time she's turned her back to me. She seems smaller. My gaze flicks to the nape of her neck, to the place where a guillotine's blade would fall, and I spy a little smudge of ink. Her Minnow. Santa Elena's words come back to me all at once, and in that moment I understand a little bit more about Swift.

If a brand on the back of her neck is how she sees the ship, we have a lot more in common than I first thought.

7

Swift's introduction to the ship is about as half-hearted as I expected. First she leads me up a ladder to the main deck and breezes through the ship's arsenal, including the two massive guns at the fore and aft. Phobos and Diemos, she calls them, then warns me never to call them that around the captain. I stare up at them, fighting to keep my expression unchanged as I remember their fury, the blaze of the guns pumping as they drove round after round into Durga's hide. My eyes burn, and I squeeze them shut before anything escapes.

Then it's on to the Splinters, the needle-like gunboats tucked against the *Minnow*'s hull by a set of pneumatic braces. Swift introduces them like a tour guide at an art museum, but her boorish accent keeps the impression half-baked.

I lean over the railing to get a good look at the Splinters. I've seen ships like this escorting vessels too small to have Reckoners. They're tiny and terrifyingly fast, and Santa Elena didn't need to deploy them to take down the *Nereid*.

I lean a little farther, letting the railing take my full weight as my gaze shifts to the night-dark ocean flying by beneath us. For a moment, I feel weightless. For a moment, I forget.

Then Swift yanks me back by the collar and gives me a warning look.

There's a beat of awkward silence. She glances around the deck, the wind whipping her hair as she searches for something else to point out to me, then shrugs. "There's more, I guess," she says. "But I'm starving, so who cares?"

She leads me back down the ladder and through the maze of lower levels, nodding here and there to indicate heads, bunks, and supply closets. I could complain about how fast she's breezing through the ship's layout, but my stomach has other matters on its mind. The promise of food has it grumbling and growling, reminding me that it's been nearly an entire day since I last ate. Back home, I miss meals left and right when I get caught up with work in the Reckoner pens— I guess I've gotten good at suppressing hunger. The idea of a hunger strike flickers into mind, but I brush it aside. If I'm going to survive on this ship, I'll need all the strength I can get, and something tells me if I refuse to eat, Swift will simply cram the food down my throat.

We finally arrive at a hatch in the fore, which Swift opens with a rough twist of the wheel. The smell of food and spices hits me like a freight train, and my eyes and mouth begin to water simultaneously. Swift steps through the hatch, and a welcoming roar rises from the crew gathered inside. Rather than climbing down the short ladder, she leaps forward, her boots slamming into the wooden floor with a heavy thud. She turns, that familiar feral grin on her lips as she beckons me.

I clamber down after her, and it's like descending into the lions' den.

In Santa Elena's lair, I knew my value, knew that the sway she held over her crew protected me from them. But here I'm nothing but meat. I forget my own hunger in the hungry eyes that follow me as I dart to Swift's side.

"Quit acting so skittish," she hisses. "They can't do shit to you. Not while I'm around." There's something uncannily warm about the way she says it.

Off to the side of the mess there's a table with a jumbled assortment of food. Most of it looks far too fresh to be anything prepared on this ship. Spoils from the *Nereid*'s kitchens, most likely. There's a stack of plastic trays next to it, and Swift grabs two. "Load up," she says, pushing the second into my hands. "This is the best meal we've had in weeks, and it ain't lasting."

I grab the fresh fruit first—it's probably my last chance to get it until this ship restocks, whether by trade or by force. There's what's left of a pork roast too, though it looks like wild dogs have ripped it apart. I shovel some of the rich meat onto my tray, and add a few of the wilting greens that the pirates have dumped onto a silver platter.

As an afterthought, I carve off a slice of the rapidly disintegrating cake that teeters near the edge of the table. The words *Welcome to Paradise* are scrawled atop it in elegant handwriting. It was supposed to commemorate our first island stop—I remember sneaking a peek in the kitchen the night before Dur—

I rein in my thoughts before they get out of hand and follow Swift to a small table where the four other lackeys sit. She shoves Varma across the bench, and I slide in after her.

"Gonna introduce us?" he asks. He flashes me an easy smile. At this range I can finally tell that the smear of ink on his cheekbone makes the shape of a small fish.

"God's sake, Varma—you've already met. Cassandra, these other losers are Code, Lemon, and Chuck," Swift says through a mouthful of food.

I recognize Code as the boy who spoke out when I wouldn't. Chuck's a heavyset Islander girl with what looks like engine grease patterning her bare arms. Lemon's all skin and bones in contrast. She twitches when Code leans over her to swipe a slice of bread off Swift's tray.

Swift catches his hand, and I notice the Minnow tattoo across his index finger. "Son of a bitch," she growls. "I can't even sit down for two seconds with you people." She squeezes hard, and Code yelps while the rest of the table collapses into raucous laughter.

They're a lot friendlier than I thought they'd be, and for a moment I catch myself hoping that their camaraderie will win out over their ambition. Swift's relaxed around them— she still postures and pushes, but there's a genuine spark in her eyes as she ribs at the other lackeys. Could it be that she actually trusts them? Only one of them can captain the ship someday, and these five are in the running for some reason or another. There's something in each of them that Santa Elena finds valuable.

Which means there's something in each of them that's dangerous.

But it's so hard to see them as a threat when they're like this. They're just a bunch of teenagers joking around, tossing food back and forth like they're in a high school cafeteria instead of the galley of a pirate ship.

On the shore, we measure pirate lives in the percentages posted every time a Reckoner takes down a ship. Seventy-six percent dead. Forty-three percent dead. The gauge of a beast's effectiveness. Durga died with an eighty-three percent average. Or something slightly less, since in her last fight she batted a solid zero. But on this ship, the monsters we created our Reckoners to fight against have faces and smiles and souls—and that makes them even worse.

And these five are the same age as me. I wonder where they all came from, what choices and circumstances drove them to a pirate ship. For most of them, I have no clue. There's some sort of inside joke circulating the table about Chuck being a runaway princess, the daughter of an Islander millionaire, but there's no way of confirming if it's based on fact without inserting myself into the conversation. And if two Reckoners are interacting, you never get between them.

It isn't until Chuck's curious eye settles on me that I get dragged into the discussion. "Hey, pet project, where you from?" she asks, and Swift shifts uncomfortably, her spine rigid.

"The Southern Republic of California," I say after a moment's pause.

"Proper SRCese shoregirl," Swift sniffs.

I don't dare correct her. It means nothing to this bunch that I've spent my whole life with one foot in the sea. They're so *narrow* that it makes me want to scream, but I just avert my gaze and shovel another bite of roast into my mouth.

"What're you doing being a trainer on a vessel like that bucket, then?" Code chuckles. "You're a friggin' kid like the rest of us."

I hesitate again. I don't know how much to give him—I know every word is a weapon that could just as easily be turned against me. "Grew up doing it," I finally say. The fact that this was my first solo mission can wait. It weakens me in their eyes, and I know I'm weak enough to start. I want them to underestimate me, but I won't be a joke to them. And I don't need Swift to have any less faith in me than she already does.

Code nods, satisfied. "You're quieter than Lemon on a good day, ain't you?"

In the blink of an eye, Lemon snatches her knife off her tray and turns it on Code, her lip trembling.

"Oh for fuck's sake," Varma yelps, lunging across the table and latching onto her wrist. "Lemon, look at me. Look at me. Code's a worthless piece of shit—it doesn't matter. Look at me."

As he tries to calm the other lackey, Swift grabs me by the arm and hauls me off the bench. "It only gets worse from here," she mutters into my ear.

I was only halfway done with my food. I make a mental note to pay more attention to eating and less attention to the company next time. Swift pulls me to the galley's hatch and clambers out of it. I follow, regretting how easy it is to just go wherever she pulls my leash.

Once we're out in the quiet of the hall, her brow furrows. "Captain didn't specify where you're supposed to sleep," she muses.

Swift's thought process is practically etched across her face. She knows I can't be stowed in the crew quarters or anywhere else where someone could get to me. If there's a chance the other lackeys might kill me just to sabotage her, she needs to put a locked door between me and them. But the last time she left me locked away in a closet by myself, I nearly got away with taking that pill. There's no way she'll risk me finding another way to off myself.

We arrive at the inevitable conclusion at the same time.

"You're bunking with me," Swift declares.

And I swear, there's a part of her that almost enjoys it.

Before I can protest, she's started off down the hall. I jog after her, trying to form a counterargument. Swift can't be serious about this. She can't actually expect that I—

But no, she's hauling open a hatch and stepping into a dimly lit, cramped room. It's consumed by the bed built into one wall, the floor carpeted by scattered clothes, a few drawers jutting out haphazardly. The room couldn't look more like her if it tried.

"I'm not sleeping on your nasty-ass floor," I warn her.

"No," she agrees. "You aren't."

My gaze drops to the bed.

I hate how much sense it makes. No one's going to cut my throat with Swift sleeping three inches away. And if she's scared I'm going to try taking the easy way out again, there's no way I could get away with it without her noticing.

But first I have to change out of the wetsuit. I tug at the zipper on the collar, and Swift catches on. "I grabbed some stuff from the sunk bucket," she says, nodding to a sack in the corner. "Was supposed to be for me, but I guess it'll do the trick for you too."

I somehow doubt that. Swift's definitely a size bigger than me. I peer into the bag of clothes, pulling out a striped T-shirt and a pair of gym shorts. That might work. But underwear is another matter entirely—every bra Swift grabbed is two cup sizes too big.

She rolls her eyes when she sees me wrinkle my nose. "Didn't know I was shopping for two. Don't blame m—"

"I blame you."

I decide to just go without, for now. Turning my back to Swift, I unzip my wetsuit and peel it off. The neoprene feels like it might take some of my skin with it, and I wince. I probably shouldn't have left it on for so long, but I didn't have a choice. I strip off my bikini top and cram the shirt hastily over my head, glancing over my shoulder when I've got it safely on.

Swift stands with her arms folded, her back to me.

I didn't expect her to be considerate.

I guess she's just a walking, talking division of self. In front of her peers, in front of the captain, she's an entirely different person. She puts on this big-shot persona to scare off anyone who dares run up against her. But it seems like I'm not a threat worth her mask.

I finish changing and ball up my wetsuit. This used to be

my uniform, a sign that I was trained to command monsters. Now it's just a hunk of neoprene and fabric that smells of sea and blood. I pitch it into the corner, adding to the heaps of dirty laundry.

Swift doesn't bat an eye when she turns around and sees it. It's probably not the worst thing cluttering her floor. Her gaze shifts to me. "You look like a deflated balloon," she sniggers.

Maybe I'm at the end of my rope. Maybe this day has been too goddamn long and started with my favorite Reckoner getting her innards spilled into the NeoPacific. Maybe I'm stuck on a goddamn pirate ship with my life tied to raising a monster to do the exact opposite of everything I stand for. Maybe I'm done being quiet and small and underestimated.

Maybe that's why I punch Swift.

She staggers backward, catching herself on the bed. My fist feels like it's on fire, but it's nothing compared to the sheer triumph that floods through my body. The imprint of my knuckles is rapidly fading from her cheek, but it's *there*.

Of course she lunges, her hands slamming into my shoulders, throwing me against the half-open drawers. I wait for the next blow, but none comes. She hesitates, every part of her body held in tension, then crawls into bed and rolls over, facing the wall. Doesn't pull the blanket up over her, doesn't say anything. From a typhoon to stilled seas in the blink of an eye.

Adrenaline took me over for a second, but I'm getting my body back bit by bit, in bruises and aches that I can feel forming everywhere. Out of options, I sit on the edge of the bed, testing to see if she'll snap at me. But Swift is drawing long, slow breaths now, the kind that bring you teetering over the edge of falling asleep. My gaze lands on her Minnow tattoo peeking out from behind her uneven blonde hair, on the ink that marks her loyalty and what it means to her.

All of a sudden it strikes me: I wouldn't be here if it weren't for Swift. I wouldn't be alive if she hadn't held me back when I was ready to tackle Santa Elena. If she hadn't told the captain to bring me along. If she hadn't caught me as the pill was on my lips. If it weren't for her, one way or another I'd be another bloated corpse staining the NeoPacific.

So when I lie back and roll onto my side, I decide I'm not bunking back-to-back with the girl who kept me from sparing Durga or the girl who dragged me aboard the *Minnow* and threw me into a janitorial closet. She's not the girl who slammed me into a wall a minute ago or the girl who called me a shoregirl like it was the height of insult.

I'm just going to sleep next to the girl who saved my life.

8

The next morning, I wake up to the girl who saved my life shoving me out of her bed. "Captain said you're hatching the beast today, since you're all rested up," Swift grumbles, stepping over me as she staggers to her feet.

I prop myself up on my elbows, watching as she rummages through the drawers. I've got no earthly idea what time it is, apart from "not night." There's no window in Swift's bunk, and it strikes me now that the janitorial closet might have been roomier.

When she strips off her shirt, I don't spare her the way she spared me. Her body is laced with scars, but that's not the only thing marking her skin. Inked across the bottom of her rib cage is a bird, its pointed wings curving down toward her hips, its head covered by the bottom edge of her bra. A swift.

Of course.

"So did your mom give you that name, or did people just see your tattoo and start calling you that?" I ask.

"Mom." She says the word like it's eggshells that she's dancing over. "Now quit staring, jackass," she snaps, and throws her shirt in my face. "Get off the floor. You've got shit to do."

Five minutes later, we're jogging through the halls on the ship's lowest level. Down here, the engines groan and grumble as if we're passing through a giant metal heart, and the smell of saltwater winds through the air. The upper part of the *Minnow* is stitched together from mismatched pieces, the halls bleeding from metal to wood and plastic in a train wreck of bolts and glue. But down here, the comforts of the yacht parts melt away into the cold, industrial womb of a warship.

We round a corner and step through a hatch into what I should have known the ship possessed from the start. The *Minnow* already has a built-in trainer deck. There are two huge cutaways with roll-up doors on either side of the hull that open out to the ocean, and a runoff trough that takes in whatever seawater washes over and sweeps it into a channel that feeds out the back of the ship. A massive cutaway dominates the rear wall, with a similar set of roll-up doors which have been pulled up to give us a wide, sweeping view of the morning sea. The floor is damp under my bare feet, and I take care not to slip as I pick my way after Swift. Santa Elena waits at the edge of the trough, four of her crew beside her and the pup's tank at her side.

On the back wall, a knot of cabin boys and girls takes me in with wide eyes. None of them look older than thirteen, and Santa Elena's boy is among them. I can't tell which is the bigger spectacle for these kids: the monster pup, or the shore-girl dragged aboard to hatch it.

A pit of dread builds in my stomach. The pup's in its purse, which keeps it in stasis. It's safe and warm, fed by the rich fluids that cradle it. The second it's exposed to the outside world, it needs constant care and attention. We usually have a rotating staff when the pups hatch back home—a night shift, an early day shift, and a late day shift. Twenty-four hour supervision.

With my life tied to this baby monster, I can't afford to do any less than that.

"I've collected the tools you need," Santa Elena says as we draw near. She's dressed in sweatpants and a track jacket, her hair bound back in a ponytail, a far cry from the elegant woman who lounged in the throne room last night.

For a second, I hold the captain's gaze, and I'm sure she sees the questions in my eyes: *How do you know what we need? How did you get this equipment? How did you get this pup?*

But she only smirks. "Your knife is there. Turn it on any of my crew and I'll have lead in your skull faster than you can blink."

She gestures to a bank of instruments spread out on a workbench. Whatever her source, she's clearly done her research. There are tubes and bellows for clearing the baby's airways, towels for wiping it down, an adhesive thermometer to monitor its temperature. And then there's the blade, gut-hooked and wicked looking, designed to carve the leathery skin that forms the sac.

I take it in my hand, testing its weight. I've only ever been the one holding the knife once, a year ago. I remember what Mom said to me as she hovered over my shoulder, ready to swoop in the instant my wrist twisted the wrong way. "Make the cut along the lower edge of the purse," she told me. "Let the fluid drain before the pup does."

But we had Tom with us, holding up the other end of the purse while Mom guided me through the work, and technicians on the sides, ready to swoop in with the care the pup needed. I need more hands than I have here, but no one's stepping up to help. Swift's fallen back to the captain's side, and none of her crew look interested in anything but watching me struggle.

"Put up the dams," Santa Elena barks. Two of her crew, a man and a woman, move to the edges of the drainage channel and haul up partitions that catch the water, creating a miniature tank that fills to knee-depth in a minute.

My hands are shaking.

"Dump the purse," the captain orders the men to her left. They wrap their arms around the tank that holds the Reckoner pup and tilt it over slowly but surely until the amniotic fluid drains into the pool, the sac sliding out after it. The waters flush a muted orange, and the pup convulses in its purse.

I grab the rest of my tools and step over the barrier, shuddering as the chill of the seawater sinks into me. The amniotic fluid forms a thin, slimy skin on the water's surface, one that the pup will have to fight once it's free-breathing. I set the tubes, bellows, and towels down on the other side of the partition and move toward the purse, my fingers curling tighter on the knife.

The purse is about four feet long and three feet wide. By my estimates, the pup's probably around two hundred pounds, almost twice my weight. As soon as this thing gets free, it's going to have a mind of its own, and it's up to me to get out of the way before it gets any ideas.

Santa Elena seems aware of this. I can see it in her smirk as she declares, "Have at it."

I kneel, the water seeping into my shorts, and grab the sac by its bottom. The pup's awake—its paws press at the leathery womb that surrounds it. Still trembling, I press the blade into the purse until its point punctures the skin. A bubble of amniotic fluid oozes out, and I press harder until the knife's hook makes it inside the sac. I yank back.

The blade's sharp, but the membrane is tough. It doesn't make a clean slice like it ought to. The edges are ragged. I grit my teeth and pull harder until I've sliced all the way across the sac's bottom. The syrupy fluid gushes out, drenching the front of my shirt as I lean over the sac and reposition it, this time so that I'm kneeling at the top.

This is the part I've been dreading. This is why it takes so many hands, why my own two won't be enough, why I stand a good chance of losing one of them.

I hook the knife in the middle of the first incision and start to pull back, carving a T-shaped gash in the membrane. I try my best to lean back, to get out of the way. The pup twitches, and one of its—*his*, I can see that now—rear legs stretches out into the open air, kicking for the first time without any resistance.

I glance down to find that his reptilian eyes have slid open. His gaze is fixed on me, and for a moment he reminds me far too strongly of Durga. The lines that shape his body are unfamiliar—clearly he isn't one of my mother's constructions—but he's a terrapoid through and through, and it's enough to rattle me. She's gone. She's really gone.

Breathe, I remind myself. *What comes next?*

"Make it fast," my mother told me. "The quicker the cut, the slower he'll react."

I pull too hard. The blade dips against the pup's skin, flaying the purse membrane wide open as he rushes toward me, and all of a sudden the baby Reckoner is free.

And he's *pissed*.

He lunges up, his beak snapping, and before I can react, he's got a chunk of my hair locked in his bite. The deck behind me comes alive, Santa Elena shouting as her crew draw their guns and point them at me and the pup. He twists viciously, his stubby limbs flailing, and the sharp edge of his beak shears off some of my hair.

The rest rips right out of my scalp.

But I'm free. I stagger backward as the baby continues to thrash, rolling off his back and into the water. He lets out a nasally squeal as if the world he's been born into has already offended him.

"Lower your guns," I shout, using the partition to haul myself to my feet.

The crew doesn't obey me—of course they don't—but

after a nod from Santa Elena, they stand down. The baby Reckoner runs up against the tank's barrier and bounces off, still squalling. His stumpy tail thrashes against the water.

I lunge for the bellows and the thermometer. I've got mere seconds to get this done before the pup locks onto me again. There's some part of me that's gone raw and wild and animal, and I let it loose as I rush toward the beast. The Reckoner wheels, but I hook my fingertips under his keratin plating and swing myself around onto his back before his jaws can reach me. He bucks and screams, his eyes rolling. I drive the bellows into his primary blowhole and squeeze them, forcing the noise back down his throat and then sucking it right back out.

I toss the device to the side, not caring where it lands. But before I can get the thermometer placed, the pup rolls on his back, plunging me underwater. I choke on the putrid mix of saltwater and amniotic fluid, and the baby's weight slams me against the bottom of the pool.

For a moment, stars dot my vision.

Then he rolls right back over, and I'm up—I'm free just long enough to rip the adhesive off with my teeth and slap the thermometer down on the beast's neck, where neither his jaws nor his stubby arms can reach it.

The Reckoner lunges predictably when I let go, but I dance out of the way and run for the opposite end of the tank, crawling over the barrier as I try to catch the breath I lost. To my surprise, there are hands there to meet me, hands that guide me out of the dangerous pool and onto the damp deck. Santa Elena passes me an approving nod from the other side of the tank, and my stomach twists.

I don't want her approval. I want to get out of here. My head throbs—I raise a hand to it, and it comes away bloody. Oh. Right.

Now that I'm safe from the pup's temper tantrum, I can finally take stock of what he's done to me. About half of my hair is missing or shorn. I probe carefully at my scalp until I can be sure of it. I drop my blood-soaked hand to my chest and press carefully against each rib. I've seen trainers with their chests crushed get right out of the tank like nothing's wrong, fueled by the adrenaline that comes from being in the water with a killer beast. For all I know, I could be dying right now, so I'm not taking any chances.

I press on my sternum, and three sharp pains cut through my sides.

They all must see it in my face. The captain strides over to me, Swift on her tail. "Get Reinhardt down here," she barks to one of the cabin boys on the back wall. I cough, and her attention snaps back to me. "Sit down. Stay as still as possible."

"Looks worse than it is," I gasp.

Her eyes flash. "Don't lie to me, Cassandra. It doesn't benefit either of us. Now *sit.*"

And I guess I'm still just a dog on her leash, because I sink down onto the damp floor.

Swift crouches next to me, her brow furrowed. "Why'd you go back in there?" she mutters. "After it got hold of you— why'd you go back?"

It's starting to hurt to breathe. The adrenaline is wearing off. "Had to—" I hiss. "Had to make sure the airways were clear... and get the thermometer on. Temperature has to be... monitored."

"Right, but that thing was about to kill you."

"If that thing dies, I'm dead anyway," I shoot back, as loud as I can manage. "And you are too, so you'd better be thanking me."

"Not on your life," she says, but there's a smile teasing on the edge of it, and a little spark of hope flutters through me, hope that she might actually be on my side.

At the very least, I hope I've convinced her I'm no longer suicidal.

———————

Reinhardt turns out to be the ship's medic, a weasely looking man who prods at my ribs with long, bony fingers and comes to exactly the same conclusion I made ten minutes ago. Three breaks, but nothing horrible enough to put me out of commission. "I can medicate you, but I can't fix fractures like this," he says, pulling a bottle of pills out of the satchel on his hip. "Two of these a day, no more. And watch them carefully. We got a lot of addicts on this crew."

I nod, taking the pills from him and immediately popping one. There's no instant relief, but the fact that I have something to manage my pain is more than I expected. My gaze shifts to the tank, to the Reckoner pup who's poking his snout up over the barrier and warbling. I've been taken care of enough—now it's time to see to him.

I check the thermometer's reading on the companion

device. He's running a little hot. No surprises there. I've never seen a birth this violent, but the pup's temperature isn't high enough to get me worried. I wave to get Santa Elena's attention, cringing as my ribs twinge. "He needs to be fed," I say.

"How much?"

I frown, trying to remember the conversion chart Mom keeps pinned to the wall of the nursery. "For a pup this size, twenty pounds of meat should do it," I tell her, trying to keep the uncertainty out of my voice. "And we'll need to swap out the water in the tank." Over her shoulder, I spy two of her crew reaching for the empty purse floating in the pool. "Watch it!" I yelp, just as the Reckoner lunges.

His jaws snap shut, missing them by inches. He's the most aggressive newborn I've ever seen, though admittedly I've never seen a pup get nicked by a knife during a birth. Most terrapoids are sluggish out of the purse. I was swimming in Durga's pool mere hours after we hatched her. But this one's already a monster without the training.

And I hate him.

He's my charge, and he's the reason I'm being used by a bunch of pirates. My life is tied to a beast that's already done his best to end it, and for a moment I find myself wishing that they'd just killed me on the *Nereid*.

But that wouldn't have done any good, because the pirates would still have this pup, this equipment, and no one on shore would be the wiser. It's on me to survive. It's on me to get this information back home, even if there's no place for me there anymore.

And then something comes to me, something I can *use*.

These pirates don't know what Reckoner pups are like. They've only been on the bad side of the fully-grown beasts.

I could play this to my advantage.

And the idea is so deliciously present that I can't believe I didn't think of it before. Anything this pup does will be blamed on his nature before my training. One little slip of the knife made it so that they see him as a wild beast that I'm taming rather than a blank slate that I'm programming. They gave me a shield when Santa Elena tied me to Swift. Now they've given me the sword. They want me to teach him to hunt.

But they also gave me the power to turn them into the prey.

9

That night, Santa Elena locks me on the trainer deck. I roll down the three massive doors to keep the sea winds from ripping through the space and make a small nest out of towels on the counter where I keep my tools. The pup watches curiously as I hop up on the ledge and curl up. "Go to sleep, you little shit," I tell him.

If I'm not careful, he'll start thinking that's his name. I've already called him that at least twenty times today. I do actually need to name him, need to give him something that identifies and differentiates him. I've never gotten to name a Reckoner before. Usually that's up to the shipping company that commissions them. The *Nereid*'s owners were Hindu; they named their beast after a goddess famous for killing demons. But what do you name a creature meant to rip the NeoPacific apart, to upset the equilibrium we've worked so hard to establish?

My thoughts jump to villains, to demons and devils, to

ancient monsters and evils that never sleep. That's the kind of name this Reckoner deserves.

But I'm not going to give him what he deserves.

He's small and fat and round, and my mind lands on the steamed buns my mom makes on the days when she needs to get out of the lab. A smirk twists my lips. I'll name him something small and harmless. I'll give him a name that will contradict every gene hacked into him.

"You're Bao," I tell him.

Bao snorts.

———————

The next days pass in a haze. The trainer deck hatch is kept locked tight, and my twenty-four-hour supervision begins. I sleep in bursts, woken by the pup whenever he gets hungry and starts to squall. As my scalp starts to heal, I cut the rest of my hair short to even out the damage. My ribs ache constantly.

Every morning the ship's cook, a giant Islander woman named Hina, comes down with a new barrel of fish caught by the *Minnow*'s trawler. The entire trainer deck starts to reek of what goes into Bao and what comes out. I have to flush out his filthy tank water every day.

It's hell. There's no lighter way of putting it. I realize after the first week that I wouldn't have a chance if someone decided to come and kill me. I'm too exhausted to put up a fight.

And if Swift was on my side after watching me birth the pup, that ship has sailed. She brings me food and escorts me to the head on my breaks, but I can tell that her patience with this game is running thin. If her life didn't depend on it, she'd probably be first in line at my throat.

Once a night, I let myself grieve Durga. I let myself imagine that I trusted my instincts, that I never let the *Nereid* depart with a dying Reckoner as its escort, that I'd figured out what was wrong with her. I don't know what caused her body to fall apart like that, but it's clear as day that the pirates were behind it. Someday I'll figure out exactly what they did to her.

Until then, I curl up on my counter with my head in my hands and cry until there's nothing left.

———

One night, I wake up to the hatch swinging open, and for a second I'm certain that a bullet is about to find my brain. In the darkness, I can't make out the figure that steps through the door.

Bao sleeps on. The little bastard is actually snoring.

Only three people on this ship have the key to get into the trainer deck. One of them just drops off fish, one doesn't want anything to do with me, but the third…

"Captain?" I ask.

"Just checking in on things," Santa Elena replies.

I want to ask her why that's necessary in the middle of the night, but if I've learned anything on this ship, it's that Santa Elena is beyond questioning.

She hits the dim lights, filling the deck with a warm glow as she approaches the pup's tank. The captain is dressed in a red bathrobe, which she hugs tighter around herself as she peers over the edge at the slumbering baby Reckoner. "It's always hardest at the start," she says.

I should probably warn her to step back from the tank. I've seen pups pretend to sleep, just to trick people into coming closer to them. Bao's playful side is still developing, and I don't know if he'd take Santa Elena's arm off or just try to startle her. But I want to see how this plays out, so I hold my tongue.

The captain's lips curve into a soft smile. "When I had my boy, I don't think I ever really slept for the first month. People always tried to tell me that motherhood was this beautiful, sacred, precious thing, but god as my witness, motherhood's nothing but a hot mess."

"I'm not a mother," I say as I sit upright, pushing off the musty towels that cover me.

"You sure as shit look like one, Cassandra."

It's not untrue. My scalp is still patchy and misshapen from where Bao tore out my hair, my shirt is covered in stains from fish guts, and though I haven't seen a mirror in ages, I can feel the weight of dark circles under my eyes.

"I miss the days when my boy was small, though," she continues. "I was stranded out on a floating city with a new-born baby, but it felt like the beginning of something, you know? When I took this ship, it was with him strapped on my back. People will tell you differently. They want me to be a demon in their stories, and a demon carrying a baby doesn't fit that image, right? Now it's the middle of the story, and it's monotonous."

I can't wrap my head around monotony in a life of piracy. I can't understand how she could consider raising a Reckoner pup that could upset the balance of the NeoPacific monotonous. There are so many ways she could have an unfortunate accident on this deck, and I know the triggers to at least three of them.

"You're thinking about killing me right now, aren't you?" she asks.

My head snaps up.

"Don't look so surprised. I developed an instinct for this sort of thing years ago. You'll find it's a very useful skill on a boat like this."

"I'll work on it," I deadpan. Bao chooses that moment to heave a snore so thunderous that he wakes himself up. Santa Elena leans out farther over the tank. Some sort of thrill lights up in her eyes, and I wonder if this is her break in the monotony.

Bao regards her with one beady black eye, stretching his stubby legs until his keratin plates creak. *Go on, you little shit*, I urge him. *Do it.*

But he doesn't.

Of course he doesn't. She's doing nothing to provoke him, nothing to make him see the worth in lunging for her. And somehow I doubt Santa Elena is slow enough to let herself get caught by him.

I know what really stays Bao, though. It's something that's instinctive to every monster I've ever worked with—the recognition of when you're overpowered. Bao sees the hurricane behind Santa Elena, and he respects it. He sees no storm in me.

Not yet.

"You're going to do great things someday, you little beast," the captain tells him, She leans back and grins. "You and me, we're going to take the seas for our own." Her gaze flicks to me. "You named him after steamed buns."

"If you'd like, you can call him Bao Bao instead," I tell her, shifting the vowels slightly as I speak.

"Is that any different?"

"It means 'precious baby.'"

Santa Elena nods, her teeth bared in a smile that edges on consternation. She knows I'm playing games—she's watching all the little tricks I pull. They're nothing compared to the grand game she's set up that ties me with this Reckoner and with Swift, but they're enough to get under her skin, and that's all I need from them.

"Enjoy motherhood," Santa Elena tells me as she turns and shuffles back for the hatch, her bathrobe swishing around her.

"I'm not a mother," I repeat.

"You're living to keep something else alive, Cassandra. What else could that make you?"

10

My next set of visitors comes crashing onto the trainer deck a few days later, lead by Swift's vicious smile. I'm in the middle of measuring Bao, which is a monumental task on its own. He squirms away from me every time I try to yank him close enough to the tank's edge to loop the measuring tape over the back of his shell, and I've just about lost my patience when all five of Santa Elena's lackeys tumble through the door.

"What—" I start, but then falter. They're a pack of wolves, all tooth and bond, and even though they've just intruded on my world, any word toward them feels like I'm intruding into theirs.

Chuck holds something huge and flat and plastic over her head, and it takes me a second to recognize it as a cobbled-together wakeboard. "First ride's mine!" she declares as she throws it down on the deck.

The clatter makes Bao snort, and I jerk my hand away

from him as his beak snaps shut. Varma slides up to my side, a curious twinkle in his eye. "What're you up to?"

"Nothing, now," I huff as Bao shies underwater. Reckoners get testy when they feel crowded, and five new people on the deck is more than enough to make him retreat.

Swift leans hard on the control panel, and the back door rattles up. She flips her hair out of her face and stretches her arms out over her head, a smirk teasing over her lips, and for one shining moment, she's the leader that the captain sees her becoming. Then the moment passes; she slouches her shoulders and pads over to where Code and Lemon are tying down lines to the deck's handholds.

I retreat to my counter while Varma helps Chuck into the straps that bind the wakeboard to her feet. Lemon tosses a buoyancy vest over her shoulders, then clips a bungee line to it. Clutching Varma for support, Chuck waddles over to the edge of the deck, where Code waits with a set of handlebars attached to a rope. The whole operation is smooth—they've obviously done this hundreds of times before.

"All set?" Chuck asks as she takes the handle from Code.

He replies with a tug on the lines and a curt nod.

Chuck screams and launches herself off the back of the boat. She turns over once in the air, her mane of wild black hair whipping behind her, and plunges into the waves three feet below the deck's lip. The lines on the deck snap tight, and a moment later, her head bobs out of the froth. She cuts through the water as she heaves against the handlebars. A breathless second passes, and then the board is under her.

Varma's fists are the first in the air. He whoops and howls

like a wild dog, and the rest of the lackeys join in. The sun cuts through the spray the board kicks up, silhouetting the four of them against the bright afternoon. They're wild, they're dangerous, they're reckless.

But they're free, and that's what matters. That's what sends a little twinge of jealousy vibrating through my muscles as I press harder against the wall behind the counter, fingers crimped on the edge.

"Hey, pet project. You want a ride?" Code shouts back over his shoulder. He comes up and leans against the counter, peering out between his dark bangs. "It'll be fun, I swear. On my honor as a pirate."

I glance at Swift before answering, unsure if it's even my place to be talking to him. She doesn't seem to object—her attention is fixed on Chuck. "Ribs are still healing," I tell Code, which is only half true. It's been long enough that I only get the occasional twinge when I stretch myself a little bit too far. I'm less worried about what the strain of wakeboarding would do to the healing process and more worried about who's offering. It would be so easy for something to conveniently break in the harness, for something to go horribly wrong in a way so innocent that anyone on this deck could be implicated.

"Code, quit bothering the shoregirl," Varma says as he approaches us. "Doubt you're even her type."

He's not wrong.

"Just seeing if she wanted to have a bit of fun, yeah?" the other lackey replies.

I glance down at the measuring tape, at the other training accessories scattered across the counter. They've all been chosen so carefully, but it's more than that. They've been chosen with specific knowledge of what it takes to raise a Reckoner pup, knowledge beyond what they'd pick up from rumors, research, or observation. Santa Elena has a source in the industry—that much I know for sure.

I wonder how much these guys know.

As the captain's lackeys, they must be privy to her dealings. Maybe even present for them. And even if they have good reason to want me dead, they're friendly and happy right now. There's a chance that if I ask about this, they'd answer.

And I almost do.

Before the words escape my lips, I catch myself. There's a lot I can gain from this information, but there's so much more I can lose. If they get an inkling of the plan that's curdling in the back of my head, my chances of enacting it will plummet. I need them to continue underestimating me. I can't draw attention to myself by asking questions.

But Varma has noticed that I nearly said something. His eyes sparkle expectantly, waiting.

"Why do you call him Code?" I blurt. A harmless question, one that gets me nowhere.

Varma chuckles. "It's 'cause that's what he thinks in. He gets to sit up in the navigation tower with Lemon all day, whispering to the little machines while the rest of us are out here busting our asses."

Code's lips twist into something that's not quite a smile, but not quite a scowl either. He tolerates Varma's easy grin for a second, then crosses back over to where Lemon and Swift are hauling Chuck back in by the bungee lines.

"You don't gotta act so skittish around us, shoregirl," Varma says, giving me a playful shove on the shoulder.

"Yeah," I tell him. "I kind of do."

He shrugs as if it's my loss and jogs over to the edge of the deck, stooping to offer a hand to Chuck as she crawls out of the churning water. She's doing most of the grunt work herself, but she takes it to humor him. He pulls, yanks, and tugs until she rolls onto the deck, cackling like a lunatic. Swift and Code are already at her feet, prying the board off while Lemon unclips the bungee lines.

"My turn," Swift declares, wrenching the board out of Code's hands. There it is again—that little note of authority, like she might actually be cut out for leadership. The rest of the lackeys get her suited up in seconds flat, and something else strikes me. From the way Swift talked before, it seems like they shouldn't trust each other with this. Anything could go wrong. Something *should* go wrong. But the five of them ignore the fact that they're supposed to be cutthroats in competition.

They're just here to have a good time.

Swift leaps off the deck, and when she lands on her feet, that stupid hair whipping in the wind as the bungee lines snap tight, it's really no surprise.

11

Weeks pass. I become practiced in the art of quick naps, stealing sleep whenever Bao will let me. I forget what the rest of the *Minnow* looks like. All I know is the trainer deck, every inch of it. Bao eats voraciously, and it's not long until he's the size of the leatherback turtles that make up part of his genetics. He's finally big enough to swim alongside the ship.

Santa Elena claps me on the back when I tell her.

We flush him in the morning, just after the sun rises. Two pirates haul down the partitions separating Bao's tank from the channel that washes out into the sea, and out with the bathwater goes a seven-hundred-pound, monstrous baby, squalling almost as loudly as the day he came into the world. He plunges into the NeoPacific and bobs up immediately, his blowholes flaring as he takes in his new environment.

I toss a fish at him, hitting him in the side of the head. Bao blinks, snaps it up, then looks to see where it came from as I scoop another one out of the bucket at my side. When he spots me, fish in hand, he gives an impatient thrash of his tail. At his current size, a single fish is enough to get his attention, but that will soon change.

"Give it to him," Swift mutters from behind me, but Swift doesn't know shit. Now that the trainer deck is vacant, she's been assigned to full-time guard duty, and she's probably pissed because tonight she'll have to share her bed with me again.

Santa Elena's somehow furnished a working beacon for me to train her beast on—no surprises there. It takes some fiddling to get its signals off the factory defaults and on to something unique. There's one signal set I know by heart, one that no other beast on the NeoPacific is going to respond to, so I futz with the dials until the device communicates in those low tones and pulsing blues that make my heart ache with loss.

The beacon hangs on hooks that jut from the edge of the trainer deck, allowing me to stand over it as I issue commands. I kick on the homing LEDs and hold the fish out toward Bao, wiggling it back and forth. He pumps his stubby legs, swimming closer until his nose brushes the flashing patterns of lights. *Then* I drop the fish.

And that's lesson number one. Come to the beacon, get a reward. I snap off the LEDs and step back into the recesses of the trainer deck, waiting to see what Bao does. Some pups don't take kindly to sharing waterspace with their companion vessel, but this is an interesting case, since the *Minnow* is the only thing he's ever known. So far, he seems to be comfortable. He knocks his beak against the ship's hull a few more times, then turns and begins nosing farther away.

Now comes the real test of whether he's ready to start bonding training. I nod to Swift, and she plucks the radio off her belt. "Swift to navigation, get us moving at a slow clip," she orders.

The *Minnow*'s engines are right below us. They roar to life, kicking up a steaming froth in the water as the boat crawls forward. Bao lifts his head, shuddering as the heat hits him, then starts to paddle after us. It could be simple curiosity driving him, though. We need to set a pace and see if he keeps it.

———

Most of Reckoner training is a waiting game, and it's one that makes Swift steam at the ears. She sits on the counter where I've grown used to sleeping, knees drawn up to her chin, tossing the radio back and forth from hand to hand. I would have thought the monotony of ship life had prepared her for a couple of boring days, but apparently there are better things to do today aboard the *Minnow* than watch a beast pup swim.

Bao keeps the pace that the ship sets, and for the first time this morning, I allow myself to relax. If he continues to follow these instinctive patterns, his imprinting behavior will engage, bonding him to the *Minnow*, and the part that's up to him will be over.

Which means the part that's up to me is days away.

Bao's cunning. He'll learn quickly. He's a Reckoner, bred to be trained. And I'm going to train him to kill. Not to defend a ship, no—this beast is going to be taught to hunt down and destroy innocent vessels. To ravage the NeoPacific, just like Santa Elena wants.

And if I can't escape, if I can't get myself back to shore, it will all be by my hand. The possibility of failure hits me like a bullet to the chest, and all of a sudden I can feel it—I can feel the slug that'll be put in me if I do anything to sabotage the captain's plans. My heart thunders and my jaw locks tight. If it comes to that, I'll have to keep going along with her orders. I'm too scared to do anything else.

I slump to the floor of the trainer deck. Dampness soaks into my shorts as a small wave breaks against the side ports.

"What's eating you, shoregirl?" Swift drawls from her perch.

A twinge of annoyance rattles through me. "Don't play that game. You don't want to know what I'm feeling."

"I'm bored as shit—I'll listen to anything."

I consider. She's the closest thing I have to a friend on this boat, even if she does want to gut me most of the time. And after today, I have to move back in with her. "I'm thinking about home," I lie.

"You're SRCese, huh?"

"Yeah," I say, crossing my arms. "We're based just outside of New Los Angeles."

"Never been," Swift shoots back.

"It's nice. Good beaches. Of course, it's empty three quarters of the year. The coast's lined with summer homes and hotels, so there's not much in the way of permanent residents. But during summer it comes alive."

She wrinkles her nose. "Gimme open sea any day. Couldn't stand living on a beach."

"Oh yeah? You've never tried it?"

Swift grins, stretching her arms behind her head. "Nah, shoregirl. Flotilla, born and raised. Didn't touch solid land until after I'd started my bleed."

Of course she's from a floating city. Now that I think about it, that's the only place that a crew like this could come from. Those behemoths thrive on piracy, unregulated by any state as they drift with the currents cycling the NeoPacific. They're too big to be taken down by a military force, and no state has the balls to try. The last attempt was twenty years ago, when a Filipino armada tried to blockade a floating city and starve out the pirates supplying it. The retribution was ruthless. Pirates across the NeoPacific began wrecking any ship flying the flag of the Philippines, and their ocean trade is still struggling to put itself back together in the aftermath.

It suits Swift to be from such a volatile place.

"How long have you been on the *Minnow*, then?" I ask. My gaze flicks to the ocean outside, and I'm relieved to see Bao continuing to keep pace.

"Captain took me on when I was thirteen, started me off as a deckhand. So, uh, five years?"

Confirming that Swift is, indeed, about my age. I nod. "And when did you get appointed one of Santa Elena's ... trainees?"

"Christ, is this a job interview? I've been in the running for a good year and a half now. My turn to ask a question."

I roll my eyes.

"You go by anything shorter than Cassandra?"

I wasn't expecting a question like that. I sit there blinking for several seconds. "Uh ... I mean, most people call me Cas."

"One syllable. Nice."

"Ooh, syllable. Big word for a Flotilla kid."

The smile drops from Swift's face, but her teeth remain, bared and ready to bite. "You're a piece of shit, you know that?"

I don't dare say anything.

Swift pushes off the counter, padding over to my side. She crouches until she's nose to nose with me, her blue eyes unblinking as she leers into my face. "You think the SRC's the peak of civilization, huh? You think the little bubble you live in is as good as the world gets, that the rest of us are just hanging onto the fringes." She's close enough that I can feel the soft push of her breath against my cheek. "You've thought it for so long that the idea's just a *joke* for you to banter with. And then you get all hurt when we call you shoregirl, as if there aren't a thousand worse assumptions rattling around inside that empty head of yours."

She doesn't touch me, doesn't scratch my still-healing scalp or shove me in the ribs. I have hundreds of vulnerable points right now, but Swift isn't looking to hit me there. She wants me to feel guilty.

But I don't.

Everyone on this boat is complicit in taking everything I hold dear from me. They're killers and captors and thieves, and if I hurt their feelings, so be it. It's not my aim to play polite with a girl who can't hurt me any worse than the damage I've already taken.

So I just keep still until she stands up straight and goes back to sulking on the counter.

———————

Bao homes to the ship for the rest of the afternoon, and by the time Hina puts out the all-call for dinner, I'm certain that he's completely locked onto the *Minnow*. For the first time in weeks, I'm allowed off the trainer deck and into the main body of the ship. I follow Swift to the mess, realizing that I've already forgotten the twists and turns of the *Minnow's* halls.

She doesn't invite me to sit with the other lackeys when I get my tray, but I do it anyway. When I'm not on the trainer deck, the safest place on this boat is glued to Swift's hip. I haven't said a word since this afternoon; at this point, I think pretty much anything out of my mouth will offend her.

The lackeys all seem too happy to see me. Even Lemon lights up a bit when she spots me tailing Swift over to their table.

"Welcome back to the land of the living," Varma says, grinning extra wide as I slide onto the bench next to Swift. The guy probably gets kicked out of funerals for looking too pleased with himself.

I eat in silence and leave with Swift. We go back to her room, she throws a change of clothes at me, and it's just like the first night, minus the punching. She just collapses in bed, rolls over, and I follow.

But this time I don't let her drift off. I have questions, and the first is, "Why do you guys like each other so much?"

Swift startles. She lifts her head, her half-there hair flopping over as she twists to look at me.

"You and the other lack—trainees," I continue. "Only one of you is going to be captain in the end, right? Shouldn't you all be at each others' throats?"

For a moment I think she's not going to respond, but then she rolls over to face me, and something seems to soften in her.

"We've been through a lot of shit together," she says. "When you work like we do, when you hunt side by side—it's something that bonds you. Sometimes the captain does stuff like this. She sets up situations where someone's clearly getting special treatment, and yeah, it gets messy sometimes. But when you suffer with someone, you learn them. And it's hard to kill a person you've learned."

I nod. I've seen that kind of suffering-bond firsthand every time we have a pup in the stables—the caretakers of the newborn Reckoner become caretakers of each other. "But it can't last, right?"

"It might have," Swift sighs. "But then you came along."

I don't know what to say. Does she expect me to *apologize* for being dragged bodily aboard this ship to raise a beast I want to destroy more than anything?

"You still on those pain meds?" she asks. "You're awfully talky today."

I wrinkle my nose. "Reinhardt weaned me off them a week ago." My ribs still twinge on occasion, but I don't want Swift to know that—she'd probably jab them if she knew.

"Ah, so you're just getting more comfortable."

"Well I *am* sleeping in your bed," I grumble.

She grins, and for a moment her eyes light up in the same way they do when she's joking with the other lackeys. "Don't get too chummy with me, Cas. I'll eat you alive."

I can't help it. I snort, and it gains momentum until I'm cackling. "Was that a *threat*? God, you're the least intimidating pirate I've ever had the misfortune to meet."

"Then clearly you haven't spent enough time around Varma."

It's like Swift's room is a whole other world, a subdimension of the *Minnow* where Swift isn't a pirate and I'm not a prisoner. Here, away from the gaze of the rest of the crew, we're talking and laughing together as if we're something like normal. There's something that unlocks in Swift when she's sealed away from the rest of the ship, something honest. Something I actually can respect.

12

The next morning, the captain wants to oversee my training session with Bao. She paces along the trainer deck as I lure the pup back to the ship with the homing LEDs. There's a spark of excitement in her eyes, and it's keeping the tension in my muscles.

Bao's blowholes flare as he approaches, blasting a fine mist into the air that hangs over the morning sea. A piece of fresh meat hangs out of the corner of his mouth, the twisted remnants of some fish he's caught. At least he's figured out how to feed himself on his own. That's a weight off my shoulders, and the fact that he's eaten recently makes me much less apprehensive about what's about to happen.

I'm dressed in a brand-new wetsuit that Santa Elena furnished. It's made of some of the most breathable fabric I've ever encountered, but it's snug and warm around my torso.

A new, top-of-the-line respirator hangs around my neck. If it weren't for the circumstances, I'd feel utterly pampered.

Bao's had a night to adjust to the ocean, which means today's the day I start water work with him. If he's going to be in my charge, I have to get him comfortable with having me in the sea at his side. Mom and Dad never let me do this stage of training. It always went to the most experienced, the bravest. I've only ever watched first contact from behind the glass of a tank.

But now that's going to change, because I'm the only one on this ship who knows how to make a Reckoner comfortable with human presence. I haven't told Santa Elena that I've never done this before, but I think she senses it somehow. She's so intent on watching this part of the training process that she's forgone her other duties on the ship just to be here.

She probably just wants to see me get eaten.

I toss Bao a few fish when he noses up to the beacon and then wipe my hands down on a towel. Reckoners have keen noses, and I don't want him to mistake my fingers for anything they aren't. With the beast pup distracted by the food, I slip into the water feet first.

I haven't swum in so long that for a moment I hang beneath the surface in shock, the NeoPacific's gentle rhythm cradling me back and forth. I blink, then slip the respirator up over my nose, my gaze fixed on the monster next to me. He's still pointed toward where I threw the fish—the little idiot hasn't noticed that anything's changed.

This is the hardest part. I have to touch him to get his attention, but there's a sweet spot I need to hit. If I go too fast,

I might trigger him, but if he's aware of me for too long, that gives him time to think, to plan a move that might rip my arm off. He's at least five times heavier than me, and his personality is as changeable as the winds.

I kick forward and reach out, fingertips stretching toward his foreleg.

When I make contact, Bao's muscles twitch underneath my hand. His eye flicks toward me, and I can see him calculating, deciding exactly what this means and exactly what he's going to do about it. I hold my breath, the respirator whining, waiting for the air that I'm bound to expel.

He turns, his head looming toward me as I push myself backward, doing my best to avoid making sudden movements. *Come on*, I plead, releasing my breath in a slow hiss that fizzles out of the mask in tiny bubbles. *Come on, little shit. You know me.*

Bao puts his nose right up against my chest, and I'm acutely aware of the razor-sharp beak that nudges at my wetsuit. Cautiously, as slowly as I can manage, I bring my hands down and place them on top of his head. He snorts, a stream of bubbles blasting out of his blowholes, and I jerk my head back enough to startle him.

My breath's caught in my throat again as Bao tenses, his mouth hanging open. All he needs to do is push forward and bite down, and he'll have my guts decorating the ocean.

But he doesn't.

The little monster—no, for the first time I think of him as *my* little monster—blinks at me, waiting. His eyes are huge, the crinkles at the edges of his eyelids making him look much more wizened than he has any right to be. He's curious. He wants to know why I've joined him in the water.

I let my hands slip down around his head until I'm cradling his jaw, my grip snug on the bones that jut out there. I kick my feet once, twice, urging him to follow me upward. So long as I hold his jaw, he can't bite me. So long as we're connected, I'm safe.

And Bao follows my push until we break the surface. He blasts air out of his blowholes and squalls, tossing his head. I let him lift me just a bit, my respirator crackling as I laugh through it. I glance up at the trainer deck, where Santa Elena towers over us. There's a flash of disappointment in her eyes that a savage grin quickly replaces.

That's right, bitch, I think, my fingers crimped so tightly on Bao's jaw that they've gone bone-white. *If you want me dead, do it yourself.*

Just beyond her, I catch the quick motion of Swift lifting her head, but the smile she wears is nothing like the captain's. It's the smile that cracks through right when you're on the edge of tears, the smile that comes in the wake of sheer, numbing fear. I lived, and so Swift gets to live too. I see another flicker of movement, this time the flash of a middle finger that jabs up toward the captain's turned back.

"Swift, put out an all-call for the rest of the crew. I think this'll be good for them to see," Santa Elena snaps, and Swift stows the gesture just as quickly as she whipped it out.

———

Ten minutes later, the *Minnow's* brethren are packed onto the trainer deck, all leering out at me in the water. In the front of the crowd, I spot Varma dangling a bill over Chuck. She has to jump to swipe the money from him, but there's a self-satisfied grin that accompanies it and lets me know that I just helped her win a bet. And it seems like Varma bet against me. That's interesting.

Bao's large eyes flick back and forth, taking in the crowd staring down at him. He hasn't been around this many people since the day he was born, and I worry that it'll throw some switch in him, something that will make him dangerous. Already he's starting to lean away from my grip, and I can feel the tension in him building, like a wound-up spring ready to burst forward.

Santa Elena's got one arm wrapped around her son, the other resting easily on the gun in her holster. She looks like a founder of a city, meant to be immortalized in bronze. "Well done, Cassandra," she says, her tone musical.

Her praise stings, but I can't let it take my focus.

There's an urge building up inside me, and I don't realize quite what it is until I release my hold on Bao and slide one of my arms across his back. When I'm out in the water, I'm free from the *Minnow* and everything it stands for. I'm my own entity, with all the power that a Reckoner can give. And I want to show them just how powerful I am.

I've tried this trick with a few terrapoid pups, but Bao's no ordinary terrapoid. His eyes roll when he realizes what I'm doing, and he beats his forelegs against the sea, a growl of protest building up in his throat. I shift my weight on top of him, push my torso up, and bring my leg swinging around so that I sit squarely on top of his keratin-plated back.

Bao tenses. I can feel his intention to buck me off building in the coils of his muscles, but before he can act on it, a wave of noise paralyzes him. The trainer deck erupts into cheers.

It comes all at once, in a cacophony of shouts and hollers and slaps on the back. But the pirates aren't cheering for me. They're celebrating what I've done, and a horrible, sick feeling rushes over me as I realize exactly what that is. I've taken a monster used to destroy them and tamed it in their favor. I've hatched the enemy's tool and shaped it into something they can wield. And here, sitting squarely on his back, I'm the very image of a conqueror, my full weight thrown on the subjugated.

I'm not a girl. I'm a symbol.

And I represent everything that I shouldn't.

The shame burns from the back of my eyes and I feel tears start to well up. But I can't let them see how this is affecting me. I've got to keep playing the part they want me to play. So I wind my fingers tight around a plate protruding from Bao's neck and thrust my fist in the air, swallowing back the salt water threatening to drown my eyes.

I force myself to smile when the cheers get louder.

13

Swift pretends she's not interested in the training process when she knows I'm looking at her, but I catch her curiosity out of the corner of my eye. Whenever I change around the patterning in the LED beacon, I can feel her leaning over to get a good look at what I'm keying in. She reminds me of a cat who used to lurk around the pens back home. He'd try to steal fish right out of our feed buckets, but if you ever caught him looking at one, he'd feign disinterest and start preening himself. Swift's not out for fish, though—she's just morbidly curious about the way a Reckoner becomes a fighting machine.

"You can ask questions, you know?" I tell her one afternoon while I work with Bao on the "stay" command. It's slow going because he's already got it so ingrained into his system that any LED signal means come to the ship and get fed. I have to start getting him to notice the nuances of the lighting patterns.

Swift ruffles her side-swept hair and folds her arms. "Fine. Why's he such a slow learner?"

"'Cause he's a terrapoid. His brain's not as suited for this kind of stuff. Anything reptilian is a brute-force sort of animal. Cetoids are much faster—mammalian Reckoners have more logical capabilities. And..."

Swift catches my pause and mulls it over before prompting, "And?"

"Simioids," I tell her, and even saying the word brings a shudder up my spine. "Simioids are the fastest learners, but that's what makes them so terrifying. You guys ever run afoul of one?"

"I don't even know what 'simioid' means."

I kick on the LEDs with the "stay" patterning and Bao wavers, still puzzling whether he's supposed to keep where he is or come in. "Monkey-type. They're much smaller animals, but their intelligence is through the roof. I never want to be a simioid trainer. It's the one type of Reckoner I've always refused to work with."

"How come?"

"People aren't even sure if we should be making simioids. They've been shown to have really advanced language capabilities, and there's an argument in the Reckoner development community that by making them, we're engineering a new intelligent species. We've had a few simioids in our pens, and... I don't know, you look in their eyes and you can see it. See them as thinking beings. And it's never felt right to me."

Swift scoffs. Her hand drops to the pistol in her holster,

and I steel myself. She always touches the gun right before she starts a fight.

"What?" I ask. There's no avoiding a spat, but if I play along, maybe we won't waste much daylight on it.

"Thinking beings, huh? You're all soft over a bunch of genetically engineered monsters, but those same monsters go out to kill thousands of people and you're fine with it?"

My lip twitches involuntarily, and for a moment I forget Bao, forget training, forget anything but meeting Swift's fiery gaze. "The people Reckoners kill are pirates. Murderers who sack ships and steal from the innocent. Excuse me if I have more sympathy for a trained animal."

There's something Swift wants to say. I can see it in the way her lips tense as if she's about to spit the words out, but she curbs herself and instead mutters, "Can I try the thing with the lights?"

It's the first time she's ever asked to be involved in something related to Bao, and it throws me off. I don't realize that I've frozen until she checks me with her shoulder, crouching to the level of the LED's controls. "I, uh … sure," I manage to say.

We're in the beginning stages of training. There's no harm in her learning the basics of the beacon, though I'd hesitate to teach her anything beyond things like "stay" and "come." And it could be useful—if I'm out in the water with him and he gets rowdy, it'd be handy to have someone on deck who could throw him a signal.

"How do you make it change?" she asks, her hands already prying at the switches.

I take a knee and slap her fingers away from the controls.

"Opcode. Basically throwing down the right switches. You memorize the switchboard and hit the ones that give the right command." I can't show off every combination without confusing Bao, but I've had the board memorized since I was ten. "First switch is the basic 'come' command. It's the easiest to key in, so someone can bring in a Reckoner and put them to rest no matter what." I flick off the other active switches, and the LEDs flash with the homing signal.

A plume of steamy breath jets from where Bao floats, and the pup swims right for us, the water cutting in a neat V-shape around his snout. When he reaches the beacon, he knocks it once with his nose and then tilts his head back, his mouth hanging expectantly open.

"Toss him a reward," I press, elbowing Swift.

She reaches into the bucket, pulling a face as she squelches a fish in her grip. Then she straightens and holds it out over Bao, her other hand resting casually at her hip.

The pup's eyes flick upward.

"Wait—" I start, but there's no time for warning. I leap for Swift and wrap my arms around her waist. She shrieks as I haul her backward. Bao lunges.

He surges halfway out of the sea, his eyes bulging, his razor-sharp beak snapping shut with a wet *crack*. His body slams against the trainer deck, sending a tremor through the metal floor below us as we hit it. Bao bounces off the rim of the deck and slips back below the waves, bellowing once before the water closes over his head.

Swift lies paralyzed beneath me, the pulpy remains of the fish stuck to her hand. It's fallen on the deck in two pieces, cracked in half by the sudden impact. But her hand's still there, not down Bao's throat, so at least something's gone right for a change.

"I said *toss*," I hiss through my teeth, my face pressed flat against the deck.

"Sorry," she groans.

"Do you have to taunt every living being you come across?"

"I think you broke something."

"At least you've still got your arm," I spit. "Moron."

Swift claps me on the back with her gut-soaked hand. I elbow her in the stomach and roll off her, landing flat on my back.

And then somehow we're both cackling. Not the quiet chuckles at each other's expense that we've shared from time to time, but the raucous laughter that comes from sheer relief and the adrenaline in our blood gradually slipping away. A flush fills my face.

Swift catches my gaze, and she laughs even harder. "You look like a tomato!" she crows, trying to wring the slime from her hands.

"At least I don't snort when I laugh," I wheeze between breaths.

This only makes her snort harder. She picks up half of the fish and throws it at me. It hits me in the shoulder with a wet slap. "You're so good at it—why don't you give him the fish?"

I sit up, ready to leap on her again, but then the second half of the fish comes flying at my face. "Jesus Christ, Swift!" I yelp, swatting it away.

"Yeah, that's right, here's your uncivilized pirate wench," she cackles, rolling on her side and pushing herself to her feet.

A bellow from the water marks Bao's impatience. I pull a fish from the bucket and pitch it out into the sea, not caring where it lands.

As I sit there, taking in the bright world around me and the damp deck beneath me and the blood that's rushed to my face, I finally take stock of what's just happened. I was in a situation where I was completely safe, where Bao couldn't touch me. And I threw myself headlong into his path, just to save Swift from her own stupidity.

Swift, my captor. But Swift, the reason I'm still alive.

Swift, my guard. But Swift, my guardian.

She's saved my life, and I've saved hers. Well, saved her arm, at least. Bao probably would have ripped it clean off if she'd left it there a microsecond longer. I acted without thinking. Maybe there's some instinct deep inside me that wants to save people; maybe that's why being a Reckoner trainer feels right, why I leapt for Swift the instant I realized she was in danger. Maybe I'm a good person at the core.

But in the back of my head there's an insidious little voice telling me, "You're part of the ship now."

The laughter we shared sours in my memory, and I fight to keep my face straight.

Then the all-call crackles on.

"This is navigation," an unfamiliar voice drawls. "We've picked up a bucket on our instruments three leagues to the North. Unescorted. The captain says we're hitting it. Prepare accordingly."

14

A change comes over Swift as soon as the all-call snaps off. The dog is gone; she's all wolf now.

"Bao can't keep up," I tell her.

She doesn't seem to care. She strides for the door into the *Minnow*, her shoulders squared, her right hand on her pistol as she cranks the hatch open with her left.

"Swift, wait—*Bao can't keep up.*" I stagger to my feet and lunge after her, but she slams the hatch just as I hit it. There's a click beneath my fingers, the click of the lock sliding into place.

She's gone mad with power or fanaticism or *something*. She can't possibly be thinking straight by locking me down here.

But it's about to get worse. If the ship takes off without Bao and leaves him far behind, he won't catch up. It's a rule of Reckoner training. You don't leave a pup unattended in open water. Without supervision, a Reckoner pup could wander off into the wild or submerge, never to be heard from again. We take careful precautions to ensure that none of our beasts go missing, installing tracking tags on all of them at the minimum. But Bao doesn't have that luxury. If he's gone, he's *gone*.

Which means I have to act fast.

Swift didn't leave me a radio, so I can't hail the captain and tell her what's happening. All I have at my disposal is what's left on the trainer deck...

And the deck itself.

I know what I have to do. I swallow back the knot of fear building in my throat and step up to the deck's edge. Above me I can hear the pounding of feet as the ship prepares for battle, and below the engines are starting to hum. I haul the beacon up over the deck's lip and drag it backward until I've positioned it in the middle of the deck.

Bao lets out a confused bellow. He knows the engines are firing up, knows that he should be backing away to a safe distance, where the subthrust won't scorch him, but we were right in the middle of training. His pattern's been interrupted; he's looking for guidance.

And so I give it to him, slamming my bare foot down on the LED beacon. The lights flare under my foot as the homing signal snaps on.

The pup groans, his beady eye peering up onto the trainer deck.

"C'mon, you little shit. I know you can do it," I mutter under my breath, but Bao's not having it. The engines are spinning up now, sending a deep rattle through the deck below my feet.

If I'm going to get him up on the deck, I'm going to have to do something really stupid. I thrust my hand in the bucket of fish and come up with a bundle. As the noise beneath my feet builds to a roar, I hold them out over the edge, right over Bao's head.

His nostrils flare.

I'm ready for it this time, and I dive backward when he lunges, his powerful legs scrabbling against the deck. His claws leave dents in the floor as he heaves himself forward, his belly shrieking against the metal.

I stumble and fall, but I can't let that slow me with a Reckoner pup the size of a Jeep bearing down on me. I toss the handful of fish at his snout, and he opens his jaws wide, catching two of them on his lolling tongue. Water seeps off him, nearly flooding the deck, and it strikes me that if the tank he hatched in were set up, he wouldn't be able to swim in it. Bao's eyes roll as he swallows, his legs kicking half-heartedly as he tries to slide himself closer to the beacon.

"You're fine, you little idiot," I huff, throwing another fish to distract him. I roll onto my belly and crawl over to the LEDs, hitting the off switch before Bao starts to confuse himself.

The all-call crackles on again and the voice declares, "Engines report ready. Brace for ignition in three."

Shit.

"Two."

I scramble to my feet and throw myself toward the switch that closes the bay doors.

"One."

There's a scream beneath my feet and a rattle from the mechanism. The *Minnow* leaps forward like a horse from the gate, the deck rearing up just as the rear bay doors slam shut. I wind my fingers tight around the nearest handhold, my muscles burning.

Bao slides backward, squalling the whole way until he crashes into the bay doors. The spray from the boat's wake washes through the side ports as we accelerate, and after a few seconds I can loosen my grip without worrying about flying into Bao's reach.

I didn't think this through. Bao can only handle being out of the water for so long. His skin will dry out, his own weight will sag against his internal organs, and he'll only get more stressed the longer he's out of the water. But he's alive for now, and I can work with that.

I grab a mess of towels and wet them in the puddles that have accumulated in the rear of the deck. I can't do anything about his weight without refilling the pool, but I can at least keep him damp. Bao's beak bobs and weaves, following me as I work my way around him, draping the soaking towels over the crucial areas of his skin where the water will seep between the keratin plating.

I've left the side ports wide open. The harsh wind rips at my face, and flecks of seawater fly off the *Minnow*'s hull and into my eyes. It's a bright, sunny day, and I can feel the power of the hunt shuddering through the deck beneath me.

"All Splinter pilots to stations," the all-call demands over the roar of the passing air.

I can only imagine the chaos that must be unfolding in the

abovedecks. A knot of fear builds inside me, a quiet thing that starts at the back of my throat and grows until it burns at my eyes. We're going into battle.

We're going to kill some people.

The ship rocks against a wave and I crouch next to Bao, keeping one hand latched onto the plating on his back in case he tries to make a move. The all-call mentioned that the ship was unguarded. No Reckoner escort means that the ship we're about to hit is going to be armed to the teeth. There will be crossfire, and Bao and I will be right in the thick of it.

His hide's still growing, and it's nowhere near tough enough to stop a bullet. I have to crank down the side ports before the shooting starts or else we're both dead.

I squint against the wind and reach for a handhold, dragging myself along the deck until I reach the switches again. Before I hit them, I take one last look at the open waters, at the wide sky above me and the early autumn sun.

The all-call crackles on again. "Splinters away on my mark. Three. Two. One."

The pneumatics release with a harsh *snap*, and two bright white hulls split from the ship, plunging into the NeoPacific just ahead of me. I lean out over the water, craning my neck to catch a glimpse of the Splinters as they drop back behind us. I spot Swift's wicked grin as she hunches over the controls of one and Varma's easy smile as he slouches in the cockpit of the other.

"Splinters away," the all-call announces.

There's a scream like a jet engine and the white hulls take off, their needle-shaped forms skimming over the tops of the waves like gulls as they shoot ahead of the *Minnow*. Three others join them, one circling wide from the aft of the ship and two cresting out from the other side of the stern.

They're our herding dogs. When we get within range of the ship's sensors, it will bolt. The Splinters are the ones that'll slow it down. Any decent-sized Reckoner could snap a Splinter in half with a single bite, but an unescorted ship would be hard-pressed to hit one with their artillery. The guns aboard the needleboats are weak—nothing hull-piercing—but they're enough to bring most other ships to a standstill.

And that's when the *Minnow* will pounce.

This is going to get messy fast, and I need to keep out of it. I crank down the doors as quickly as the mechanism will allow and slide my way back over to Bao. With a layer of metal between us and the waves at our hull, it sounds like we're in a washing machine, surrounded by the muted churning of the sea.

Bao hates it. I can see the stress eating away at him. He's got his head drawn back into his body, his chin rocking back and forth on the floor as he lets out a long, keening groan. His blowholes flare in and out rapidly, and all I can think right now is how lucky I am that he's not an ichthyoid or a cephalopoid or anything that couldn't handle a stint out of the water.

But he's still a Reckoner, and they're meant to swim. His body is designed to rely on the water's support, and though his keratin plating shields him on the outside, it also weighs against him in ways that I can't fight for long with the tools at my disposal. I've got the wet towels, but that's about it.

All I can do is wait and pray.

If Swift had waited three seconds before running off to kiss the captain's ass—if she'd just *listened* to me, the only person on this boat who knows how to keep the damn beast alive—we wouldn't be in this mess.

She's not on my side. I'd almost forgotten, what with the sleeping in her bed and the joking around and the lessons about Reckoner training. Her life may depend on mine, but she's only interested in saving her own skin. For a few minutes there today, when we were both earnestly laughing, I'd forgotten what she was.

The *Minnow*'s pace slows. We must have caught up to the ship. The engines' pitch descends until their low thrum rattles the deck beneath us, matching Bao's groans. With the partitions down and the engine noise masking his complaints, we've managed to almost completely disguise the fact that we've got a Reckoner onboard.

It hits me. This is the first time in weeks that we've come into contact with another ship, the first time since we left the *Nereid* to sink that there've been good, decent people nearby. People with radios and uplinks. People who could tell my parents that I'm alive, who could get an armada on our tail, rescue me, and confiscate Bao.

People whom Santa Elena is about to butcher.

I want to throw up the partitions and toss Bao into the water. I want to dive in after, to flail my arms and scream for help. I want to get aboard that ship and find their radio, call home, get someone to come *save me*.

But there's a flaw with that plan. I'm on the *Minnow*,

coming from the *Minnow*. They'd see me as a pirate before anything else, and they'd shoot me on sight.

I'm all by myself down here, locked away from everyone that might hear me, so I feel no shame when I suck in a huge breath and scream like I've been stabbed. Bao jerks his head at the noise, but he's too weak out of the water to do anything about it. I let my lungs empty until the sound chokes off, and when I draw my next breath I feel lighter.

So I scream again.

But this time I can't get it all the way out before a loud explosion rocks the ship, causing the deck beneath my feet to lurch. Bao kicks, his claws scrabbling against the metal floor.

It's starting.

Muffled thuds ring out from the upper decks as the *Minnow* returns fire. They'll target the ship's engines first, taking out any chance of it fleeing. That's part of the reason Reckoner trainer decks are positioned right over the engines. A boat that's dead in the water is so much harder for a beast to defend, so we keep the Reckoners' focus close to the thrusters.

My first solo battle, on the *Nereid*, was so atypical. I'd been utterly focused on Durga back then, and I'd seen nothing but the *Minnow*'s victory in the aftermath. A sick sort of curiosity grips me, a frustration that I can't see the attack in progress. Dad taught me the basics of pirate tactics when I was little, and I want to see them put into practice.

Once they take out the engines, they'll target whatever artillery's trained on us. I'm guessing that starts with whatever shelled us in that opening shot. The Splinters are probably already seeing to that. When they disable those guns, they'll pull up alongside the ship and throw down the ladders.

And then comes the part that I don't want to think about, but I *have to*, because of Captain Carriel and all of the dead crew I left behind when Swift dragged me off the *Nereid*. They're going to swarm this boat, and they're going to kill everyone onboard who fights back. Bullets will find brains, knives throats, until the decks are wet with blood. I saw the bodies last time, the crew that had put up a fight laid out in the open. This time, I won't know what they look like. I'll just know that they're all dead.

Once they've eliminated the crew and disabled the communications, they'll loot the ship. They'll take every last piece of valuable equipment, tear out the tech, strip out the wires. Hina and her team will raid the kitchen, and tonight we'll feast like kings.

No, *they'll* feast like kings. I'll be fighting too much nausea to take from the spoils.

Bao's my only comfort as the fight grows louder and louder. He's breathing slower now, his blowholes flaring, his sides heaving in and out. I kneel next to him and press one hand flat against the towels, feeling the steady pounding of his massive heart beneath them.

Another shell hits the ship.

I replace my hand with my head, letting the thunder of his heartbeat drown out the noise of the *Minnow*'s wrath. *We're alive*, I remind myself. My cheek is damp against the towel, my hair plastered to my head. With my nose this close to him, I can smell the faint carrion stench he carries, and it reminds me of Durga. Of the last time I saw battle.

Of the time I was ready to do anything I could to save that ship.

Have my weeks aboard the *Minnow* changed me? When the *Nereid* was under attack, my very first thought was not for myself, but for Durga's well-being and the passengers on the ship. But the situation I'm in is so far removed from anything I trained for. My Reckoner's life is synonymous with my own now, and there's a pirate girl thrown into the mix. When I forced Bao to board the ship, who was I saving?

Who was I supposed to be saving?

Another shell.

I curl up against Bao, folding my arms around my knees. I don't want the other ship to win. I just want it to be over.

15

Finally the noises of the fight fade away, replaced by the sound of heavy footsteps above, laden with the take from the ship. I roll up the trainer deck doors and dive into the sea behind the *Minnow*. The sun's gone down, but the waters are lit with dancing flames. My stomach churns as I take in exactly what Santa Elena has done to the ship we hit.

It's burning from the inside out.

They fought back viciously, and this is how they paid for it. I shudder, imagining what would have happened to the hundreds of people aboard the *Nereid* if I'd thrown Durga into battle instead of reining her in.

Bao perks up once he realizes that the water is within his reach again, and this time he needs no signals or encouraging. He kicks and scrabbles against the deck until he topples back into the NeoPacific with a shriek. The water paralyzes him and for a moment he simply floats, catatonic. After all the stress he's been through today, he's as at-risk as he was when he first hatched, and I realize with a sinking feeling that I'm going to have to sleep on the trainer deck to keep an eye on him for the next few days.

With the flames from the ship heating it, the water's unnaturally warm for a night in the middle of the ocean. I let myself hang for a moment, watching as the hull blisters and crackles. We'll be underway soon. If the ship managed to get out a distress call, there'll be aircraft inbound to pick up the pieces.

If the wreck wasn't so... on fire, I could find somewhere to hide. Somewhere the pirates wouldn't realize I'd slipped away, where I could wait for the searchers to come. Provided they're coming.

But the ship is on fire. Just a blazing ruin, a star of heat in the middle of the ocean. The closest thing I had to a chance at escaping is now a smoldering heap of metal, waiting for the sea to consume it.

I could probably construct it as a cosmic sign, a flashing neon banner emblazoned with the words *YOUR LAST CHANCE AT FREEDOM*. I'm not likely to get another.

The trainer deck hatch is still locked, but there are other ways of getting into the *Minnow*, and now that Bao's back in the water, there isn't much more that I can do for him. A righteous anger crackles through me as I swim around the ship's portside and find a series of handholds built into the hull. My grip is unsteady, and several times I plunge back into the water and have to start all over again, but I'm on a mission. I'm not going to let some slippery ladder be the thing that stops me tonight.

When I finally manage to swing myself onto a deck on the ship's lower levels, I can't help but pause. I've never walked these halls without Swift escorting me. Theoretically, there are several people on this ship who want me dead, and now's their perfect chance. I can hear the thunder of celebrating pirates from all the way down here. No one's concerned about the captive Reckoner trainer, and no one would notice if she disappeared.

But I've got business to deal with, so I start off toward the mess, leaving a trail of water in my wake.

———

I burst into the middle of the celebrations without anyone noticing. The entire crew seems to have packed themselves into the mess hall. There's food flying, stringers injecting, and a thrumming beat blasting from speakers as the pirates relish their victory. When they took down the *Nereid*, the feast was reserved. But this was such a vicious fight that they can't help but go a little wild. I didn't even realize I was starving, but the sight of the fresh food laid out has me salivating within seconds. The air is thick with sweat and the bitter scent of stringlets, which the pirates pass around like candy.

I spot Swift tucked away in a darkened corner with a girl on her lap and Code slumped next to her, nursing a bottle. He perks up when he sees me, one eyebrow arching. "Hey, Swift, your wife's here," he says as I approach, his words scarcely audible over the din. "And she don't look too pleased."

Swift startles. Her arms slide from around the girl's waist and she almost stands, then seems to think better of it. "How the hell'd you get here?" she asks.

"Took the long way 'round."

Her eyes are rimmed with red, and a stringlet needle dangles from her elbow. The girl pushes out of her lap and disappears back into the crowd, leaving Swift looking rumpled and flustered. "You're lucky," she slurs. "You could have been killed coming up here."

It's taking everything I've got to keep myself from punching her again. "You want to talk lucky? Your worthless ass is lucky that I got the damn beast on this ship before it took off, that I had the sense to take care of the thing that both our lives depend on after you *locked me on the trainer deck.*"

"Can't hear you," she mouths. "Too loud."

I grit my teeth and lean in, propping one foot up on the bench next to Swift as I tower over her. A satisfied smirk curls over her lips, but I can't let that throw me if I'm going to make her understand just how pissed I am at her. "You almost got us both killed," I start, yelling right into her ear. "If you had just *listened* to me instead of rushing off at Santa Elena's whistle, we could have kept Bao in the water, and you'd still have taken the ship."

I draw back, searching her for any sign of guilt or worry or any of the things I want her to be feeling, and for a second I think I see it in the glint of her eyes as they wander. Her expression shifts, and I can see her on the cusp of spitting something out, see the gears in her brain churning as she tries to process this information.

And for a split second, just when the light shifts, I stop seeing and start noticing. I notice the muscles in her jaw pulse as she bites her lip, notice the curve of her collarbone where her tank top has shifted, notice the imprint of teeth on her earlobe.

Something lights inside me.

It's not like with the girls I've dated at school—no, she's too much of a disaster for anything like that. She's a *pirate*. But there's a hunger in Swift, and maybe it's just my trainer impulse that makes me want to feed it for a moment.

Then her attention flicks back to my eyes. "When an all-call goes out that we're about to hit a bucket, I'm at the captain's side no matter what. If I'm not there for her, I'm as good as dead anyway. It's your job to save my skin when the beast is concerned."

Moment's over.

"Also, you're dripping on me," she adds.

I push away from the bench and catch Code's eye. He sniggers, taking another swig from his bottle. "C'mon, have a stringlet or something. You need to relax, girl."

"No thanks, my life's a living hell already," I snap back at him. "Swift, I'm sleeping belowdecks tonight. Bao needs to be observed after today's ordeal. No need to come get me."

She shrugs, her hungry eyes roaming over the crowd of pirates. "Was probably going to need the room to myself tonight anyway."

I don't have anything left to say to her after that. I scoop some of the spoils onto a tray and carry it with me down into the bowels of the ship. Since I'm still locked out of the trainer deck, I find the closet full of cleaning supplies where I spent my first hours on this ship. I close the hatch behind me and feel around for the switch. When I flip it, a bare bulb flickers on, filling the closet with a dim, sickly light.

In the thick of the fighting, I thought I'd be too nauseous to eat the food we took today, but the dead aren't using it, and my stomach is growling. I eat with my hands, running my fingers over the tray until I've scooped up every last bite. The meal sits heavy in my stomach, but not on my conscience.

It should horrify me. It doesn't.

16

I get used to sleeping on the trainer deck again. Santa Elena's liable to burst in at any time, but it's the closest thing I have to a space to call my own on the ship, and with a few extra pieces of bedding ferreted out of Swift's laundry carpet, I make the counter comfortable enough that I no longer wake up sore.

Autumn deepens, and in bits and snatches of conversation that I catch from the crew in the mess, I discover that it's the last week of September already. If all had gone right, if the *Nereid* had continued her voyage, I'd be back in school now. I'd be a high school senior, trying to convince my parents that I don't need to go to college, that I can be a trainer full time, that my future is in the industry.

Given the circumstances, I think that future's been dragged out back and shot.

But I've fallen into the *Minnow*'s rhythm so easily. I sleep with the trainer deck doors wide open, listening to the sea against the ship's hull as I drift off and rising when the sun crests over the horizon to glare murderously into my eyes. In the hours before Swift comes to drag me to the galley, I hop into the sea with Bao and give him a once-over, and it's in that moment each day that I let myself pretend all of this isn't happening. In the cradle of the NeoPacific, with the *Minnow* to my back, I imagine that I never left home, that this massive, round baby is just one of the new additions to our stock and I've been assigned primary care on him.

I slip a respirator over my nose, dive under his belly, and check for any abnormalities, making sure that his keratin plates are fusing properly as he grows and ensuring that he hasn't run afoul of anything that might hurt him. I make a mental checklist of everything I notice, imagining that when I turn around and swim back, I'll be pulling myself up onto the meridian between the observation bays and logging all of my data in a logbook. But it's always the keel of the *Minnow* that greets me when I leave Bao's side, and I always haul myself up onto the trainer deck, disappointment gnawing at my stomach.

But it might just be hunger, since I don't get to eat in the morning until Swift comes. She's almost always late. On the one hand, I want to accuse her of doing it purposefully, but she always looks so disheveled when she forces her way through the hatch and slumps in the door frame, waiting for me to get my act together. I think she just always sleeps in.

I'd buy her an alarm clock, but I don't exactly have the means.

I start to get more privileges as the days wear on, and finally Santa Elena presents me with a key to the trainer deck that was formerly Hina's. "You've learned the ship well enough that I think it's time you get some say in your protection," she says when she presses the little sliver of metal into my hands. "But just remember—if you get yourself killed, my girl goes too."

I want to tell her that Swift's well-being has no bearing on the risks I take, but I know the captain can smell lies.

It's not that I care about Swift; she's one of my captors, one of the people who makes my life a living hell on a daily basis. But I slept next to her for a month and learned all of her little quirks, and when you know a person to that level of detail, you can't get them killed.

Since she doesn't have to escort me to meals anymore, I see less and less of Swift. As one of Santa Elena's lackeys, she's part of a rigorous, strange training program that I observe from afar. Each of the five has their own unique focus, which they learn at an advanced level and help pass down to the others. For Chuck, it's the mechanics of the ship. She spends all day in the engine room, and, from rumors I hear tossed around the deck, she sleeps there most nights rather than in her own bunk. Varma trains with the helmsman, learning the art of maneuvering the ship. It's occasionally his fault that we lurch against a poorly placed wave, and once I almost chew him out when the *Minnow* clips Bao under his command. I'm fairly certain it wasn't an accident. I don't dare speak up, though; anything that calls attention to myself and what I'm doing makes me a target.

Code has the job that I least understand, maintaining the ship's navigation systems. The computers are complex, artful things, and he has an uncanny way with them. Lemon's apprenticed to the lookout, and of the five of them, I'm convinced she's the smartest. She has a strange intuition for the sea and somehow feels the squalls before we ever see them. Of all the lackeys, she seems like the one most on my side—she always passes an alert down to the trainer deck when we've got something bad on the radar, and I've been able to get Bao to dive every time.

Swift's apprenticeship has her maintaining the ship's guns, Phobos and Diemos. When the captain isn't on deck, she climbs up on top of the barrels and suns herself like a big cat.

Bao's training crawls along. With fewer resources and only one trainer, he can't pick up things as quickly as most of the pups in our stock back home, but he gets by. We usually have a robotic sub to tote around beacons for teaching dive commands, but I take its place, the massive LEDs strapped to my chest and a buoyancy vest locked around me to prevent the extra weight from taking me to the depths. I start to introduce more audio signals to the visual training—things that draw Bao's attention to the beacon so that no matter how distracted he might be, the lights still call him, still have him under their command.

By mid-October, he's clearly recovered from the ordeal that left him beached on the trainer deck, and his repertoire has grown to include sustained dives, staying absolutely still, and even basic fetching, which we practice with a life preserver until the day he grows too big to hold it properly in his jaws.

But the harder stage is still to come, and it's something the *Minnow* is woefully unprepared for. Back home, the owners of the Reckoners in our stock buy ships that have been decommissioned: tugs at first, but eventually even aging yachts and warboats. Those skeleton ships become practice targets for baby beasts that need to cut their teeth. First we train them to ram the ships, then to target their guns, Finally, when they're big enough, we teach the Reckoner pups how to crack a tug in half, and everything from then on out is instinct. But I doubt Santa Elena's going to let me loose Bao on one of her precious Splinters, and until I come up with an alternative, his training will stagnate.

But the captain won't notice. Not for a while.

And that's what I'm counting on. It's a risk, but it's worth it if it will keep Bao harmless. It gives me more time to unravel the mystery of his origins and figure out how I'm getting myself off this boat.

All the same, I fear the day the captain finds out what kind of games I'm playing.

———

We stop at islands from time to time to trade for fuel and food. I'm never allowed to accompany the landing party, of course. I always get stuck in a Splinter with the homing beacon on my back, left out at sea with Swift to watch over me and Bao. Santa Elena wants to keep her pet Reckoner under wraps—show people something they've never seen before, and they're bound to talk. The captain can't afford word getting out about Bao while he's this young, when he relies on the ship to defend him and not the other way around.

So we wait.

This afternoon, the *Minnow*'s gone to do business with some Islander millionaire who's staked out turf on a chain of artificial atolls, and so once again Swift and I load into the Splinter and put out around a league away, using the LED beacon to keep Bao in place as the ship jets off to the welcoming dock. Bao gets antsy the second the *Minnow* leaves his eyeline, his imprinting behavior taking over, but the lights and noise from the beacon keep him rooted next to us, bobbing at the surface with his blowholes flaring in and out.

I climb out of the Splinter and drop into the sea, leaving Swift to twiddle her thumbs and fiddle with the controls. She's not too happy about this either. She hasn't gotten shore leave since I got on the boat, and as much as she disparages people who live on dry land, she's itching for a chance to get away from the *Minnow* for a bit. "Can't wait for the day when we can just roll into port with this guy," she grumbles, rolling her head back. Her eyes are hidden behind a pair of mirrored aviators.

"I'd say the same, but the captain would probably just lock me in a closet on days like that," I shoot back as I climb onto Bao's back. His keratin plates flex beneath my feet as I scramble to the ridge above his head, where he's grown accustomed to me sitting. The Reckoner pup makes an exasperated noise, but he doesn't shy under my weight.

Swift's grown a little colder after our encounter the night that the pirates took down that other ship. She doesn't try to joke around with me, doesn't try to participate in Bao's training or anything. I shouldn't be too bothered, but before that day it felt like at least I had an ally on this boat. Now I have nothing.

Well, I have a fat baby sea monster. But Bao doesn't tell jokes, and somehow I need that.

I hate how I need that.

"How heavy is he?" Swift asks.

I want to shoot back "Hell if I know," but that's not constructive—it's not what she's looking for. I shrug, glancing over my shoulder at Bao's length. Reckoners are designed to mature unnaturally fast so they'll be ready to serve as soon as possible. Bao's growth has accelerated so quickly over the past few weeks that he's now large enough to take down a neocete. He never finishes his meals, though, and often ends up following the *Minnow*, dragging a carcass behind him like a pull toy. It's disgusting, but also sort of adorable.

"Maybe fifty tons?" I hazard. It's difficult to judge by sight, but he's around the length of a semi truck. "He's been gaining weight like crazy, now that he's got neocetes in his diet."

Swift nods, then lets her head roll back against the headrest, her fingers tightening on the controls. "I remember someone telling me that neocetes are just fleshdumps for Reckoners to eat."

"I mean, they're genetically engineered, just like the beasts. They're meant to be extreme omnivores so they'll survive in any climate, and they have to be slow-swimming enough that pretty much any type of Reckoner can take them down."

She lets out a low scoff. "That's super messed up."

"You ever had beef?" I counter. "Same thing, except meat cattle live in packed conditions and get slaughtered en masse. At least the neocetes live a natural life."

Swift pauses, considering the perspective like she's testing the taste of it on her tongue. "I just like neocetes. Like 'em lots more than cows, that's for certain."

"They're smarter than cows. They're in a similar class with most toothed whales. Orcas, dolphins, you know. Social creatures."

"Yeah, that's why I like 'em. Stop making me sympathize with them—you're just making it worse," she grumbles.

I laugh. It's pure nature that Reckoners eat neocetes. If we hadn't created a prey animal to feed them, they'd have devastated the NeoPacific's biosystem within months of the first beasts' creation. We gave the Reckoners an easy target, and in the process spared pretty much every other animal in the ocean. It's one of the reasons that the IGEOC regulations exist. Only a certain number of Reckoners can exist at a time without depleting the NeoPacific's stock.

Of course, Bao throws a wrench in that plan.

Unregulated Reckoners aren't supposed to happen. If Bao's the only one, it might be okay, but if a whole ocean of pirate-grown Reckoner pups crops up, it will wreck the biosystem. I don't know what circumstances led to Bao being in Santa Elena's possession, but whatever they were, they were orchestrated perfectly. He hasn't shown any sign of growth defects—in fact, he's grown far faster than any Reckoner I've ever raised. He had to have been created in a lab at some stable, because no independent lab without IGEOC support could produce a beast so perfectly made. He came out of the purse with no obvious defects, so whatever journey brought him from that lab to these circumstances had to have been carried out flawlessly.

Could he be stolen property? I've never heard of a stable

reporting theft of a pup, but then again, the IGEOC would shut down any stable that admitted to theft of their stock. Maybe someone's covering for a missing pup, reporting him as unviable on paper. It'd certainly explain how he showed up out of nowhere. But the infiltration of a Reckoner facility would involve an elaborate heist, not just the brute force I've seen the *Minnow* display. Maybe Santa Elena hired out some independent contractors to pull it off.

I almost ask Swift. When I glance up at her, the words building in my throat, her gaze is fixed on the distant horizon. Not toward the shore where the ship's disappeared to, but somewhere farther than that, out on the open sea. Her lips are set in a bitter line.

Better not to show my hand now. Better to let her dwell on whatever it is that has her thoughts.

We wait out the rest of the afternoon, me on Bao's back and Swift in the Splinter, until the *Minnow* appears on the horizon again. I stay on the pup while Swift jets back toward the ship, but Bao can't resist his imprinting. He swims after her, nose pointed directly at the boat he's come to identify as his home and charge. I watch from his back as claws on tethers descend from the ship, scooping the Splinter back up into its resting place. Swift gets out to meet Code and Chuck, who wait for her on the deck with packages in hand. She snatches the goods roughly from their grasps, and something clenches inside me as she moves out of sight.

17

I always knew the *Minnow* kept its looted treasures locked up somewhere. What I didn't know—at least until today—is that the place doubles as a training ground.

"Welcome," Swift says in that half-baked tour guide voice, "to the Slew." She claps me on the back, and a jolt runs up my spine. Recently, she's been trying to make up for the way she treated me in the days after we hit the unescorted bucket. Most of the time, it's by inviting me along whenever the lackeys do something dangerous. It's sort of unnerving, but I can't deny that these little excursions past the trainer deck make me feel... well, at home.

It's weird to say that about a pirate ship, but embracing that sort of weirdness is the only way to keep going around here.

The curve of the ship's hull bows out around us as we descend the steps to the mats, which have been nailed in haphazardly amid stacks of cargo. My gaze fixes on a bright floral suitcase tucked behind a crate, and on the wads of cash stuffed in its pockets. It's child-sized.

The hold is packed with crew. Swift makes for a corner, where the four other lackeys are gathered in a knot. As we approach the wall, I spot a familiar face among the crowd— the girl who was in Swift's lap the night we sunk the bucket. For a moment, I fear that we're headed for her, but then she spots Swift and glares. And Swift glares back.

And something triumphant lifts inside me before I can stop it.

As we reach the lackeys, Code taps Chuck on the shoulder and a feral grin curls its way across her face. "Fists?" she asks.

"Anything for you, princess," Code simpers.

Varma's lip curls, and Swift jabs him in the ribs as she takes her place next to him. I hang back, a nervous energy humming through me. When Swift invited me to see the best show on the ship, I didn't anticipate anything like this.

As Code and Chuck step onto the mats, they tip salutes upward, and I spot the captain perched on a stack of crates in the ship's prow, her son at her side. Santa Elena bares her teeth and salutes back. The boy sits up straighter.

"Slew fights," Swift mutters over her shoulder, beckoning me closer. "First rule: if the captain says it's over, it's over. Second rule: if a crew member calls it, the captain has to finalize the call. Third rule: if you break someone bad, you fight the captain. Rest of it's pretty straightforward."

"You ever fought the captain?" I ask.

Swift snorts. "If I'd fought the captain, I wouldn't be standing here."

Varma's lips twitch another notch upward, though his eyes never leave the lackeys on the mats. "Captain took this ship single-handedly. You fight her, you come out in pieces."

I can feel Santa Elena's gaze on me even before my eyes flick up to meet hers. She flashes me a wicked grin and tilts her head toward the mats, a question in the quirk of her brows. A hollow, sinking feeling floods me as I understand exactly what she's challenging me to do.

I pull back into the shadows.

Under the harsh glare of the industrial lamps, Chuck and Code square off. There's no opening bell, no whistle, no countdown. Code simply leaps forward, and Chuck's forearm is there to parry. The crack of knuckles on flesh snaps through the hold, and the fight is on.

But I soon learn that a good fight is mostly about waiting. They dance around each other, Code with quick, elegant steps, Chuck with smoothness and deliberation. When one of them makes a move, the other matches it. Chuck has power, but Code has speed. Chuck has endurance, but Code's reflexes are faster. Her shirt stains with sweat before his does, and on the sidelines, Varma's muscles wind tenser and tenser.

"Don't look so moon-eyed, loverboy," Swift growls, nudging him with her shoulder. "Your princess still has gas in the tank."

Because the captain's attention is fixed on the fight, I feel bold enough to speak up. "Is she ... is she actually a princess, or are you guys just saying that because she's ... "

Varma raises an eyebrow, but Swift shrugs and says, "Chuck was the only daughter of the man who owns Art-Hawaii 5. Took to mechanics early. Father didn't take too well to that—Islander princesses should be running businesses, not sneaking off to repair engines, you know? So when it got to be too much, Chuck stole down to the docks and begged aboard the first vessel she found with an engine that . . . what was the phrase she used?"

"Felt like home," Varma fills in.

"Right. Captain didn't want to take a big spoiled princess onto her crew, but then Chuck got in the engine room. No more doubt after that."

"You were there?" I ask as Code ducks into an opening and lands a flurry of punches. Chuck staggers backward, then swings with a vicious uppercut that grazes his chin.

Swift nods. "Chuck was the last of us. Lemon came a year before. Captain picked her up from an Aleutian colony after she heard the local gossip about a girl who could speak the ocean's language."

Before I can confirm that Lemon speaks *something*, a burst of action on the mats draws every eye in the Slew. Code's made a misstep, Chuck lunges, and a hiss rises from the crowd.

Her fist drives into his temple.

The cheers that echo through the hold swallow the sound he makes when he hits the mat. Varma throws his hands in the air, and up on the crates, Santa Elena leans forward. "That'll do," she thunders.

Chuck steps back, running her hands through her hair as a grin cracks over her face. My lips curve involuntarily, and pride flushes through my body as Varma rushes to her side. I can't resist it. The celebration sweeps me in, and I find myself trailing in Swift's wake as she hops up on the mats to congratulate Chuck.

But then Code is crawling to his feet, his eyes narrowed, his face flushed, and the first words out of his mouth are "I'm not finished." He fixes Swift with his pale stare and lifts his chin. "You. Knives this time."

Swift freezes, her gaze flicking up for the captain's approval. Santa Elena nods back.

One of the crew members on the sidelines tosses two rubber training daggers to Code, who offers one to Swift blade-first. She takes it with a scowl, flipping it over once and catching it by the hilt. "You sure?" she asks, and no one in the Slew misses the way she hesitates before bringing her knife up.

"I'm just getting started," he snarls. "Clear the mats."

I follow Varma and Chuck back to our corner, where Lemon is still lurking. Under the lights, Code and Swift circle each other, the tips of their blades dancing back and forth. He makes the first move.

A good fight is mostly waiting.

This isn't a good fight.

Code comes at her with an animal's voracity, his knife plunging straight for her throat. She catches his wrist and twists, but he flows with the movement, bringing his elbow down hard on her sternum. Swift chokes out a gasp, staggering back, but Code keeps coming even as she raises her blade and slaps it hard across his forearm. He doesn't slow.

Then Varma's voice is in my ear. "All you need to know

about those two is they came on this boat on the same day. Him in slavers' chains, and her of her own volition."

It's a harsh reminder of how far from home I am. Out here, beyond the regulation of any state, people can be bought and sold. And it makes me reconsider everything I know about Code. A boy who started with nothing, and now he's clawing his way to the top of the *Minnow*'s food chain. No wonder he fights so viciously.

My nails dig into my palms as Swift hits the mat with a thud that drives the air from her lungs. Code's free hand latches around her neck just as her legs swing up. She punts him over her head, and he collapses in a seething heap.

Swift props herself up on her forearms, her eyes darting to the captain.

Santa Elena ruffles her son's hair and smirks. She won't call it. Not while they're both still fresh.

Murmurs roll through the crowd as Code and Swift stagger to their feet. The fight's hit its first lull at last, leaving them catching their breath and rolling their shoulders. Code adjusts his grip on his knife and raises his eyebrows, daring Swift to make the next move.

She sweeps her hair out of her face, sticks the hilt of her blade in her mouth, and grabs the hem of her T-shirt.

Oh no.

Swift peels her shirt off, and the crowd collapses into whistles and hollers as she balls it up and pitches it to the side. Her back is already slick with sweat, shimmering in the harsh glare of the industrial lamps overhead. Her lips twitch devilishly upward around the knife's butt, and for a moment—a horrible moment—she catches my eye.

I blink and stare at the floor, wishing I could drain the blood from my body just to keep it away from my cheeks.

Swift is hot. It's a fact, simple and scientific and unnoticed until the day you think too hard about it, and then it's everywhere.

She plucks the knife from her mouth, licks her lips, and lunges forward. But even as she twists in midair to dodge Code's swipe, it's clear she's miscalculated. Or he's calculated more. His free hand snaps out, latching onto her hair. He gives it a brutal yank, wrenching her backward as his blade comes down hard on her bare stomach.

But he doesn't stop there. The rubber knife tumbles from Code's hand as he hauls Swift upright. His fist drives into her jaw, and the Slew erupts with shouts from the crowd.

The captain doesn't call it.

Swift's too busy trying to pry his hand from her scalp to block the next punch. It splits her lip. His knee smashes into her stomach, and she lets out a bloody gasp as Code shoves her backward, sending her sprawling on her back.

His leg is halfway into the kick when Santa Elena snaps, "Enough!"

Code's toes stop just short of Swift's ribs. He scoffs, rolls his shoulders, and turns his back on her, trotting over to rejoin us. At the edge of the mats, he pauses. "Hey Swift," he calls.

She groans, still flat on her back.

"How about you try something a little more your speed."

And before I can pull back, Code lunges forward, grabs

me by the wrist, and yanks me onto the mats. A murmur of surprise rises from the crowd. He steps around behind me and shoves me in the back, sending me stumbling toward Swift.

The brightness of the lights is paralyzing. Up above, the shadowy figure of Santa Elena has risen to her feet. When she speaks, it feels like her words surround me. "Do you have any combat training, Cassandra?"

The mutters in the crowd complete her sentence. *Or do you let your monsters do all your fighting for you?*

I tell her exactly what she wants to hear. "None whatsoever."

Swift crawls to her feet. She swipes at her busted lip, drawing a thick red line across the back of her forearm. Her hair is a ruffled mess, half of it flipped the wrong way over, the other half hanging in her eyes. "Boss—" she starts, still a little winded.

Santa Elena cuts her off with a wave and says to me, "Land a hit on her and I'll call the fight."

It might be the most generous thing the captain has ever offered me. There's still a part of me that balks, that wants to jump off the mats and retreat to the safety of the trainer deck. But after almost three months of making myself as small as possible on this ship, I can't pass up a chance to be a little big again.

And I've landed a hit on Swift before.

I bring my fists up and square off, and immediately the Slew echoes with shouts of glee. I meet Swift's eyes.

But she's laughing at me as she sweeps back her hair. "You

hit me like that and you'll break a thumb for sure," she snorts. "Fists with thumbs on the outside."

I frown, adjusting my hands.

"And keep your weight back. That's where your power comes from."

"You sound like you want me to hit you."

"You look like you need all the help you can get." She brings her own hands up, palms open, and takes a step forward.

My first swing is downright embarrassing. I aim for her shoulder, but she sidesteps me easily and swats my hand to the side. I expect her to counter, but the hit doesn't come. Instead, she circles around and squares off again, waiting for my next move.

When I catch her gaze again, her smile is utterly teasing. There's heat rushing through me now, and it's not just the industrial lights above. My whole body is coming alive, and as I raise my fists again, I let my own grin curl across my lips.

I can play at being part of this.

I can have *fun* with this.

At my back, the noise of the crew has grown louder. And it's not just cheers for Swift. Cries of "Get 'er, shoregirl" rise from the shadows, and when my eyes once again turn upward, Santa Elena passes me an encouraging nod.

I take another swing. And another. Swift slaps them away, but I keep a rhythm going. She favors her right hand, and so I try coming from the left. Her reaction is slower—I almost make it through. Our eyes meet.

She winks.

Swift steps around me, and I nearly trip over my own feet trying to reorient myself. Chuck cackles from somewhere in the crowd, but I let it blend with the rest of the noise. Everything else falls away until it's just me and Swift and the steady, predictable rhythm of trying to break her defenses. Every time I swing, she's there to meet me, catching or deflecting each punch I throw.

I catch the shift in her smile before the shift in her strategy, but it's too late. She aims a kick at my knee that takes my feet out from under me, and I crumple onto the mat. A flush of humiliation rushes through me. I shouldn't have fooled myself into thinking she'd stick to pure defense, not with the captain and most of the crew watching.

Swift grins out at the crowd as if sharing a joke with them. Grins for a moment too long.

I push off the mat with every ounce of energy left in me and lash out at the leg she's leaning on. My heel strikes true, and Swift collapses on all fours.

The Slew goes wild. But over the noise of the jeering pirates, I hear the soft words that mean the most. "That'll do," Santa Elena says.

I roll my head and once again find Swift's eyes. I expect her to be furious, embarrassed, or somewhere in between, but as she pushes herself to her knees, there's nothing but pride in her smile. "You might just fit in here after all," she says.

Three months ago, I would have hated those words. But today, under the bright lights with a crowd cheering at my back, I'm starting to like them.

18

With Bao's training stagnated, I start to follow Swift around during her training exercises. As long as I don't directly interfere with anything, I lock up the trainer deck, and the captain doesn't notice my negligence, I figure it's only fair that I get a better sense of how things work on this ship. Plus Swift seems glad for company that isn't in direct competition with her.

One overcast afternoon in the second week of November, I watch from the back wall as she and the other lackeys gather around the helmsman for lessons on piloting the *Minnow*. My attention constantly flicks backward to check on Bao. He's big enough that he hunts during the day and homes back to the ship at night, so he doesn't always roam within sight of us. Still, I rest easier knowing that he's there. I don't know what might happen if his imprinting behavior mucks up, if he suddenly wanders off and never returns. Reckoners don't usually do that, but there's a first time for everything, and Bao is full of surprises. Briefly I wonder how long it would take Santa Elena to notice if he vanished.

I let my focus shift back to the five trainees crowded around the helmsman, a stout old man named Yatori. He's spitting out some lecture about the ship's mechanics, his voice stuck in a nasal drone that nearly puts me to sleep. Chuck and Varma look bored too. As an enginesmith and a helmsman's apprentice respectively, they've heard this spiel about powering the *Minnow*'s engines at least a hundred times before.

Swift, on the other hand, looks like she's about to pop, like everything the helmsman is saying is completely over her head. I can understand most of it—stuff about currents, about the way the ship handles in different types of water—but Swift looks like she needs to be taking notes to get all of it down, and I start to feel sorry for her. I *know* she's clever, but this kind of learning just isn't her style, and she has so much riding on her ability to memorize this stuff. Any good captain should be able to pilot her own ship, and if Swift ever wants to fill Santa Elena's shoes, she'll have to be passable at helming the *Minnow*.

I watch the little tattoo on the back of her neck snap up as Yatori calls on her.

"Take over," he instructs, lifting his hands from the controls.

She slides into place, her shoulders squared and tense as she takes the helm. One of her hands rests on the wheel, and the other slaps the radio on the dash. "Swift to engines, report when ready," she says. She's trying so hard to sound authoritative.

"Engines ready," the engineer's voice declares a second later. "On your mark."

Swift nods. "Minimum thrust on my count. Three. Two. One."

The ship lurches forward, and I glance over my shoulder again to catch the jets of mist as Bao surfaces behind us, already nosing forward to keep up. It doesn't take much. A few strokes of his legs, and a hundred and fifty tons of young Reckoner is on our tail. He's been growing at an alarming rate, and he's nearly half the size of the ship now. For a moment, I feel a flash of pride surge through me, like my kid's just won first place in a fifth grade track race.

Swift rolls her head until her neck pops, and I notice Chuck and Varma exchanging glances. This is usually where things go south. When Swift has manual control of the engines, she can't keep them steady.

Her hand shifts from radio to throttle, then back to radio again—she's forgotten to hail the engine room and instruct them to make the switch. "Swift to engines, prepare to transfer control to me on my mark."

"Ready," the radio cracks.

"Three. Two. One."

The *Minnow* bucks so forcefully that I stagger forward, grabbing a handrail to stop myself from stumbling into Lemon and Code. Our pace slows to a drift, a low rumble shaking the tower beneath us.

"Engines to helm, adjust to match engine spin immediately or relinquish control, confirm decision," the engineer demands.

Swift lunges for the throttle and throws it down. The machinery underneath us groans, but the engines catch, and the ship lurches forward again. "Swift to engines, adjustments made."

The ladder from the belowdecks rattles, and two seconds later, Santa Elena clambers up into the navigation tower to join us. She's got her hair pulled back and that one coat on, the long black number that makes her look especially commanding.

"Captain on deck," Code mutters to Lemon, and there's a joke inside those words, something that makes her mouth twitch into a tiny smile.

"I had a feeling it was you," Santa Elena says as she circles around Swift. She folds her hands behind her back, peering out the rear window to catch a glimpse of Bao.

Swift keeps her head down, her gaze focused on the controls.

I can feel myself tensing up in the captain's presence. I press back against the wall I'm leaning on and pray that her attention doesn't swing my way, that she doesn't question my presence on the bridge. We haven't talked about Bao's training in weeks. Any time she feels the need to give orders, they come through Swift. I don't know if she's noticed the stagnation, and I know I'm going to pay dearly on the day that she does. But until then, Swift's bad driving is more than enough to distract her.

"Orders?" Swift asks the captain, letting one hand slip from the wheel.

Santa Elena glances down at the compass on the dash. "Eastern heading, cruising speed."

We're heading West right now. Swift grits her teeth and yanks the wheel hard. Everyone in the tower reaches for a handhold as the ship swings around, its hull plunging deeper into the ocean as we lean into the maneuver. Swift pumps the throttle forward a tad, giving us a boost of extra speed that sinks us hard and sure into the turn.

I would have thought that the captain's presence would throw Swift off, but she's piloting better than ever with Santa Elena breathing down her neck. I guess there's something about the pressure that she exerts on her crew. When the captain's not around, they don't feel as compelled to perform. But when Santa Elena's eye is on you, you're at your best or you're out, no questions asked.

Swift hauls the boat straight as we line our sights on the eastern horizon. She cranks back the throttle and lets the engines spin down to cruising speed.

Then a plume of mist jets out of the sea in front of us, and a primal fear grips me so tightly that I almost lunge forward and wrest the wheel from her.

We're headed straight for Bao.

Swift's hands shake on the wheel, and Santa Elena leans in close. "Graze him," she says, like it's a joke.

"No," I breathe, before I can think better of it, and the captain's attention snaps around to me.

"Problem, Cassandra? Your beast not smart enough to get out of the way?"

"He hasn't been trained to respond to threats—I don't know how he'll respond. I don't know *if* he'll respond." It's a fight to keep my voice even, a fight I'm desperately losing. I can't give orders, can't tell Swift to deviate or slow or anything that I want to scream into her ear. I can only stare down Santa Elena, doing my best to hold her fiery gaze, and pray that she doesn't extrapolate from what I just blurted.

"Swift?" the captain calls.

"Yes, boss?"

"Hold course."

I push myself off the wall and dive between Code and Lemon, stumbling up to Swift's side. I'm waiting for someone to step forward and yank me back, but no hand lands on my shoulder and no shove comes to push me away from her. "Slow down a little, at least. Could you do that?" I hiss.

She glances at Santa Elena, who nods back.

Swift strains against the wheel, her grip sliding just a bit as she reaches for the throttle and cranks the ship back into a drift. We're still bearing down on Bao, but we have time on our side now. "I'd appreciate it," she grunts, "if you didn't breathe right in my ear."

"You hit him hard, we're dead. You glance off him, we might live, but it's doubtful." I watch Bao out the front windows, see him stop and wait, his head weaving back and forth as he tries to make sense of his imprint ship heading straight for him.

Reckoners aren't born with fighting instinct. They're trained into it. He won't attack the ship. He wouldn't—it's not in his nature. But a spark of doubt ripples through me as I see him snap his beak and blast another spurt of air through his blowholes. Bao's always fallen on the less predictable end of the spectrum. Maybe today's the day he shows us what an unregulated Reckoner truly is.

Grazing him wouldn't be enough to put a dent in the ship, but his claws are razor sharp, definitely strong enough to slash the hull. Nothing that will sink us, but Santa Elena's put us on a collision course that could get the *Minnow* crippled.

We're seconds away from impact as his head disappears below the boat's stern, and we're bearing just a little too far starboard for my taste. "Port," I snap at Swift.

She doesn't adjust. Her hands are frozen on the wheel.

I slam down my hands over hers and yank left. The floor lurches underneath us as the ship swings, and out of the corner of my eye I spot Santa Elena flailing for a handhold. An indignant squall echoes out from below us, but there's no thud of impact and no shriek of claws on metal. We've steered clear.

But I haven't.

Santa Elena grabs me by the throat before I have time to flinch. My feet lift off the ground as she twists and slams me back against the wall, and my world goes dark for a second. A wave of pain crashes over my head, but through it I can see the captain's bared teeth leering in my face.

"Maybe I've let you get too comfortable," she hisses, fingernails digging into my skin.

I struggle to breathe, my throat convulsing under her grip.

"You don't touch her controls. You *never* touch my ship like that again. Next time it happens, I cut a finger off. Each time you go against me, you lose another finger. When you're out of fingers, you're out of luck. Am I clear?"

I nod, just a twitch of my head. "Perfectly," I choke. "Ten chances it is."

She blinks, and then the sharp-toothed smile is out. She's impressed. Her hold loosens, and I slump against the wall, my lungs working like bellows to heave in the air that I've lost. For a moment, my vision spins.

I find Swift's eyes when I've recovered, and she looks like something's shredded inside her. But when my gaze meets hers, she blinks and stows the expression, her face settling back into that hardened mask that she always wears for the captain. Her hands are still locked tight around the wheel, keeping the ship on the course Santa Elena ordered her to take.

"Yatori, take over," the captain instructs the helmsman. "Put us back on our old heading. I want us at the Flotilla in two days. The rest of you, clear out. Lesson's been learned."

She hops back down the ladder, and her lackeys follow her one by one until it's just me, Swift, and the helmsman left in the navigation tower.

Swift moves for the ladder, then pauses. "Are you getting up?" she asks me, but she's masking something with that question.

"I have to ... go make sure Bao's uninjured," I rasp.

Then she does something unexpected, something she definitely wouldn't do in sight of the captain. With a furtive glance over her shoulder to check that Yatori's distracted by the controls, she reaches down and offers me a hand. "C'mon, quick," she hisses.

Though the pain in my back is screaming for me not to, I take her hand and let her drag me to my feet.

Everything's happening too fast for me to take it in. Maybe the captain's right. Maybe I've gotten too comfortable in my position aboard this boat. Maybe I *deserved* to get slammed into the wall like that, and the pain that rattles me now is a reminder of my place. I catch myself. It's disgusting, letting her make me think like that. I don't *deserve* any of this. I deserve freedom and safety and a thousand other things that aren't available on this ship.

I must look particularly woozy, because Swift's still holding on to me. I steady myself and let go, tottering toward the ladder. It's a miracle I make it down in one piece.

After what just happened, I don't feel safe wandering the halls of the ship alone. Every corner is a risk, and the shadowy light doesn't help. I descend into the bowels of the *Minnow* by myself, making my way back to the trainer deck and vaguely wondering if Reinhardt is allowed to treat damages inflicted by the captain.

I round the corner that leads to the trainer deck and freeze. A chill floods my veins as I take in the sight. This isn't possible. This can't be happening.

The hatch, which I left locked, is wide open. Someone is on the trainer deck.

19

If I hold my breath, maybe I can fade back into the shadows. Maybe I can escape without being noticed. But someone is on the trainer deck right now, someone who isn't supposed to be. And if they're making a pass at Bao, I need to do everything in my power to stop them.

But I'm not brave enough. My head is pounding, my breath is coming in little ragged gasps, and it's taking everything in me to lift up one foot after the other and creep closer and closer to that open door. The LED beacon hums to life, and I recognize the homing command that rattles through the deck. They're summoning Bao.

If I don't stop them, I'm dead anyway. That seems to be the only reason I do anything these days. So I creep forward until I'm right on the other side of the entrance, my fingertips curling around its harsh metal edge. I have to force myself to crane my neck forward until I catch a glimpse of the figure standing in the middle of the trainer deck, staring out at the Reckoner's approaching bulk.

It's Code. And in his hand is a massive syringe filled with a syrupy, cyan liquid.

Cull serum. I'd know it anywhere.

When Reckoner pups are still embryonic, there's an evaluation period that ends one of two ways. If the pup is deemed healthy, it stays in stasis until someone commissions it. But if an IGEOC agent marks it as unviable, the pup gets an injection. One little syringe is enough to kill a fetal pup. Cull serum is designed to dismantle them from the inside out, and it's one of the only reliable ways to kill a Reckoner.

Bao is massive, but there's no telling what a dosage that strong could do.

There's a clatter of noise, the thunder of footsteps behind me. Someone else is coming, and if I know my odds, it's someone with the same goals as Code.

I jump, pressing myself back into the shadows just as Swift skids around the corner and bounces off the wall. She barrels onto the trainer deck, letting out a primal roar as Code whirls to meet her. He tosses the syringe to the side and whips out his knife, but Swift doesn't slow. She twists away from his reach as Code slashes, and the blade carves a neat red line in her side.

I should step forward. I should help. Swift can't take on Code alone—he beat her in the Slew. But I'm frozen.

I'm not a fighter.

Swift grabs his other arm and yanks hard, throwing him back against the wall. Something's been unleashed inside of her. She's an absolute animal. Code tries to raise the knife, but she slams her elbow down on his wrist, and the weapon pops from his grip.

"You son of a bitch—you thought I wouldn't notice my keys were missing?" she gasps as the knife clatters to the ground.

"You picked up on it much faster than I'd have thought," he spits, straining against her hold. For a moment they shudder, locked in tension. Then Swift's arm slips, he kicks her legs out from under her, and all of a sudden she's on the ground, scrabbling for the knife. Code throws himself on top of her just as her fingers close around the hilt, and she gasps, trying to swing the blade around. He catches her and twists her arm.

Swift bellows in pain. The wound on her side is starting to stain her shirt. "Where's Cas?" she hisses through gritted teeth. "What did you do to her?" The muscles in her arm strain as she tries to bring the knife around.

"I didn't—" Code chokes.

I force myself to stop thinking. I'm not going to sit here and let Swift save me all by herself.

I'll save me too.

And so I plunge from the shadows and sprint for them, grabbing Code by the shoulders and yanking back with all of my might. He lets go of Swift and swings at me, but she lunges up and locks her free hand around his throat as together we shove him back against the trainer deck wall.

"Please," he croaks, but Swift presses the knife against his neck, and he falls silent, his arms going slack.

"You stupid little shit," she growls.

My arms are shaking, but I keep them fisted in his

windbreaker, ready to hold him back if he tries to make a move again. I'm not sure if I can. He's skinny and wan, but he's bigger than I am.

"Kill me now then," Code whispers, and he starts to lean forward against us, letting his throat jut into the knife.

Swift tilts the blade so that it presses flat against his skin. "I'm not going to do that. I'm going to march you right to the captain, and we're going to see what she does with you."

I didn't think it was possible for Code to get paler, but he does.

She nods down to the radio on her belt. "Cas, call her up."

I let one hand slide from Code's jacket and pluck the radio from her hip. Still shaking, I skim past the all-call channel, bring up the captain's private line, and hold the device up to Swift.

"Hey, boss. Just caught Code trying to kill our pup. Had the serum and everything. I'm bringing him up to you in a minute."

"Is he subdued?" Santa Elena asks, and I can't miss the pleased note that echoes in her voice.

"Yeah, I've got him."

"Bitch," Code spits.

"I sincerely hope that wasn't aimed at me," the captain says. "Bring him on up. We'll have a little chat." The channel clicks off, and Code slumps. He's finished.

Swift yanks him off the wall and shoves him toward the trainer deck door. I wait until she's slammed the hatch behind her before sinking down onto the floor, the strength evaporating from my legs.

I should have seen this coming. I've let myself get so comfortable aboard the *Minnow* that I nearly got myself killed twice in one day. If Santa Elena hadn't been quite as forgiving, if I'd walked onto the trainer deck without noticing something was amiss, I'd be just another corpse floating in the ship's wake.

If it hadn't been for Swift, that definitely would have happened.

I find myself wishing the captain hadn't muddled the waters by tying Swift's life to mine. I have no idea who Swift's saving at this point. Obviously her own skin is her top priority, but when she charged onto the trainer deck to catch Code in the act, she thought he'd already done away with me.

And she was going to *kill* him for it. Of course, if I'm dead then she's dead anyway. She fought like she had nothing left to lose, and she bled for it. But the way she asked about me, the venom in her voice when she thought Code might have killed me—it makes me reconsider what I know about her.

The facts are these. Swift has saved our lives on several occasions. The only thing I've done for our lives so far is not get eaten, shanked, or shot.

I'm still not sure if I'm in debt or not.

The engines beneath me fade to nothing as the boat slows. Santa Elena's probably decided to stop while she sorts out Code. I don't want to think about what that entails.

Bao bellows from the far end of the trainer deck. I get on my knees, crawl over to the LED beacon, and snap it off. He presses his beak against the still-warm lights, and I feel the deck shudder just a bit underneath me. At half the boat's size, he's easily powerful enough to push us around. If he were in a proper training environment, he'd be deemed ready to start escorting his imprint ship.

He's probably big enough to take down the *Minnow*.

I peer into the water, watching as the trunks of his forelegs sway back and forth in his shadow. They're huge against his body, now that he's grown into his adult proportions. The sun is setting on the other side of the boat, and the long shade of her guns stretches out into the sea like ragged claws. My heart still thunders in my chest, and Bao watches me with eyes the size of dinner platters.

I don't care that I'm not in my wetsuit, that I don't have my respirator around my neck. I jump into the water headfirst. Bao shies away from me, the suction in his wake almost pulling me beneath the waves, but I fight against it, keeping my head over the water. Once he settles, I swim forward and grab onto his plating. *I'm here,* I will him to understand. *Don't forget.*

I move down his side, checking for any signs of damage from the hull. Every time he draws a breath, his flanks swell out several feet, pushing me away before drawing me back in again. If I close my eyes, I can pretend that it's Durga. I can pretend nothing's changed. I can pretend I'm safe at home. It's the same ocean, after all.

There are no wounds in Bao's hide and no sign of bruising. I circle him twice, just to be sure. By the time I settle back by his head, clinging to a plate on his jowls, the sun has sunk below the horizon and my heart has stopped thundering. I haul myself up until I can stare directly into his eye. "Hey, little shit," I mutter, and Bao pulls his head up, lifting me halfway out of the water, just like Durga used to. A bitter smile twists my lips. "Saved your ass today, and what do I get for it?"

Bao only blinks.

I shake my head and haul myself higher, slotting my bare feet into the gaps in his armor until I can clamber out on top of his skull. He's used to my weight there. He keeps absolutely still, waiting for me to make my next move. There's still a glow on the horizon that lights the sky afire, and I turn my face toward it, wincing as Bao releases a rancid breath from his blowholes.

They can try to kill me all they want, but I'm the girl who stands on the backs of the beasts of the NeoPacific. The *Minnow* blazes from within, promising life and warmth and villainy, but out here I'm mighty.

Or at least Bao's mighty, and I'm with him.

I stretch my arms up toward the sky, where the first faint lights of the stars are starting to peek through the hazy cloud layer that's settled over us, and remind myself of what's important. I have to survive. Bao has to survive. And, after what happened today, I think it'd be kind of nice if Swift survived this mess too.

My clothes are drenched, and the chill of the night is settling in. I leap off Bao's head and plunge back into the water, swimming to the trainer deck in a few quick strokes. The Reckoner turns tail as soon as I'm clear and submerges, his dark form plunging deeper and deeper below us. If he were still a pup, I'd be worried, but Bao's fully bonded now, and he always comes when I call. I haul myself up onto the trainer deck and drag the LED beacon back to its usual resting place.

My eyes fall on the syringe of cull serum. Santa Elena had this on the ship the whole time. Only IGEOC agents are supposed to have this stuff, and somehow it ended up on the *Minnow*. And Code stole it. He knew what it was, what it was for.

And there's something more, something I noticed that's itching at the back of my mind. Swift knew what it was too.

I pick up the syringe and pitch it out into the inky November sea. One more mystery to unravel later.

I need dry clothes, so I lock the trainer deck's hatch behind me and make my way to Swift's room. She still isn't back yet, and for a moment I worry that Code overpowered her before she could get him up to the captain's quarters. I've got to start having more faith in her if I'm ever going to pay her back for saving me. I pull open her hatch—unlocked, like she always leaves it when she's not there—and step in.

Swift's room is starting to smell like home. There's always that scent—the one that sticks in your memory but doesn't really surface until you find it again and all of a sudden it's crashing over you like a wave. I guess I've collected a lot of these scents over the years: the sickly sweet smell of amniotic fluid from Mom's lab; the rough, earthy tones of a Reckoner's hide; and now this, the sort-of-musty, sort-of-woody odor that characterizes the little nest Swift's carved for herself in the middle of a den of pirates.

Her floor's still carpeted with dirty clothes. I've yet to see her wash them, but I know she must because there's definitely some sort of rotation going on, and there's always clean stuff in her drawers. I nudge one of them open and root through it until I find a tank top and a set of shorts that I quickly swap into, dumping my soaking wet clothes in a less-than-convenient heap by the door. I shake out my hair while I'm at it. It falls in my eyes now. Maybe I'll live long enough to grow it back to shoulder-length.

For a moment, I consider going back to the trainer deck, but all I can see there is Code with the knife, wearing the invincible grin of a boy who's trapped an animal in a corner. Tonight, that place is haunted. Here is safe.

So I sit on the edge of Swift's bed and wait until I hear the shuffle of her bootsteps in the corridor outside.

"Cas?" she calls as she sticks her head through the door. She rolls her eyes when she spots me perched on her bunk. "Should've known. You *are* aware that you leave a trail of water pretty much anywhere you go, right?"

"What happened to Code?" I ask, drawing my knees up to my chin as she pushes into the room and closes the hatch behind her. Suddenly my chest feels tight, like I've dived too deep and the pressure is crushing my lungs.

Swift pauses, and something bitter flashes in her eyes. "Captain's having a long chat with him. She threw me out after a point. I dunno what she's going to do, but I don't think I wanted to be around to see it anyway."

I don't know how to tread here. She's been on this boat for five years, and so has he. And they've been working closely together for at least a year. The night after we took down that bucket, they were celebrating together. Code with a drink in his hand, and Swift with a girl in her lap. But then that afternoon in the Slew a month later, Code had it out for Swift. He wanted to humiliate her, to make her suffer.

And today he wanted to kill her.

I remember how it felt in the Slew, with the crew's support at my back. That invincible, top-of-the-world feeling—to have that all the time, to have the loyalty of the *Minnow*. For a moment, I let myself crave it.

For a moment, I understand why Code would do anything to captain this ship.

"I'm sorry," I tell Swift, figuring it's the best I can do.

Swift shakes her head and pulls up her shirt, revealing a fresh bandage that's been slapped over her side. She catches my eye. "Tried to tell the captain it was nothing, but she insisted on having Reinhardt patch me up."

"It looked pretty bad. Are you sure it's okay?"

She shrugs, yanking her shirt over her head. "It'll be a scar, that's all."

"Just adding to the collection?"

"It's yours, I guess," she says, then draws a sharp breath as if the words came out wrong.

I wrinkle my nose. "That's hella weird, Swift. It's on *your* body, for Christ's sake."

She chuckles, grabbing an oversized T-shirt from the drawer. "It's my body, but I don't let it get carved up by meaningless marks. Every one of them's got a story, and every one of them is for someone. This one's for you. Deal with it."

"Am I supposed to say thank you?"

"You can if you want," she says, grinning impishly as she starts unlacing her boots.

"Well, I did kind of want to thank you—not for naming your weird scars after me, but for, y'know, saving my life back there. Even if you were just saving your own life, I mean...what I should...thanks. Just...yeah, thanks."

Swift freezes, her mouth slightly parted, and for a moment I think she's going to tip over with her boots half off.

"Also, can I sleep here tonight?" I blurt before I can think better of it.

The impish grin is back. "Knew you weren't buttering me up for nothing," she chuckles. "Yeah, it's fine. Dunno why you sleep out on the trainer deck anyway."

"Bao grew out of his snoring. You haven't."

Swift throws a boot at me, laughing as I bat it away. "He's okay, right?" she asks as she turns her back, works the other boot off, and shucks out of her pants.

I keep my gaze lowered, pretending that I have no interest in her bare thighs and what lies above them. "If you're going to kill him with your driving, you'll have to try a little harder."

Swift rolls her eyes, steps into a pair of shorts that she plucks out of one of the laundry carpet's corners, and climbs into the bunk, crawling past me to take her usual spot along the wall. But this time she settles facing me, folding her arms and letting out a long breath. "I guess I should thank you too," she says, her voice low and quiet.

"For?"

"Basically the same thing."

I scoff.

"No, seriously. If you hadn't jumped in...I mean...both times..."

"You aren't too good with words, are you?" I rib at her, lying back and propping my head up against the wall as I swing my legs into bed.

"Captain put me on guns for a reason."

"Mhm."

She kicks the light off, and it takes a second to adjust to the sudden black and the glow seeping in through the hatch. I drop my gaze to the pirate girl curled up next to me, but Swift's eyes have already slid closed. Her shirt has ridden up a bit, enough for me to see the stark white of the bandage peeking out.

I think about what she said, about each of her scars being "for" someone. It sounds stupid. I've got scars, sure, little ones that dot my body from a lifetime in one of the most dangerous environments a child can grow up in. I've even got faint sucker marks wreathing my ankle where a cephalopoid pup got hold of me once, and I sure as hell didn't get those "for" anybody. But if Swift wants to name her wounds and count her scars, so be it. I guess it's not my business, except for where that one scar is concerned.

I wonder what it will look like when it's healed. I let myself imagine the future Swift, with a neat white line slashing across the slab of skin that the bandage now hides. As much as I hate to admit it, a part of me wants to stick around and see how it turns out. If Swift's decided it's going to be mine, I can play along.

I drift off slowly, listening to the thrum of the engines and the hiss of Swift's breathing until some combination of the two lulls me into unconsciousness.

In the middle of the night, I wake up to find that Swift's shifted, one of her arms thrown lazily over my waist.

I decide that I kind of like it there and let the rhythm of the sea rock me back to sleep.

20

The next morning, we wake to Chuck throwing the door open, slamming it into the wall with a thunderous crash. She's got a manic grin plastered on her face that only gets wider when she sees me in the bed and Swift's hand trying to sneak back over the crest of my hip.

"I thought you sleep on the trainer deck," she says, glee sparkling over her round features. For a moment it seems she's forgotten why she came bursting in, but then her brow shoots up. "Captain's ordered everyone down below. Apparently we've got a traitor in our midst."

Something horrible is about to happen. There's a beast in my stomach, clawing to get free, and the sensation persists as we get dressed and sprint down to the trainer deck, joining the throng of crew packed in there. Swift immediately plunges into the crowd, heading straight for the captain. I reach out, hook my fingers in the back of her jacket, and let her guide me forward.

Of course it's Code that's caused this commotion, but I still gasp when I see him. His skin is patterned with bruises. Some must be from Swift, but others dot his body in places I know she didn't hit him, and I'm sure they belong to the captain. He keeps his left hand clenched around his right, and when he shifts, I can see why. His index finger, the one that used to bear the inking of a little fish, has been sliced clean off.

Santa Elena stands behind him, one hand clenching his shoulder, and I'm convinced it's the only thing keeping him upright at this point. The captain's eyes glint when she spots me and Swift heading straight for her. "Glad you could join us, kids. Didn't want to start the show without you."

"What's going on, boss?" Swift asks. I let my hand drop from the back of her jacket before Santa Elena notices it.

The captain shrugs. "Spectacle, mostly."

Swift and I slot in next to Varma and Chuck. I glance over my shoulder to find Lemon hanging back against the wall, pressing herself as far away from the crowd as possible. Her eyes never leave Code, and I feel a twinge of sympathy for the lookout trainee. She and Code spend all day in the navigation tower together, and I get the sense that he's the closest thing she's ever had to a friend.

I set my gaze back on the boy who tried to get me killed, shuddering when his electric-green eyes meet mine. Even though he's bruised and battered, Code shows no signs of remorse.

"Right, you bastards," Santa Elena thunders. "Got a bit

of news for you. I figured you'd all inferred that any attempt to mess with my beast or his trainer wouldn't end well for you. Well, this scrap of meat here decided to risk it. And, as you can see, it didn't pay off." She shakes Code's shoulder, and a vicious tumult of laughter rises from the crew.

My heart rate is rising, the anxiety prickling at the back of my neck. I glance at Swift, but she's got her arms folded, her jaw set, and the hint of a cruel smile edging in on her expression. She wants him to suffer, and she's enjoying every second of this.

"Got anything to say for yourself?" the captain asks Code.

He nods. "Not for myself. To her." His eyes fix on Swift, boring into her. "If the captain had put you on the other side of this, you'd have done the exact same thing. You don't get to stand there looking all smug. You'd have come down to that deck with a knife and a needle, same as me."

"I'd have come down to that deck with a gun, you moron," Swift spits through her teeth, and her fists clench as if she's thinking of giving him a new bruise to match the old ones.

"God, can you really blame me, Swift? Like Captain would've picked a nav as her replacement."

"So you decided to try to knock out the gunner kid, because you felt the most threatened by me?" she says. "That's sweet. Really, I'm flattered. But it was stupid, Code. You deserve this."

"What does he deserve?" the captain prompts.

"Whatever you see fit, boss."

My heart sinks, my chest feeling like it's shattered again as Santa Elena smiles, showing enough teeth to put a shark to shame. "Cassandra, weren't you just telling me yesterday that Bao's not ready to fight—that he hasn't got any aggressive impulses because he hasn't been trained?"

This leads nowhere good, nowhere I want to tread. I swallow the knot of fear in my throat and nod.

"I've had this theory about Reckoners for a while, you see. About most beasts, really. Everything fights to survive. Everything's got a base instinct locked away inside it. You and yours train the beasts to release it, but I think you guys give yourselves too much credit. I think he can do it on his own."

No. She can't do this. She can't—

Swift gives me a worried glance.

Code's shaking, but Santa Elena's grip on his shoulder is as strong and true as ever. "Cassandra," the captain says. "Call your beast."

She'll shoot me if I don't. I can see it in the way her hand drifts right to the gun at her hip. She probably wouldn't kill me outright, but if I don't start moving for the homing beacon now, there's a world of pain in my future. Still, I'm rooted to the deck beneath my feet, and I feel like my skin will tear away if I take that step forward.

And then a gentle hand presses into the small of my back, and it's as if my stomach's sunk to the depths. Swift pushes me forward, urging me until I can't resist, until I stumble. I pad over to where I left the beacon last night, feeling as forty pairs of eyes bore into the back of my head and probably other places as well, since the wetsuit I wear leaves little to the imagination. I close my hands around the beacon's handle and lug it toward the open doors, toward the rolling sea sparkling in the morning sun.

I wish the crew were noisier. I can hear every bump and scrape of the beacon's bottom against the deck in the dead silence that pursues me. Careful to keep my hands from slipping, I lift it over the edge and set it on its hooks.

I could key in the wrong code. I could order Bao to dive, and it would take minutes for the captain and the crew to figure out that I hadn't followed orders. But if I bought those minutes, I don't know how I'd spend them. And the cost would be painful. A bullet in a nonessential extremity, or worse, a finger or two gone forever. I feel my own selfishness take root again, that same selfishness that kept me from killing Bao back when he was a pup, that made me hesitate to take the pill when I had the chance.

I flip the switch, hating myself a little more with every blink of the LEDs.

Santa Elena pulls Code over to the edge of the deck. Fear flashes in his eyes, and it twists something deep inside me, something I can't bear anymore. I stand up straight, my fists balled so tightly that my nails bite into the skin of my palms, and say, "Don't do this."

The captain pauses.

"He's not going to become the monster you want him to be if you give him a person. He needs boats to train on— he needs to learn to track LED signals. I've had to stop his training because he doesn't have a ship to wreck, and I'm sorry. I should have told you sooner, and I'm *sorry*. This does nothing. And it's *cruel*."

That's it. I've thrown my cards on the table. I've given her what she wants, what I've been keeping from her for weeks. *Come after me. Do what you want with me, but just leave this boy alone.*

"Swift," the captain says, her steely gaze flickering back to the other trainees lined up on the deck. "Your pet seems to have forgotten her place on my ship. I think you've given her leash a little too much slack. *Rein her in.*"

And Swift, the girl who saved my life, the girl who slept with one arm slung over me, her breathing so close that I could feel it in my hair, steps forward and grabs me roughly by the wrist. "Stand down," she hisses in my ear. "This doesn't help us."

Screw that. I wrench myself from her grip and lunge for the beacon, but Swift surges forward and wraps both arms around my waist, hauling me back deeper onto the deck.

"Don't touch me!" I shout. I don't care that everyone can see me, I don't care that I'm trying to save the life of a boy who tried to get me killed yesterday. I scream and kick and pull at her arms, but her grip is like iron and her will like steel.

Santa Elena laughs. It starts as a chuckle and builds until she's howling, and the crew's laughing with her, their voices a barrage of tiny knives that slash at the strings holding me up. I fight against them, but they keep coming, keep cutting. I've been surrounded by these cutthroats for months, but I've never felt less safe than I do now. My breath's almost choked out of me by Swift's grip, and I realize that I'm crying. Ugly, fearful tears plunge down my neck to join the saltwater of the spray that kicks off the *Minnow's* stern.

Out in the ocean, through the haze of water that clouds my vision, I can see the dark form of Bao approaching, only this time I can't see him as a Reckoner, as my charge. He's a monster, an ancient horror emerging from the depths and coming for blood.

There are only two other people on the deck not laughing now—Swift, who's got her nose buried in the crook of my neck as she tries to restrain me, and Code, who's finally stopped shaking. He's got his head hung, as if he's finally ready for what the captain's about to do.

"Don't," I choke, clawing at Swift's hands. "Please. This is gonna ruin *everything*. You don't know what you're doing."

And for some reason this makes Santa Elena laugh even harder. "Cassandra, this is unbelievable," she chuckles once she's calmed herself. "You raised this beast to do exactly this. You've always raised these beasts to do this."

"I raise ship-sinkers. Not *maneaters*," I sob.

"Eaten, drowned, crushed. Dead is dead. And you raise monsters that deal death because you're too clean to do it yourself. That's shoregirl thinking, kid. Won't do you no good out here."

"Please," I call out again.

"Muzzle her," Santa Elena orders, and then Swift's hand is over my mouth and I'm screaming against it, thrashing, trying to bite, but I can't wrench my jaw open wide enough. I can only taste her skin and see the captain as she turns to face Bao, who's drawn up alongside the trainer deck. His huge eyes roam over the crowd, and his beak rolls lazily open as he leans forward to nudge the beacon, just like I trained him to do.

There's nothing I can do at this point, and it's only now sinking in. Swift must feel the fight leave me. Her arms relax, but she keeps her hand over my mouth, the other clenching my wetsuit. "Cas," she warns, dropping her voice low. "He deserves this."

Those are the last words I hear before Santa Elena pulls out the knife, and the trainer deck erupts into incoherent noise as the pirates cheer on their captain. But the trainees aren't cheering. Lemon's still folded up against the wall, Chuck and Varma are leaning close to each other, their faces set in stoic masks that hide what must be an ocean's worth of turmoil, and I can feel Swift's pounding heart against my back. This is their companion, their comrade who betrayed them and shattered the trust that had grown between them.

This is their traitorous friend, and he's about to die.

I can't look away.

Santa Elena takes Code by both shoulders and leans in close, whispering something that only he can hear. When she draws back, he's crying, his face ashen, his hands limp at his sides. The captain turns the blade over in her hand, then draws it back, and he squeezes his eyes shut.

She thrusts the blade between his legs, flaying his inner thigh open, and a wash of red pours out in the knife's wake. Femoral artery. Clean slice.

Code screams as he drains, his hands clutching the front of Santa Elena's jacket, but all she says is, "Hush," and his grip slips away until she shoves him backward. His arms don't pinwheel—he flops into the NeoPacific with a wet slap, but he still struggles, still tries to swim even as the waves lift him toward Bao.

Don't do it, you shit. Don't you dare.

Bao tilts his head, and I can feel everyone on the deck lean forward to get a better view of the inevitable. Code has stopped screaming. He's reduced himself to messy sobs that grow weaker and weaker with each breath he draws, and the Reckoner looms over him, beak dipping down to sample the bloodstained waters that wreathe him.

Don't do it. Don't—

My thoughts are worthless. Bao lunges forward, his jaws snapping shut, and then Code is in half. His torso disappears down Bao's gullet, and it's merciful because finally, finally, finally his sobbing stops, replaced only with the surge of the monster's body against the sea.

I've never hated Bao more than I do in this moment.

Swift's holding me so tight that she's practically strangling me. She must feel it. Must feel how I'm a beast in my own right, waiting to strike, ready to surge at Santa Elena the second her hold lets up.

She's *ruined* Bao, perverted him even more than he already is. He's been given human flesh as a reward for coming to his goddamn beacon, and I can't erase that. And even worse, Bao's proven her right. He doesn't need fancy training, with beams and noises and beacons to tell him what to destroy. He's already the monster she needs, and I raised him. I could have killed him, but I raised him.

I did this.

I let myself go limp until Swift's the only thing keeping me standing. I keep my eyes fixed on the bloody stain, on Code's legs sinking into the depths, on Bao as he plunges after them.

When Swift lets me go, I run.

21

The crowd parts. That's the first surprise. The second is that Swift takes the time to wait for the captain's approval before sprinting after me. I see Santa Elena nod to her as I glance back over my shoulder. My bare feet pound against the trainer deck as I leap through the hatch and take off down the hall.

"Cas!" Swift bellows from behind me, and it's like a spur in my side. I skid around a corner and scramble up a set of stairs.

I still don't fully know the ins and outs of the *Minnow*, but I know where I can go to escape her. It's somewhere on the ship's second level, near the stern, nested between a set of heating pipes that run down into the engine rooms below. Swift's bootsteps come thundering up the stairs just as I spot it. I open the door, throw myself inside, and slam it behind me.

The harsh scent of ammonia and other weird cleaning solvents washes over me as I clutch the handle of the janitorial closet's door. It feels so familiar, like no time has passed since the first hours I spent on this ship. If I root around on the floor, I'll probably find that little blue capsule again. It's tempting.

The handle jerks under my grip, and I hear Swift grunting on the other side of the door. "Goddamn it, Cas," she groans, but I keep my hold. "What was that shit you were trying to pull back there? Do you want us both killed?"

I'm so out of breath, so disoriented that it takes me several seconds to reply. "You held me back. You stopped me from—"

"You wouldn't have saved him. You would have just gotten us killed along with him. Jesus, Cas, he *needed* to die. He tried to kill us."

"No one *needs* to die," I gasp. "You're so messed up, all of you."

"Cassandra Leung, you're a filthy hypocrite and you know it."

"Leave me alone," I scream. I don't want to hear anything she has to say, not after what she's just done. It's like the nightmare when we hit the bucket, all over again. Swift takes the captain's side no matter what. She's killed for that woman, and she'd die for her.

"You fucking listen to me, Cas. All your life you've killed people like Code. You've sent beasts at us that shred us, that swallow us—you measure their success by the percentage of death they deal. And you do it because they attacked you first. There's no difference between what the captain just did and what you, as a trainer, do *every goddamn day.*"

"You—"

"What was I supposed to do? Let you tackle Santa Elena? Let you push her into the water with your killer beast?"

"You could have——"

There's a hollow thud on the other side of the door, like Swift's just punched it. "There was nothing I could do but save your stupid life, like I always do. Every—every single——"

I can feel a storm building inside me, a fury that won't quiet. Swift has the nerve to compare Reckoner justice to the brutality I just witnessed. She's nothing but the captain's pet, a dog at the end of a very short leash. She's seen nothing of the world I know. "You've never once saved *my* life, you piece of shit," I growl. "Everything you do, you do to save your own neck."

I expect her to scream back, but there's nothing but empty silence on the other side of the door. I keep my fingers winched tight around the handle, ready for her to wrench it open at any minute, but there's only stillness.

Then I hear her sigh faintly, the metal between us warping the sound until it rings. "Did it ever occur to you that your neck might matter to me at least as much as mine? Actually, probably more than mine?" she says.

I freeze, suddenly aware of how my breathing has slowed. I'm trying to picture her on the other side of the door in this moment, but an image doesn't settle. She could be standing, arms folded, wearing that confident smirk that she always puts on when she's teasing, but I seriously doubt that's what's going on. The Swift I picture on the other side of the door is the one that she doesn't let the captain see. Her forehead's pressed against the metal, or maybe buried in her hands, or maybe she's got one hand clutching the handle of the door, waiting for that opportune moment to twist it open.

I don't know what to say. I *knew* she cared for me, but I didn't expect her to come out and say it like this. Sleeping with her arm folded around my waist feels like an eternity ago, a frozen moment in time that I can't fathom going back to. After everything that happened this morning, what did she think this would accomplish?

"Swift," I start, but I don't know what to finish it with.

"Forget... forget I said anything. It was off base. I—"

"Swift, I'm a goddamn prisoner on this ship."

"I know. I—"

"We aren't on equal footing, not in the slightest. You realize how messed up this is?"

"Cas, I didn't mean I want to—"

"I'm in no position to be thinking about any of that shit right now. I've got bigger problems to deal with than you and your feelings."

"I know," she snaps, and there's the thump of her fist again.

I hear voices farther down the hall. People are starting to disperse from the trainer deck and move back to their stations. The *Minnow* will be underway soon.

"I'm sorry. I'm sorry I said anything. Forget it," Swift groans. And then her footsteps fade down the hallway, and I finally let my grip slip from the handle of the door.

I guess I've been fooling myself into thinking it couldn't get much worse, but clearly the *Minnow* has surprises up its sleeves that I couldn't predict. This morning, I had Swift and Bao—the girl and the beast, the beings whose lives were entangled with mine, who were completely on my side. Now Bao's a maneater, and Swift...

Well, she probably doesn't want anything to do with me at this point.

I can't go back to the trainer deck. Not after what happened today. Code's blood probably still stains the floors, and there's no way I'll be able to sleep in my nest there without nightmares of Santa Elena and a raised knife. And Swift's bunk is out of the question.

There's one room on this ship that I know is completely unoccupied, that I know locks from the inside. I shudder at the thought of it, but with no other options, it's only a matter of seconds before I've hauled open the hatch of the janitorial closet and dashed down the hall to the row of trainee bunks. Code's is the leftmost door, positioned closest to the aft of the ship, and of course the door's unlocked, because I deserve some luck at this point. I swallow the images that haunt me, step inside, and slam the hatch behind me.

Though the layout is nearly identical to Swift's bunk, the room feels nothing like hers. For one thing, Code kept his laundry in a plastic sack instead of strewn about the floor. It's organized and bright in here, an outward reflection of the guy who, up until about an hour ago, occupied this bunk. I lock the door behind me and start to poke around in the hidden nooks and crannies, breathing in the details of the navigation lackey, the little pieces that used to make up Code. His clothes are all stacked and folded neatly in the drawers. Maybe he was brought up in a civilized place, or maybe I've just gotten way too used to Swift's laundry-related barbarism.

But he didn't make his bed. The blankets are rumpled, the pillow askew, and I start to wonder if Santa Elena let him spend his last night in here. The thought seems ludicrous, but then I spot the long smear of blood trailing across the sheets, the painted marks of the stump left behind when the captain sliced off his index finger.

Code slept here right before he died.

I reach down and drag the blankets off the bed, tossing them in the corner of the room. Next come the sheets, which I strip off and let fall to the floor. My stomach twists every time I brush up against them, but I fight the revulsion and shove everything into the laundry bag. I'll probably throw it off the back of the ship later, but for now I collapse on the bare, lumpy mattress, bury my head in my hands, and groan until the noise rattles my skull.

Swift and Santa Elena both told me today that I'm no better than them, and the worst part is I'm starting to believe it. I try to remember Dad's lessons on the ethics of Reckoner upbringing, the years of scholarly debate that finally settled into wholehearted support of the industry. Reckoners aren't meant to be aggressive creatures. They only become aggressive if triggered by an attack. It's right there in the name. They're the reckoning that comes crashing down on anyone who attacks their imprint ship, the retribution that deters attacks in the first place. No one in their right minds tangles with a Reckoner-escorted ship, and the seas have never been safer because of it.

But those arguments seem meaningless now.

Dad raised me to kill and justify. I've watched Reckoners destroy ships from afar. I've been standing behind the laser projectors, pointing them at targets that I never attached to faces. Maybe Swift's right. Maybe I've lived a life of convenience. The world out here is cruel and brutal, and shoregirl thinking doesn't account for shades of gray.

What did I become when I resolved to bear whatever the *Minnow* threw at me?

And what was I, to start with? These pirates may be captors and thieves, but they only kill the people who fight back. Their murders are defensive. Every Reckoner attack I've ever facilitated was meant to be utter annihilation. I think of the cabin boys, the cooks, the people on this ship who never lift a finger against us. If I turned a Reckoner on this boat right now, they'd fare no differently than the captain herself.

Swift is right.

Santa Elena is right.

My life's a waking nightmare, and the dead boy's bed I'm lying in is just the icing on the cake.

Bao can go the rest of the day without any supervision. Sure, it's an interruption in his training regimen, but so is being fed a traitorous lackey. My stomach aches and my head is throbbing. I should get up. I should go to the mess and scrounge up some food.

Instead I curl up in Code's bed and will myself to sleep, trying to ignore the voices outside, the engines below, and somewhere off in the distance, the calls of the monster I raised.

22

I wake in a muddled, overslept haze to the all-call crackling on. "We'll be docking with the Flotilla in three hours," a voice announces. I still haven't figured out which of the crew lends her voice to the announcements. "Report to stations for instructions."

I roll over, and my empty stomach keens.

Two minutes later, someone pounds on the door. "Cas, I know you're in there," Swift calls. Her voice is choked and hollow, like she's holding something back. She's probably holding a lot back. "Captain wants you on the bridge. Got you some food and shit. Leaving it here. See you in five."

I wait until her footsteps fade down the hall before crossing to the hatch and yanking it open. Sitting outside in a neat pile is a water bottle, a few protein bars, and a set of clothes that, under closer inspection, appear to be almost folded. I gather them up and lock the door behind me.

I make my way up to the navigation tower a few minutes later, still chewing on the protein bars, which must have been sitting in the *Minnow*'s stock for all five of the years that Swift's been aboard this ship. Crew members rush back and forth around me, making preparations for the docking. They hardly notice me. I guess I've finally become part of the landscape.

When I climb the ladder into the navigation tower, the four lackeys are the first thing that greet me. Chuck and Varma seem curious, Lemon looks distant, and Swift's trying to burn holes in the floor with her stare. The captain stands at the navigation instruments with Yatori, muttering to the helmsman in low tones. When she spots me, she gives me that shark smile I've come to know so well. It repels me, but I step forward anyway.

"Cassandra, glad to see you out. Got a bit of a surprise for you today," Santa Elena says, clapping her hands once for emphasis. She's decked out in her best leathers, looking fit to swashbuckle her way back to civilization. If she's mad about me stagnating Bao's training, she doesn't show it.

My meager breakfast churns in my stomach.

"We're rolling into the Flotilla in full regalia today, Reckoner and all."

Panic floods me. Bao's unpredictable, and putting him in a busy environment is the last thing we need right now. Reckoners are introduced to the complexities of ports in stages. Even in the Reckoner-free harbors of a floating city, Bao's curious enough that there's no end to the trouble he could get himself into.

"We'll set his beacon to get him patrolling and see where it takes us," the captain continues. "If he starts to cause a ruckus, we'll rein him in. But in the meantime, I want the world to see what we've got. He's ready. It's time for a show of strength. Nothing fancy, mind you. But the fact that we have a beast bonded to our vessel's going to be enough to get everyone talking, and that's exactly what we're going for."

I can't contradict her. Any urge I have to speak out against her gets pushed back down my throat by the thought of Code's blood billowing in the water. Of the crack Bao's beak makes when it slams shut. Of the captain slamming me into the wall of this room. All I can do is nod again, short and curt, and wait for her to dismiss me.

But Santa Elena's grin widens, and I want to wipe it off her face even more. "You've been doing well aboard this ship, Cassandra. It's time you got some time off it. You'll get shore leave while we're docked. I feel like you could benefit from a day away."

She can't have said what I think she said. Santa Elena's letting me loose? In an entire city? I don't even know the Flotilla's layout—I could get lost in there so easily.

I could get lost and never return.

And just as the thought is settling in, just as the hope is kindling in my chest, I feel the chill of metal around my wrist and hear the light *snap* as the handcuffs lock into place.

Should've expected that. But Santa Elena doesn't ask for

my other wrist to bind to the one already locked in. Instead, she beckons Swift.

"Oh no," Swift protests.

"She's been your charge from day one, Swift. That isn't changing just because she's getting off the boat for a bit."

"Boss, you can trust me to make sure she doesn't run off. C'mon, this is the first time I've had leave in months. I'm going—"

"I take risks, Swift, but not stupid ones. Give me your hand."

And two seconds later, I'm handcuffed to the one person on this entire boat that I can't even look in the eye right now. Chuck and Varma whisper to each other over in the corner, and I can see them barely holding back their laughter. They stand up straight when the captain's glare finds them.

"Both of you are on treasury duty today," Santa Elena says. "Make sure salaries go out before we dock—I really don't want a mutiny on my hands in the most popular port this side of the meridian."

They accept their orders with quick, cocky salutes and plunge down the ladder. I hear a cackle float from below as their footsteps patter away.

Santa Elena turns back to us. "Report time is noon tomorrow. Cassandra, if you somehow get it in your head that you're going to make an escape attempt, know that I will hunt you down and bleed you out, and there are only so many places to hide on a floating city. Enjoy leave." She claps me on the shoulder, then disappears down the ladder.

"Well," Swift huffs.

There's not much else to say. And Santa Elena hasn't even given us the luxury of cuffing us *after* we descended the ladder. Truly her sadism knows no bounds. Swift and I end up working it so that we go down side by side, wedged together in the tiny chute, which is uncomfortable, to say the least. Several times I elbow her, and I bet she thinks I'm doing it on purpose by the end. But the fact of the matter is, it's *really hard* to go down a ladder handcuffed to someone you don't want to talk to.

When we get to the bottom, Chuck and Varma are waiting for us with several cloth bundles slung over their shoulders. Varma holds one up. Swift's name is scrawled on it in blocky, childish print that I recognize as her own handwriting immediately. "Your winnings," he says, tossing it to her.

Swift catches it with one hand, and I don't miss the slight bounce she gives it as she evaluates the weight.

Chuck nudges her as she walks past, tossing her mane of wavy hair so that it slaps Swift in the face.

"Oh come on," she yelps, but the mechanic lackey only laughs.

"Have fun, you two," Varma calls over his shoulder as the pair of them disappear around the corner.

I've never seen Swift go redder. "This can't be happening," she mutters under her breath. "Okay, look. I have business I need to take care of at the Flotilla, so you're gonna have to just shut up, play cool, and come along for the ride."

"I shouldn't leave Bao—" I protest, but Swift silences me with a jerk of her wrist that causes the handcuffs to bite into my flesh. "Ow, Jesus!" I yelp.

"This is non-negotiable. The Flotilla's our biggest stop on the trade chain—that's why we get paid here. I *have* to—" She cuts off, her face souring. "Never mind. Just work with me, okay?"

I nod. There isn't much else I can do.

———————

We go to one of the midlevel decks to keep an eye on Bao while the ship makes its approach. He spots the Flotilla looming on the horizon and swims out ahead of us, blowholes flaring curiously, but then the trainer deck beacon flashes on, and he returns to the *Minnow*'s wake like a well-behaved dog. Santa Elena is giving the signals herself this time. She wanted the feeling of rolling into port with a Reckoner at her beck and call. It gives me the afternoon off, and there's no way someone else will make a pass at Bao with the captain on deck. All that remains is for him to handle being in port like a properly trained beast.

He's never had a problem with the ship's Splinters, so it's no surprise that as we draw closer, he pays little attention to the smaller ships that dart around in the distance. Some are ferries, carrying crew to and from massive smuggler ships that anchor out on their own where their autonomy is unquestionable. Others are fishing vessels returning from the net stands, loaded with enough meat to feed a hundred families for a week. My lip curls when I spot one of them dragging a bundle of neocete carcasses.

The Flotilla towers over us as we creep closer.

I've seen pictures of this place in textbooks, usually in the context of the justification for the Schism. Dividing the world into smaller states was supposed to ensure that governments were small enough to take care of all of their people. But some people still slipped through the cracks and floated out to sea, and the currents coagulated them into the floating cities, the fringe civilizations that live off both their wits and their availability to the pirate trade.

The Flotilla's a Jenga game of shipping crates piled on skeleton hulls piled on what looks like real concrete foundation but must be something far lighter. The pile winds its way up into towers that steam and smoke in the noon sun. It's a place that's been carved out of salvage and wrought into something alive, something that rises and falls with the sea, a breathing being in its own right. Though it towers above us, it also splays out into a winding network of docks, like a cephalopoid's arms, that host a veritable armada of pirate vessels.

I've never seen so many hunter ships in one place before. They slumber right next to each other, just waiting for a crew to wake them, to take them out and blaze their guns. I can feel an old impulse rising inside of me, the one that orders me to point projections, to direct Reckoners at the largest threat. Unleash a fully grown, fully trained Reckoner like Durga on this place, with all of the ships in such tight quarters, and we'd squash a good percentage of the NeoPacific's infestation within hours. But everything here is bristling with heavy artillery, and I know that it'd be a waste to pit a single Reckoner against it.

It's not like Bao would be up for the challenge anyway.

Or me, for that matter.

There's some sort of nervous energy thrumming away in Swift. She keeps on fidgeting with the sack of cash, her eyes fixed on the looming Flotilla. If it wouldn't take me along for the ride, I'd push her over the side of the boat. In all of her twitching and glancing and picking, she hasn't bothered telling me what's eating her. I don't want to ask. Being chained to her is bad enough—it only gets worse if we have to have a conversation.

The *Minnow* prowls into the Flotilla's inner harbors. We've gotten docking permissions at a prime slot, and I have no doubt that Santa Elena paid an arm and a leg to get us such a prestigious spot, just so she can show off her new pet. Bao follows quietly behind us, and already people are lining up along the docks, scrambling over haphazard stacks of crates and rickety platforms that balance on barrels and slabs of foam. Their eyes are wide, and some are already snapping pictures with their phones. When Swift spots them, she tugs me back from the railing and into the shadow of the ship's interior.

Because of course we can march into the harbor with an unregulated Reckoner, but god forbid a presumed-dead girl turns up alive and well in the background of a viral video. It's not like anyone would recognize me anyway—all of my hair is hacked off and I'm dressed in Swift's clothes. It's been months since the *Nereid* went down. Everyone's probably given up on me by now.

When did I start thinking that?

The realization doesn't bowl me over or anything. It's something that's always been there. Everyone at home thinks I'm dead. They think the pirates killed me when they sacked the *Nereid*, or else I took the pill when I was captured. Nothing's given them reason to assume otherwise. No one's looking for me anymore.

And it's sort of freeing, being a dead girl walking. As the docking arms extend and bring the *Minnow* in, I feel lighter. There's an itch building in me, a longing for something other than the ship's deck below my feet. I want solidity and stillness and everything I've lost at sea. I want to run without running out of hallway.

That's obviously not happening with my wrist chained to Swift, but I can dream.

As the *Minnow* puts down its ramp and the crew pours off the ship, Swift guides me through the crowd, her knuckles white on the bag of money. She's so protective of it that I can't help but wonder if it's been ripped from her hands before. Swift wasn't always one of the top dogs on this ship. While she hasn't told me much about the time before Santa Elena raised her out of the ranks, looking at the way she guards her sack of cash, I'm starting to think that the captain's favor was sorely needed.

We spill out onto the dock, and immediately Swift takes off, dragging me after her. I yelp when the cuffs bite into my hand, but nothing's slowing her down now. She charges for a set of rickety steps at one end of the dock and thunders up them, climbing furiously for the upper levels of the city. I barely have time to look down, and given how much the stairs shake underneath us, I don't think I want to. I glance back over my shoulder at the *Minnow*, and then we're around the corner. For the first time in months, the ocean is out of sight.

Not out of mind, but it's good enough for now. I can feel a pressure releasing from my back, though I still have a niggling sensation that urges me to check on Bao. Leaving him back in the harbor without any sort of trainer supervision is probably the captain's weird idea of a show of force. Hopefully he doesn't wreck all of the shit before I get back from wherever Swift is dragging me.

I hook two fingers inside the cuff, trying to keep it from chafing as I stumble along in her wake, but they just pinch against the bone when she jerks and I have to withdraw them. "Swift, slow down." I warn her.

She lets her pace slacken a little, eyes still fixed determinedly forward.

Now I've got time to see the sights, but in that regard, the pirate city is sort of disappointing. True, most of the people here are packing more heat than anyone in the streets of New Los Angeles, but there's a sense of normalcy that permeates the people we pass in the streets. It's like the world out here is just a different, more dangerous flavor of the same stuff I'm used to. Even the fact that I'm cuffed to my companion doesn't bother many of the people we pass. I puzzle over it until Swift offers a solution when she notices me glancing after one man who stared too long. "They think you're a slave," she hisses, then yanks me down a side street and up another flight of stairs.

I try to keep her pace more gracefully after that.

The city gets rougher and more chaotic the higher we climb. On the lower levels, there were paths resembling roads, where rickshaws ran wild and porters with inhumanly large loads strapped to their backs wandered the streets. Up here, the buildings are balanced precariously together, supported by massive iron beams that the sea winds have turned a dull orange. The paths are either narrow walkways that jut out from the sides of the buildings or spindly plastic bridges that stretch between them. Most of the construction is done with the cannibalized remains of shipping containers that have been haphazardly welded together to create homes and little shops, shops we pass up despite the heavenly smells wafting out of them. The protein bars I had this morning feel like nothing in my stomach.

"We're getting close," Swift blurts. "Okay, no matter what, you can't tell anyone on the ship about where we're going or what you see there. Understood?"

I nod.

"Say it."

"I understand. Not a word," I spit, rolling my eyes, though inside I'm getting worried. Swift's business here is apparently so important that she practically had to run the second the ship docked. If it were an errand for Santa Elena, she wouldn't have sworn me to secrecy. All she's carrying is the sack of cash, her entire salary bound in one scrap of flimsy, well-worn cloth. Is she running some sort of smuggling job on the side, working for some Flotilla crime boss underneath the captain's nose? Or maybe there's a debt to some dangerous warlord, something where she's in so deep that her entire salary is forfeit.

She pulls up at one of the rickety hovels, and I can see the tension building in her shoulders. "This is it. Just stand back, be cool, and let me do the talking for us."

"Got it," I tell her, wishing that she was wearing more than her pistol at her belt.

Swift raises a hand and knocks three times on the door. There's a shriek and several thuds, followed by the pounding of feet. I shrink back just a bit, just in case. If this gets ugly, I guess I can try to run, but I go where Swift goes, and something tells me she's making ready to stand her ground.

The rust-tinged door swings open, and I freeze mid-flinch. Standing there, beaming wide and spreading his arms, is a middle-aged man with a baby in a sling on his chest and a child clutching his ankle.

"Welcome home!" he says, beckoning us inside urgently.

23

Swift and I step through the door. We both have to duck. The tiny shack is sparsely lit—most of the light comes from the holes that the rust has eaten in the roof. It bakes like an oven in here, the metal reflecting like a hotbox. There are random strips of cloth nailed up everywhere in a feeble attempt to off-set the effect, but I immediately feel the sunken weight of the humidity inside settle over me.

I'm still trying to process what's happening as I watch the man hug Swift, who squeezes him back, careful not to disturb the baby on his chest. When she releases him, he regards me with a curious eye, but I remember Swift's instructions and keep my questions to myself.

"Prisoner," she explains as she bends down to greet the anklebiter still clutching the man's leg.

"Ah, delightful. Hi, prisoner. I'm Saul," he says sticking

out his hand. His voice has the same easy cadence as hers, the same accent dragging at his syllables.

"This," Swift says, deflating just a bit as she lets the words out, "is my dad."

Oh.

Oh. It's all very clear now. The secrecy, the salary—everything. I grasp his offered hand, still reeling, and give it the firmest shake I can manage.

"And who the hell is this?" Swift asks abruptly, pointing at the baby.

"Language, girl," Saul warns, and she rolls her eyes. "This is Pima. She's your half-sister."

"Thought I had enough of those already," Swift grumbles as two small girls scamper from the shadows and attach themselves to her legs. "Yes, *hello!*" she says, patting each of them on the head and shooting me a panicked glance. "Shouldn't you be out of the house? Doing kid shit?"

"Swift," Saul warns.

"Sorry. Kid *activities.*"

"Xiao saw your ship on the horizon. We wanted to be here when you got back!" the larger one yelps.

"That's very kind of you, Teresa," Swift replies, her voice thick with sarcasm.

"Is it true that you have a monster with you? Xiao said he saw a big beast following your ship, but it wasn't attacking it," the other girl says, still locked onto Swift's leg. "Is it true?"

Saul raises his eyebrows.

"Yep, it's true. Captain decided it wasn't fair that all the buckets had beasties fighting for them, so she went and got us one of our own. And a trainer to go with it," Swift says, hitching her cuffed thumb at me.

The girls' eyes go wide, and the kid at Saul's side lets out a whispered "*Wow!*"

Swift grins, and it's the most honest smile I've ever seen her wear. She holds out the bag of cash to her father, who takes it without hesitation. This exchange is practiced—there's no embarrassment or wavering in her handing over everything she's earned to her dad, and I can immediately see why it's happening, just looking at this place. I can't even tell how three kids, a man, and a baby manage to get by in a living space so small, but I spot the hammocks strapped to the walls, the crib lashed to one of the beams that supports the roof, and the tiny stove tucked in one corner, and I realize that they get by.

It also does a lot to explain why Swift was so comfortable sharing her cramped bunk with me right from the start. When you come from a place like this, having your own room on a ship is a damn luxury.

"So, you're a Reckoner trainer, huh?" Saul asks as he dumps the bag out on a table in the corner that seems to be cut out of the same material as the walls of the house. "Where from?"

"SRC," I say, still lost in processing everything around me.

"Interesting. So the *Minnow* went after an escorted SRCese ship just to get its trainer?" he asks, more to his daughter than me.

"Not … exactly. Cas was a bonus on top of a good haul," Swift says, her voice struggling to stay conversational. "Our focus was on killing the beast. Seeing if it could be done."

"And how'd that go?"

Swift pauses, but when she speaks, it's the word I know she wants to use. "Magnificently," she says, and there's so much sick pride in it that I start to feel a little nauseous. Of course the attack on the *Nereid* was about killing Durga. But more than that, Swift's essentially confessed that Durga's illness was *arranged*. That suffering, that inhumane end to her life—it was all orchestrated under Santa Elena's command. A fury alights in me, but there's nothing I can do about it with the kids watching.

Pima chooses that moment to wake. She stirs in her sling and lets out a vicious, piercing cry. Saul's attention immediately shifts from the money to the squalling baby, and I feel a twinge of sympathy. I got off easy with Bao. He only took a month or so to mature to the point where he didn't need my supervision. I can't imagine years in that situation.

Saul bounces her up and down, lifting her from her sling so that he can cradle her closer and croon soft words against her head until she calms. I wish that worked with Reckoner pups. It's such a pity they aren't cuddly.

I don't realize I'm staring until Swift tugs the cuffs, snapping my attention back to her. "So, uh," she starts.

"I . . ."

"This . . . this is where I come from." She shrugs. "It's not much, but y'know. It's home."

"It's nice."

"Bullshit."

"Heard that," Saul warns. "Teresa, Eva, you two get gone.

You've gotten a chance to greet your big sister, now give her a chance to rest. Be back for dinner, okay?"

The two girls nod and scamper off, banging the corrugated metal door shut behind them. The sound startles a mound of blankets in one of the hammocks that shifts to reveal the wizened face of an elderly woman. She lifts her head, peering suspiciously from her nest. "Oh," she croaks, her lips twisting. "You're here."

"I'm here, Oma," Swift says, spreading her arms. My wrist goes along for the ride.

"Thought you'd run off for good this time and left us to starve. Like your mother."

"Mom, let her rest," Saul mutters from over by the stove as he prepares a bottle for the baby.

Swift smirks. "You know I'd never do that. If you got it in your head that I wasn't coming home, you'd get up out of that bed and do something useful with yourself."

Her grandmother sighs exaggeratedly, tugging the blankets tighter around her. I don't know how she can stand it in the sticky heat that swamps this house, but I guess this particular woman has managed to become part lizard in the face of her hardships. She narrows her eyes at me. "Did your crew become slavers? That thing's far too skinny to sell on this raft. She looks like she'd snap if you asked her to bend."

"Santa Elena's taken a prisoner, and it's my job to guard her while we're on shore. Captain wanted her secure, so she cuffed me to her."

"Doesn't look like it'd do you much good. She could slip right out of those things."

"Hush, Oma. Go back to sleep. Dream about that Islander prince who's going to take you away from this wretched life."

Swift's grandmother mutters under her breath. I catch something about horrible girls and mothers, and then she's burrowed back under her blankets and seemingly out like a light.

"Dad, do you need me to do anything?" Swift asks, moving toward the stack of money on the table. I trail her, nearly tripping over the little boy as he tries to dart between us. "Watch it, Rory!" Swift yelps, taking a gentle swipe at his wild red curls, but he dodges her and slips out the door.

"You go ahead and relax. I'll take care of everything." Saul nudges her gently to the side. He's got Pima slung against his chest again. She nurses greedily from the bottle as he reaches over to the notes from the sack and takes a bundle. "Go see a show or something. Make the most of your shore leave—don't waste it on little old me."

"I want to waste it on little old you," Swift whines, but he gives her another nudge toward the door.

"Show your captive the sights. The SRC's got nothing on this place, you know?"

"Dinner's at the usual?"

"As always."

When his back is turned, Swift sweeps a handful of cash into her pocket and tugs me insistently toward the door. We burst out into the bright sunlight, and for a moment I swear I see a tear in her eye. She stops a moment to take in the view, so I share it with her.

As I take in the Flotilla's sprawling jumble, I squint against the light and pick out the shapes of people on the farthest docks bringing in the fishing haul for the day. Seagulls glide through the network of bridges beneath us, their beady eyes fixed on the fresh catch coming in. This whole place is like a giant organism, an ecosystem that thrives on sheer willpower and the strength of the people who hold it all together.

"This place is a fucking dump," Swift groans, leaning against the railing. "And don't you dare try to tell me different, don't you give me any of that shoregirl bullshit. I can already see it in your eyes—you want to make us into these noble poor people."

I say nothing.

"Everything in this city works because of the pirate industry. I feed those kids back there with money that I earn by hunting ships full of innocents. I'm not oblivious, Cas—I know that's not right. But it's all I have, and it's all I can do. So just…don't look at me like that, okay?"

"Like what?" I ask.

"Like you have more respect for me because you know where I come from."

I try to come up with something to protest with, but I'm grasping at straws. This morning, I didn't know anything about why Swift had gotten into the pirate trade in the first place, beyond the fact that she'd done it willingly. I'd never imagined what kind of life would lead to that. I guess in my head, Swift was born into piracy the same way I was born into the Reckoner trade, and I'd never pictured her growing up outside of it.

She gives my wrist a tug and starts picking her way down a dangerous-looking path, past racks of laundry hung out to dry in the afternoon sun. We descend a few levels to a grocery store that deals in both fresh catch and the far more expensive preserved items that ship in on the vessels trading here. Swift pulls out the wad of cash she siphoned and uses it to pay for a few giant sacks of rice and some assorted staple foods that she gets me to help carry back up to her house. It doesn't do much to dispel the impression that I'm a slave. Her father rolls his eyes when we show up loaded with groceries, but he lets us store them in the baskets woven from plastic scraps that dangle in the kitchen area.

It's so *normal*, after months at sea, that I want to cry. I've been bottling up how much I miss home, how much I miss late night runs to the little corner grocery down the road and cooking with Tom and Dad and just plain old *stability*, for god's sake. What's even worse is that I'm absolutely terrible at concealing it. I let my fingers fidget, trying to subtly vent off the effect all of this is having on me, but Swift feels it. She glances down at my hand, then catches my face before I can swallow back the emotion showing there. "What's eating you?" she asks.

I shake my head.

"C'mon, Cas."

"Outside," I hiss.

I expect her to put up a fight, but Swift immediately moves for the door, taking care that she doesn't yank the cuffs against my wrist for once. We emerge into the sunlight, where the sea winds tousle her hair and the ocean stretches far into the distance. I watch her for a moment. She glows here. There's something about the sunlight and her home and the straightness in her spine that makes her radiant.

"Come with me," she says, a soft smile on her lips. "I want to show you something."

She leads me around the side of her house to the space where another roof slopes just below hers. Before I can protest, she jumps from the path and slides onto the rough corrugated metal, towing me along for the ride. I panic, trying to stop, but she grabs my hand before I can get out a word of protest and guides me into a skid that sends us flying off the edge.

For a moment, all I can see is ocean.

Then we strike the next roof below us and Swift slams on the brakes, snaring my waist with her free arm to make sure I stop with her.

My heart thunders in my chest as Swift jumps back, stowing her hands nonchalantly in her pockets. We've landed in a little alcove, a den of metal and plastic siding that looks out on a spectacular view of the Flotilla's western docks. The sun is sinking in the sky. It's only early evening, but we're on the cusp of winter.

As I look around, I realize that this place isn't accessible by any other means. Every house around us has its back turned, and none of them have any sort of door or window. It's like a little space that the Flotilla forgot, a secret it kept so long that everyone stopped looking for it.

"Was goofing around on the roof one day when I was a kid, slipped, and ended up here," Swift says. "Nearly broke my ass, but I guess it was worth it, 'cause ... well, y'know. House like that, never a moment to myself. I came here to think a lot. First when Mom shipped out. Then when Teresa and Eva's mom shipped in. And then when she shipped out, and then … well, you get the picture."

Her words echo against each other in the space, and I notice that there's a little plastic bucket sitting quite intentionally in the middle. I picture a little blonde kid sitting on it, elbows on her knees, staring out at the sea. "It's a good place to be when something's bothering me, so I thought … " She trails off, shrugging. "Want to talk about it?"

The bucket's too small for either of us, let alone both of us, so we sit on the edge of the platform, our legs dangling out over the roofs below.

"I got overwhelmed," I start. "Just being in there, being with a normal family—"

Swift scoffs.

"Shut up, your family's plenty normal. I mean, it's just … god, I don't know if I'll ever see them again. I don't have any way off the *Minnow*. When the people around here think that I'm a slave, they aren't far off. If I weren't, well … " I lift my hand, giving the handcuffs a shake. "I'd run. No question about it, I'd try to find a boat shipping off that I could stow away on and just *go*. But I'm chained to you, and … and I don't mean that in just the literal way," I say, trying not to let bitterness tinge my words. Swift's shared the truth with me. It's only fair that I do the same.

"I'd run with you," she blurts. "I'm so *sick* of who I have to be for the captain every damn day. I'm tired of her stupid mind games, of her playing us against each other like it's all a big joke and then executing us when we slip up. No lie, I'd go wherever you'd run to, if it weren't for..." She jerks her head upward toward the house we just left.

"You provide for them."

"I'm the only one who can. Oma's too weak to work, Dad has to take care of all of the kids and that's a full-time job, and... well, Mom shipped out when I was seven. And Teresa and Eva's mom left when I was thirteen. Every time Dad gets someone to settle down with him, they always end up going back out to sea, and they never come back. The second time it happened, we got left with two little kids, and we didn't have any income. So I became the income. Found a captain who'd take me, worked my way up, and every penny of that salary goes to keeping them alive. If that stops... I don't know what's going to happen. Dad's got the kids to look after. He can't work, and now there's this new baby—I still haven't gotten that story—I just—" She punches the ground with her free hand, her teeth bared in a snarl. "I didn't sign on for any of this, but I can't stop it now."

When I first met Swift, I thought she was only tense around me. I thought that I was the drag in her life, the thing that sealed her off when she was around her fellow trainees. She always seemed so carefree when she didn't have to deal with me. But that's not right—that's not who Swift is. She's been showing me who she is all along. Swift is a scared, stressed, angry girl, but she's *trying*. She's trying so hard.

And because of the way our lives have been twined together, it's only now sinking in that there's far more at stake than just me, Bao, and Swift. There are four children and two adults whose existences depend on Swift. And Swift's existence depends on me. And my existence depends on Bao. And he depends on me, and I...well, as much as I hate to admit it, I depend on Swift to keep me alive. We're all stuck together, and if any of us falls, we all fall.

"Captain's got us good," I groan, and Swift laughs.

"Fuck her," she says. "I mean yeah, she's everything I aspire to, but god, I was barely thirteen when I begged her to take me on. We scraped by in those years, but we only had two babies to feed. Then Rory came along, and I had to convince the captain to bump me up from deckhand to crew. And Dad didn't tell me about Pima. With this new baby, thank god I made trainee on this last rotation."

"Wait, so you haven't been home in—"

"Over a year, yeah. Santa Elena likes to make the Flotilla a rare thing. It's our biggest hub, so we make one big stop to trade and flaunt when the Northern fall's over. It's just one more nail in the coffin, the fact that I can only see them for at most a month out of the entire year. And this time around it's even shorter. She wants us shipping out tomorrow. Probably has something to do with Bao."

I nod, my fingernails digging into the gravely edge of the platform we're sitting on.

Swift blinks. "I've been talking about myself this whole time! This was supposed to help you, not be all about me venting my issues."

"It helps when you vent your issues," I say with a shrug. "Your shitty life distracts me from my shitty life. It's a win-win."

She gives me a shove with her shoulder, her mouth

drawn into a taut smile, and something inside me takes flight. Onboard the *Minnow*, the constant scrutiny and the balancing of power makes it nearly impossible for me to be certain of Swift's motives whenever she does something like that. But out here, in a space that was completely her own until she decided to share it with me, Swift's laid bare. I can see her for who she really is.

And I guess I really like her when she's honest.

She catches my eye. "Hey, if it'd help put your mind at ease, we can go check on Bao. I'll bet the crowds have died down, so there's less of a chance you'll end up in a video." Swift stands, reaching down to help me up with her cuffed hand. As she grabs me by the wrist, I feel her nervous energy buzzing from her palm into my arm, and for once in this whole messy disaster, I feel like I have the upper hand.

"So how do we get out of here?" I ask, searching the walls that surround us. None of them look climbable, even by a single person. With the two of us chained together, it seems impossible to reach the roofs we slid down over.

But Swift isn't looking up. Her gaze is fixed on the jungle of metal below us, on a spot that I can't quite see, and my feeling of upper-handery vanishes. Suddenly I want my wrist back. She whips around her other arm, snaring my waist again, and just as the first word of protest is leaving my lips, she topples backward off the ledge, dragging me along with her.

24

We fall.

I scream, flailing my unchained hand as if I'm going to catch something. Panic threads in my veins.

But Swift is laughing, her fingers fisted in the back of my shirt. Her idiotic hair whips into my face as she yanks me closer and says, "Brace yourself."

I don't have time to question it. Swift twists in the air, rolling me off her so that we're plummeting on our backs, and it's not a second too soon. We hit canvas with a *whumph* and get tossed back in the air, gasping to recover the breath that's been driven from our lungs. The second hit is better. We sink in, float up, and then come to rest.

"Holy shit," I wheeze.

Swift's still cackling.

I raise my free arm to hit her, but it's shaking so badly

that I can't go through with it. "*Warn* me. Jesus, Swift, I thought we were going to die."

"If I'd warned you, you wouldn't have made that amazing face."

I groan. She's high on the adrenaline rush, her cheeks pink, her hair wild. Up above I can spot the ledge we fell from, a little sliver glowing with the light of the setting sun. Internally I remind myself that even when Swift's in her natural environment, she's still a tricky little bitch who can't be trusted.

We've landed on a tent that covers some sort of shop, as I deduce from the yells of a man below us. Swift perks up. "I didn't know Vorsta still ran this joint," she says as she pushes herself into a sit. "Oh, by the way, it's time to run." She grabs my hand and yanks me up.

We leap from the roof of the stall and land hard in the street. There's a shout from behind us, and a mountain of a man comes crashing out from the racks of fruit and fish, brandishing his fists. "You!" he bellows.

"Me!" Swift shouts as she whips me into an alleyway. We plunge down a narrow flight of stairs. The shouts fade from behind us, but Swift keeps running until we've spilled out onto the lower levels of the Flotilla. My heart is still pounding in my chest, and it takes me a few seconds to realize that I'm clutching her hand as if it's a lifeline. I let go.

"Figured out that trick by accident a few years back. Shopkeeps around here roof their stalls with old sail, stuff that's supposed to swell in the wind. Nice and bouncy. But Vorsta's a real pain in the ass about it."

"By accident."

"I … slipped, yeah." Swift shrugs, but something dark flickers over her face for a second, something I know I'll never be able to ask her about. "C'mon."

We weave through the bustle surrounding the docks, dodging traders, slavers, and seemingly everyone in between. The chatter around us shifts effortlessly from language to language. I swear everyone around me is fluent in at least three. English dominates the conversations—pre-Schism colonialism at its finest—but as we slip through the crowd, I catch snatches of Spanish, what I think is Tagalog, and a few strains of Canto that I instinctively try to translate. We make our way toward the heart of the harbor, where the not-quite-sleek form of the *Minnow* awaits us.

There are still a few spectators on the dock when we arrive, but there isn't much to see. Bao sulks behind the ship, his bulk barely eclipsed by it. Reckoners are finicky creatures, and they're notoriously shy when they've got hundreds of people ogling them. They're built for the privacy of the open seas, not the speculation of ports, but the homing signal keeps him bound to the *Minnow*'s side, regardless of how bashful he feels.

"He needs a chance to get out and hunt," I say as we approach the knot of people still watching our beast. "Do you think the captain would let us take a Splinter and—"

The words die in my throat. Something's risen over the babble of the crowd, two words that need no translation:

"Cassandra Leung."

I turn so fast that the cuffs all but cut my wrist, and there's Fabian Murphy, our IGEOC agent, his cold gray eyes fixed on mine. His suit looks as out of place on the Flotilla as it did in Mom's lab all those months ago, and he seems just as startled to see me as I am to see him. I don't blame him. To Murphy, I'm a ghost made flesh, a long-dead girl who's somehow managed to crawl out of the sea.

It takes Swift a few seconds to realize exactly what's happened, but when she does, it only takes her an instant to react. She pulls hard on the cuffs, jerking me away from him as he takes a step forward, and before I can choke out a protest, her hand is over my mouth. "We need to get away from the ship," she hisses in my ear.

"Calm down, miss," Murphy says, shifting after a few uncertain syllables into the voice he always uses to negotiate. "Look, I'm sure we can talk this out."

Swift hauls me backward just as Murphy reaches out, his cold grasp latching around my wrist before she can tug me out of reach. I try to speak through her fingers, but all I get is muffled vowels.

His grip is unrelenting, and it feels like he's about to rip me in half. "Cassandra, it's your handiwork, isn't it? The beast? Please, I can get you away from them. I have contacts in the SRCese military who could—"

"Who *is* this guy?" Swift scoffs, her breath hot on my neck. Murphy pulls so hard that I feel a pop in my shoulder. I'm caught in a tug of war between savior and captor, and the worst part is that I know exactly who I'd go with if given the choice. But neither of them are giving me that choice. The people around us are starting to stare.

"I can tell your parents—"

"Cas," Swift warns.

It's all up to me. I let the stiffness go from my spine, going so limp that Swift startles, checking to see what's wrong. Her hold slips, and I lunge forward, straining against her and toward Murphy. His grip on my wrist loosens, and in that moment, I twist.

And then I'm free. Relatively speaking. Still chained to Swift, but Murphy takes a second to blink, and that's all we need. Swift's arm slips from my mouth to my shoulders as she drags me into a sprint. But we're not headed down the docks, toward the heart of the Flotilla.

No, Swift hauls me off the edge of the platform, and for the third time today, we're falling.

We plunge underwater, and immediately Swift starts swimming for the shadow of the pier, drawing me into the dark. The harbor is bitterly cold in the shade, and when we finally come up for air, my breath comes in shudders.

"Would you stop jumping off shit for like, three seconds?" I hiss between my chattering teeth. I shouldn't be joking, but I don't know what else to do. Why is Fabian Murphy on the Flotilla? What's an IGEOC agent doing in a pirate colony?

Whatever the reason, two things are for certain. Murphy's on an uplink right now, and I'm no longer a dead girl walking.

Swift treads water, reaching down to her belt and pulling out her radio. She shakes it a few times, then lifts it to her lips. "Hey boss, we've got a situation. Some random on the docks recognized Cas."

"Are they still there?" Santa Elena's voice cracks through the radio, echoing off the floorboards above us. The light that streams down between them traces dappled patterns in the waves.

"Not sure. We're in hiding now."

"Get back to the ship. I'll call everyone else in. We're off this raft in an hour."

When the comm clicks off, Swift deflates, and I know exactly what she's thinking. She's going to miss dinner. She isn't even going to get a chance to say goodbye. Her already-spare time at home has just been taken from her in a matter of seconds, and it's all my fault. In the half light that weaves through the shadows, I can see the tears welling up in her eyes as she bobs, keeping her head just above the water.

"I'm sorry," I say.

"They're gonna think I'm just like Mom," Swift croaks. Her hair falls over her face in a messy wet mop as she dips her head, trying to turn away from me.

"We could get someone to send a note to them. We could explain—"

She lifts her left wrist, marked by red welts from the cuffs, and gives it an emphatic shake, still avoiding my gaze. "Too risky. Captain would gut us."

"Fuck the captain."

Her lips twist, a smile almost escaping before she swallows it. I know she's right. I know there's nothing we can do, but I'm still struggling to find a way to make it work. We can't go anywhere on this raft with Murphy out there. He could have backup. He could snatch us and run.

And as much as I want that to happen, for my own sake, I know I can't let it. Swift's livelihood depends on her position aboard the *Minnow*. If we do anything that could compromise it, her whole family pays the price. This morning, I would have done anything to escape the hell I'm sunk in. But now, as the sun starts to dip into the sea, I realize that I'm willing to give up that chance. Not just because of the kids, but for Swift too.

I reach out for her, not sure what else I can do. She startles when my hand comes to rest on her shoulder, and her eyes flick to mine.

"C'mon," I say. "Let's get back to the ship."

Swift pushes forward suddenly and snares me in a hug so tight that for a minute I can't breathe. Our knees knock together and we sink beneath the surface of the water, unable to tread when we're so tangled.

I hug her back. I don't care. I don't care that we're on opposite sides of a war, that I'm an ocean away from everyone I love and it's mostly her fault. I don't care that she's the one thing standing between me and my freedom. All I care about is here and now, our own little world beneath the docks, where nothing from that ship can touch us. All I care about is her nose in my neck and the way her floating hair ghosts over my cheek. Her fingertips brush mine, the cuffs no longer the only thing binding us together, and I have to suppress an urge to twine my fingers with hers.

It's a moment that can only last so long, and though I wish my lungs weren't screaming for oxygen, I kick once, and immediately Swift's grip on me slackens. I break the surface, nearly choking on the water as I inhale, and Swift's there bobbing beside me, looking equally out of breath.

"I'm … sorry," she gasps. "I didn't mean—equal footing, I know, I know."

"It's okay," I tell her, but I know she doesn't think I mean it. I shake my head, pushing off one of the dock's support struts and drawing us toward the knot of hulls in the inner harbor. I don't know where I stand now. I don't know what my next move is, or even what will happen to me once we get back to the *Minnow*. But one thing's for certain: if I wasn't in over my head before, I sure as hell am now.

25

When we rush back up the ramp and onto the ship, Santa Elena is waiting for us. She keeps her arms folded, and a sleek pair of sunglasses shade her eyes. "No one else spotted you, then?" she asks, sizing us up. Lemon and Chuck lurk just behind her, leaning on a railing that looks out over the bay.

Swift nods. We're soaking wet and panting, but at least we didn't run into Murphy or any of his goons on the way back to the ship.

"Cas, you wanna explain who that was?" Swift asks, and I notice the harsh edge she's forced into her tone.

I stare at the shiny black discs where the captain's eyes should be. "Fabian Murphy. Works as a liaison between Reckoner stables and the International Genetically Engineered Organisms Council. He's an old friend of my parents."

"He's powerful," Santa Elena says, but it's not quite a question.

"He's well-connected."

"Boss," Swift says. "He made the connection. Cas to Bao. Bao to the *Minnow*."

"He'd be an idiot not to." The captain shrugs. "Welcome back to the land of the living, Cassandra. Come here." She draws the handcuffs key from her pocket, and a shudder of relief courses through me. Swift and I stick our wrists out, and she pops the metal loops open one at a time, tucking the cuffs back into her belt once we're free.

I shake my hand, wincing as the sea wind cuts across the chafed skin. I almost thank her right then and there.

"Stow her," Santa Elena snaps.

And suddenly Chuck's at my side, wrenching my arms behind my back as Lemon grabs my hair. My eyes roll back in my head as they yank, the pain searing through my scalp like wildfire.

Swift steps forward, but the captain snares her by the wrist. "You and I are going to have words. Right. Now," Santa Elena snarls.

I watch, helpless, as she drags Swift toward the bridge. Chuck and Lemon haul me into the ship's interior and throw me down a ladder. I hit the ground in a heap and pain shoots through my hip. They don't bother waiting for me to get up; Lemon takes my right wrist, Chuck takes my left, and together they tow me down the shadowy hall.

This is all feeling very familiar. So familiar, in fact, that I know exactly where they're taking me. I can almost smell the janitorial closet before I see it, and when they yank the door open and toss me in, it feels unnaturally homelike.

"You guys really need to invest in a proper brig," I say as I roll onto my back, glaring up at the two of them.

Chuck grins. "I'll put in a word with the captain." She slams the door, and the lock clicks into place. Seconds later, the engines rumble to life.

A laugh nearly bubbles out of me. I spent the whole day chained to a pirate, and only *now* do I feel like a proper prisoner. Santa Elena was counting on word about Bao getting out, but she didn't think I would be part of the news. She wanted the word to be that pirates were raising Reckoners on their own.

Murphy's changing that. He's letting the world know that the pirates didn't hatch and rear the beast—that there's a professional trainer behind it all.

That without me, Santa Elena has nothing.

I just went from an absolute nobody on this ship to its most protected resource. The captain can't lose her Reckoner after putting him on display like that. But now word's gotten out that she has a hostage, and the hunt is going to start. They can't take out the *Minnow* without attempting to extract me first. I'm both the reason we'll have a pursuit on our tail and the only thing keeping them from blowing the ship out of the water.

And somewhere in this closet, there's probably that little pill I was supposed to take, a little pill my parents now know never made it down my throat. I failed in my duty as a trainer, and now they'll see just how bad the consequences are. They'll be so disappointed.

I scoot into the corner and hug my knees, trying to preserve my body heat. Night's fallen, the cold has set in, and I'm still soaking wet.

————

I must fall asleep like that, because the next thing I know it's morning, and Varma is throwing the door open. "Rise and shine, *rani*," he says. "Big day today. Captain's got a surprise for you."

"Oh, she shouldn't have," I simper as I crawl to my feet. When I pass through the door, I notice that Varma's grin stretches the tattoo on his cheek. I wonder if the artist had to knock him out to put it on him.

Varma escorts me down to the trainer deck, where Santa Elena and a very rumpled-looking Swift wait. She lurks behind the captain, and as we draw near, I spot the bruise shining on her cheek. Whatever she and Santa Elena discussed last night, it doesn't look like it was friendly.

"So," the captain says, clapping her hands with a flourish. "The news is out. An unregulated Reckoner is escorting the *Minnow* and Cassandra Leung is training it. It's time to move our operation into its next stages." She sweeps over to the door controls and jams down the button. As the doors wheel up to let the sunlight in, a prickling sensation creeps over the back of my neck.

Chained to the back of the *Minnow* is a decommissioned tug.

"I trust you know how to make the most of this," Santa

Elena says, gesturing at the smaller ship. "And there's one more thing." She lifts a duffle bag from the counter and lobs it at my chest.

I catch it with a grunt and unzip it. Lying there, waiting for me, is a pair of Otachi. Wrist-mounted laser projectors with blazing beams a hundred times more powerful than the flashing lights of beacons. The tools of a real Reckoner trainer.

I used to dream about using them in battle. Watching my dad throw beams across the waves was like watching a swordsman at his craft, and I'd stand at his side, counting the seconds until the day that I would get to do the same. But in my fantasies, it was always Durga who followed me as I slashed the lights across her targets.

And it was always pirates at the other end.

I turn on the captain. Something's broken loose inside me, and as I meet her narrowed eyes, I finally ask the question that's been burning in me for three months. "Where are you getting this shit?" I snap, throwing the duffle at her feet. "These tools are only sold to Reckoner trainers. The cull serum, Bao—how the hell are you—"

Santa Elena raises an eyebrow. "You have all of the pieces, Cassandra. Put them together."

"What pieces?" I sputter. There's no rational explanation for why high-end Reckoner gear and a Reckoner itself ended up on a pirate ship. Even if the pirates were willing to pay through the nose. Even if the broker had access to every facet of the industry. Even if—

Cold gray eyes. A man who had no reason to be on the Flotilla. Unless...

"Fabian Murphy," I spit through gritted teeth, fists clenched at my sides. The pieces fall into place.

"When you want to run counter to an imbalanced system, you have two options," the captain says, her voice grave. "Either you find the pure of heart willing to fight for your cause, or you find the most corrupt willing to forsake their own. Fabian Murphy is the latter." She says it with a note of bitterness, as if she'd hoped for better things from him.

"Money?" I hazard.

"The only reason men of his mold do anything," she says with a nod. "Murphy is willing to sell his industry for a cut from ours."

I think back to that morning in Mom's lab. The security concerns he'd mentioned with hesitancy. He was throwing us off his scent, ensuring his access to the inner sanctum of the Reckoner industry.

And then there was the pup himself. A chill rushes through me as I remember the cyro-crate Murphy hauled out of our lab, the unusually high number of unviable embryos he'd found, my mother's hesitation. He was stealing pups right out from under our noses, under the guise of protecting the industry's investors.

Yet Bao clearly isn't one of my mother's monsters. Murphy must have been preying on dozens of stables.

"So he was the one who poisoned Durga," I blurt. Murphy had access to the observation bays—he easily could have slipped in and dosed her with some IGEOC serum. Maybe he didn't expect them to take me alive. Maybe that's why he seemed so surprised to see me.

"If you say so," Santa Elena drawls, her lips edging into a lopsided smile. It's not an answer, and I hate that it's not an answer. The agony of Durga's death is still raw inside me, and all I want, all I need to close the wound, is somewhere for the blame to fall.

My gaze falls on the duffle I've unceremoniously deposited at the captain's feet. "But if he's your broker, why would he try to get me rescued?"

"Who knows? He's a friend of your parents. He has an inkling of a conscience. He never anticipated uneducated pirates successfully hatching and training one of the monsters he sold us. Or maybe we're not his most valuable clients."

The last thought sends a shiver down my spine.

"Go ahead," Santa Elena prompts, indicating the Otachi. "Give 'em a spin."

I crouch, pull one of the devices out of the bag, and set it over my forearm. There's a set of straps that I have to adjust to keep the Otachi in place and some loops that go over my fingers. It takes a few minutes to get everything where it should be. I roll my shoulder, adjusting to the weight, then switch the device on. As the dials beneath my fingers glow to life, a rare sensation takes hold of me, something I haven't felt since that night on Bao's back.

I feel powerful.

With a few twists of the dials, I set the Otachi to project Bao's signal set and call up the homing signal. The tech responds at the lightest touch, a far cry from the heavy switches I'm used to. I step up to the edge of the trainer deck and raise my teched-up arm, pointing it at the tug's side as my fingers hover over the triggers.

I pull them, light blazes from my wrists, and the tug's side lights up with the familiar pattern. Speakers on the Otachi ring with the low noise that draws our Reckoner to the ship, and somewhere off in the blue, a puff of steam rises as Bao hearkens to the call.

The devices are heavy. The beams waver in the air as I keep them fixed at the spot I projected to. I duck my elbows down to compensate.

A minute later, Bao surges out of the sea, his nose pointed right at the projections on the tug's side. I draw them down the ship's hull, and he follows. It's like a cat with a laser pointer, but with a beast the size of a house. Varma chuckles from somewhere behind me. I click off the projections and let my arms fall to my sides.

"Optimistically, we've got about three days before some sort of shitstorm comes raining down on us," Santa Elena says. "Less, if SRC politicians by some miracle deliberate relatively quickly. Either way, whenever our reckoning comes, we'd better have a Reckoner of our own."

Swift snorts, and Santa Elena aims a kick at her.

"I'll … " I start, but I don't know what to say. It takes months to train Reckoners into aggression, but then again, that's with safety considerations. That's with standards and regulations, with pacing that avoids stressing out the beasts. If I push Bao, maybe we can get somewhere in three days. Maybe I can make him lethal.

He's already lethal, I remind myself, thinking of Code's bright green eyes.

"You'll do your damndest, Cassandra, or dear Swift will be that thing's next meal," Santa Elena snarls.

For a moment I think she's kidding, but I see the way Swift's jaw clenches, the way her body leans slightly away from the captain's side. That must have been what they talked about last night, and suddenly I feel stupid—so completely and utterly stupid—because this was Santa Elena's plan all along.

When I was alone on this ship with nothing to lose, she could barely control me. It was a stroke of luck for her that I felt the need to uncover the mystery behind Bao's origins. But she gave me a companion, a protector, a friend, and she bided her time until it became clear to her that I'd been snared by her trap. That's why she didn't seem bothered by my revelation that Bao was still docile. It wasn't because she thought that he'd instinctively fight when the time came.

No, she knew about that idea stewing away in the back of my head. The one where once I'd gotten what I needed to know, I'd take the beast she gave me and turn him on the ship that had taken everything away. The one where I used Bao to crush the *Minnow* into oblivion.

The one that's impossible now, because I care too much about Swift. I can't take her life, her livelihood; I can't let her family starve.

And not once in this conversation have I questioned using Bao to fight the pursuit. Not once have I doubted that I can turn my monster against the people coming to rescue me. Santa Elena has worked her magic.

"I'll do everything I can," I tell her, hating how much I mean it.

26

In the first few hours with the Otachi, I've been able to bait Bao into ramming the tug enough that he now associates the flashing pattern with charging. When I project out against a wave, the beams cutting into the murky ocean waters, he surges after them, throwing the full force of his body after the bright lights.

My arms are sore. I've been switching between them, trying to keep myself going, but by noon I've hit a point where I can barely lift either of them.

Swift brings down a tray of food from the mess just as the sun reaches its high point in the sky. She avoids my gaze when she hands it to me.

"Hey," I say when she turns her back without a word.

Swift freezes. Her neck stiffens, as if the tattoo branded there has nailed her in place.

"Captain says we've been getting too chummy," she mutters. "Says we shouldn't talk as much. Says we'll both pay if we do."

Telling her exactly what the captain can go do seems unwise in this situation, so I simply say, "Shame," and try to mask the fact that her words have set something boiling in my stomach. I guess there's no need for me to be guarded on this ship anymore, not after what happened to Code. Everyone's too afraid of the captain to try anything, Swift included.

The bruise on her face has gotten a little bit worse. It must have been fresh this morning, and it makes me wonder just how long the captain interviewed her. I want to ask her what they talked about, but she's already through the hatch, slamming the latch in place behind her.

I eat slowly, the food tasteless in my mouth. Out across the waves, I spot Bao rising out of the water, a neocete held delicately in his jaws. Seems I'm not the only one who needed a lunch break.

When I call him back, he's sluggish to respond. I can see the tension that coils and uncoils in his muscles when he draws up alongside the trainer deck. He's already feeling cranky and overworked. If I push him, he might push back in a way I can't control, but I can't afford to lose any time.

"Sorry, little shit," I tell him, and strap on the Otachi again.

I try to go easier on him in the second round, letting him take a few minutes to shake out his limbs before calling him back in to have another go at the tug. With each hollow thud of his plated snout against the ship's metal side, I can feel the frustration building inside him. He can't make sense of why he's being asked to repeat the action, and he's gotten too big for any sort of reward to be effective every time he strikes true. I can't exactly furnish a host of carved-up neocete carcasses like we do back home, and red meat is the only sure way to get a Reckoner's favor. As his frustration mounts, I start to worry that he'll remember Code, that eventually he'll just stick his head onto the trainer deck and snap me up.

But I'm frustrated and overworked too. It doesn't mean he gets off the hook. I blaze the lasers again, and again, and again, conducting a hundred-and-fifty-ton orchestra with wrists trembling from exhaustion. There's something I want to try, something I've never been able to attempt within the confines of regulated Reckoner training.

I want to see how far he'll go to get me off his case.

So I keep on throwing up the same signal. The lights I project are so bright and sharp that they leave streaks across my vision in their wake, and I know they must be burned into Bao's retinas by now. The lasers mounted on the Otachi are powerful enough to scorch things that get too close, and though the smudges in my vision make it difficult to tell, I think they've already started to wear a dark spot on the tug's hull.

I wait for the moment I feel certain.

It doesn't come until nearly evening. When I throw the Otachi's beams against the tug's side, Bao lets out a groan so loud that the ocean around him vibrates, and when he wheels, it's with a burst of energy far stronger than anything he's done in the past hour. He cuts through the waves like a freight train, his thick limbs kicking up a froth in his wake. I wait until he's half a body-length from the tug's side.

Then I twist one of the knobs, switching the signal from *charge* to *destroy.*

He doesn't know what it means. He doesn't need to. Something clicks, something falls into place, and his fury unlocks. Bao hits the tug with a roar, but instead of glancing off, he keeps going. His forearm crashes down on the deck as he locks his beak around the cockpit, and the shriek of tearing metal echoes across the waves.

I stagger back a few steps.

Bao's neck muscles snap taut as he wrenches his head back, ripping the cockpit from the ship. His weight crashes down on the tug's deck, and the boat's hull warps. With a high-pitched keen, he thrusts his head back down, and when his jaws snap shut, it's like a thunderclap. The tug cracks cleanly in two, the pieces bobbing up on either side of him as he sinks between them. Bao chases one of them, locks it in his beak, and starts swatting at it with his foreleg. His massive claws shred the hull like tissue as both he and the fragment of the ship sink into the depths beneath us.

My work here is done. A pup's training ends when they devastate their first tug. From here on out, it's instinct. It takes months to properly train a Reckoner.

But I did it improperly, and I did it in a day.

There's a sudden roar from the decks above me, and I realize that we had an audience all along. Somewhere up there, Santa Elena must be watching. Somewhere up there, she's seeing exactly the kind of beast she has on her side.

I hope she's impressed.

As for me, I'm terrified and just a little bit proud. A Reckoner's strength comes from careful practice, from routine and comfort and precision. What I just saw Bao do was nothing like that. Proper training is tai chi; this was a backstreet knife fight. Now not only does our beast have a taste for blood, but he's also got a knack for savaging ships that's unlike anything I've ever seen.

Bao is, without a doubt, the most dangerous thing in the NeoPacific.

And he answers to me.

27

Chuck escorts me back to my "cell" minutes later. I guess now that there are people out there looking for a prisoner, Santa Elena's decided it's time to start actually treating me like one. I settle into my nest of mops and sprays, wondering if anyone actually uses any of this stuff. I've seen some of the younger kids in the crew on deck duty, I suppose, but everything in here always seems like it's exactly where I left it.

My arms feel like jelly, and I'm so exhausted that I fall asleep almost immediately. When I wake up, there's an air freshener can digging into my back like a wedge. I can't believe I passed out right on top of it. I pull it out, squinting at the label.

Lavender Meadow.

I haven't smelled anything remotely like a lavender meadow since the day I got dragged onto this ship.

With no windows in the closet, I lose track of time.

Occasionally a crew member will toss a meal through the door and escort me to the head, but I sleep so much in between that I can't tell if they're coming at regular intervals. It's never a lackey, never Swift, never someone I can ask how long it's been, if there's pursuit on the horizon, if the captain's said anything about letting me out of this room.

All I can do is wait and listen to the rumble of the engines beneath my back. We're always fleeing now. The captain must be trying to put as much distance as possible between us and the Flotilla, to get us out in the open sea where we'll be nigh impossible to reach. But there are satellites in the sky above us, the last gasps of pre-Schism space programs that watch the oceans with hawkish eyes. If the SRC commissions a sat to track us down, there's no way we can hide.

I keep waiting.

————————

And finally the door opens, and it's Swift standing there, but it's not the Swift I've known. That spark, that hunger I used to see in her is gone. She looks like an empty shell, her hair limp, her eyes hooded, and all she tells me is, "It's time."

As we jog down to the trainer deck, the all-call crackles on. "Radar has picked up an aerial attack inbound. Four SRCese quadcopters. All hands on deck. Let's knock these birds out of the sky."

The pursuit has caught up.

"The *Minnow*'s artillery will handle the brunt of the attack, but we want you prepped just in case there's an opening," Swift explains as she unlocks the hatch and lets me scramble through ahead of her. "We also need Bao near the ship. We don't want him to take too much damage, and they can't fire anything heavy at us when we have a hostage onboard."

I cross to the counter where I left the duffle with the Otachi. Swift watches me, her fingers drumming on her biceps as I strap on the devices one by one.

"Don't you have somewhere to be?" I ask as I winch the velcro tight around my wrists.

Confusion flickers over her face, as if she doesn't know the answer to my question. Then she steps forward and draws an earpiece from her pocket. "I'll be on Phobos, on the main deck. If you need me to do anything, this is a direct line, okay? I . . . I promise it won't be like last time."

I take it from her palm, shivering a bit when my fingers brush her skin. "You're on my side."

"You're the only one on my side. What else am I sup-posed to do?" she says, and she's only half-joking. She jogs back to the door, then glances over her shoulder.

Our eyes meet.

I want to say something, want to wish her luck or make her stay. I want to make these seconds count, because if some-thing bad goes down here, they could be our very last. And Swift seems on the cusp of spitting something out too. Her lips twitch, but she inhales sharply before any words start to form, and then she bolts out the door without even saying goodbye.

I call Bao in with the beacon and slip Swift's earpiece on, wincing as I adjust the moldings to the shape of my ear. It's silent now, but if I press against it and speak, the device will read the vibrations in my skull and pipe my voice straight to her. No matter how much chaos surrounds me, she'll hear me loud and clear, and there's a little bit of comfort in that.

A blast of sea wind hits me, and I shiver. It's an overcast day. Maybe that's why the quadcopters have chosen now to strike. I squint up at the clouds, as if I could spot a four-rotored shadow creeping up on us from above. But the only shadow approaching is Bao's beneath the waves. I spot him circling deep below us, drawn upward by the light and noise of the beacon.

The earpiece buzzes to life, and I almost lose my grip on my handhold. "Keep him submerged for now," Swift tells me. "Only bring him up if we need him."

"Got it," I tell her, and kick the beacon, flipping the switches to order Bao to dive.

"Inbound is less than a minute out. Splinters away at my mark," the all-call snaps. "Three. Two. One."

Two sharp cracks echo out on either side of the *Minnow* as a pair of sleek white hulls fall away. I stick my head out the port-side door just as Varma wheels past with Chuck sitting primly in his copilot seat. They swing wide around the back of the ship, and as they come back around, the guns slide out of the Splinter's needle-like nose, poised and ready to kill. The second Splinter comes flying around the *Minnow*'s keel, and I realize that they're circling us. The ship may corner like a speedboat at a good clip, but the agility of the smaller craft can't be matched, and Santa Elena knows the Splinters are our best defense.

There's an awful stillness settling over the sea, and again I look up at the clouds, hoping to spot some sign of the impending attack.

"Inbound on starboard," the all-call screams. "Engines to full, all crew brace for immediate ignition."

The *Minnow* surges forward, and I dive for the nearest handhold. We're running, running far faster than I've ever seen the ship move. The engines below my feet scream, and when I lean out over the edge of the deck, I spot Bao's figure keeping pace with us in the depths. *He's gotten so big*, I marvel.

Rotors scream to my left as four glistening black quadcopters drop from the sky in formation, their hulls streaked with SRCese gold and red. A screech echoes from a set of speakers embedded in them, and in one voice the four declare, "Unregistered vessel, on the authority of the Southern Republic of California you are being ordered to stop and transfer the citizen you have unlawfully kept aboard your ship. Failure to comply will be interpreted as an act of aggression and will be met with uncompromising force."

The all-call screams back, in a voice that's unquestionably Santa Elena's, "Suck my dick! Here's your compliance!" and the whole ship rattles as the big guns unload.

The Splinters weave across the waves, rounding out on the other side of the quadcopters, their barrels pointing skywards just as the pursuit opens fire.

The quadcopters' guns blaze as a clatter of artillery fire rains down on the *Minnow*'s upper decks. I roll away from the open doors, pressing myself against the wall by the hatch. Out of the corner of my eye, I spot the flash of hundreds of brass casings pouring into the sea.

The Splinters' barrels light up, crosscutting the *Minnow*'s fire, and the copters' engines shriek as they drop back. Their formation changes—they spread out around us, two of them shifting their fire to chase the Splinters, but Varma's a step ahead of them. He disappears around the prow of the ship.

Is he using us as cover? I wonder.

Then a thud rolls through the deck beneath my feet. Phobos fired, and the copter chasing Varma takes a direct hit to one of its rotors. The whole bird screams as it tries to compensate, spinning wildly and sinking so low that its underbelly skims the top of the waves. Another shell slams into the water, and the third strikes the cockpit, exploding with a blast that casts long shadows across the trainer deck floor.

I sneak a glance outside, just in time to catch the twisted wreckage of the craft disappearing beneath the waves. One down.

But the other three are shifting their attention to the *Minnow*'s engines, and I'm about to be in some serious shit. The chances of a stray bullet finding me just got a whole lot better. My heart thunders in my chest, and the engines shudder below me. I raise one hand to my ear and press down. "Swift? Still alive up there?"

"Miraculously. Hold on a second." Another thud rattles through the ship, but there's no explosion in its wake; the shell must have missed its mark.

"If I give up my position to them, their paradigm will shift. Their infra will recognize that I'm unguarded. They'll stop shooting at the engines and start trying to bring me in."

"Cas—" Swift starts.

There are children on this boat. There are people on the *Minnow* whose only crime was being born on the fringes. The people on the copters aren't trying to spare them, and even if they do bring me in, they won't waste the opportunity to take out a pirate ship. There's only one way to save everyone on the *Minnow*.

"I think I can get all of them right up against the water at the back of the ship," I tell Swift. "And then I'll light the Otachi."

There's a long pause. Then Swift laughs, as if she can't believe what she's hearing. "I'll tell the captain. Give me a second."

"I don't have a second," I hiss. The guns are swiveling around, the barrels pointing straight at the engines beneath my feet. "Make sure she doesn't shoot me for this."

Swift yells, "Cas, wait—"

But I'm already pushing off the wall, sprinting for the edge of the deck, my fingers fumbling with the straps of my right-hand Otachi. I strip it off, toss it over my shoulder, swing my arms up, and dive headfirst into the sea.

The water thrums with the beat of the rotors overhead, and I turn end over end, my fingertips scrabbling for the dials on my wrist. I twist them, the device comes to life, and a beam of light blasts down into the depths as the sound of Bao's homing call rattles out after it. With the saltwater burning my eyes, I can't keep them open long enough to see if he responds.

I can only pray now.

With two quick pumps of my legs, I break the surface again and immediately fling up my bare arm, waving it wildly back and forth. "Here!" I scream over the roar of the quadcopters. "Help! I'm here! Please!"

Their infra must detect me; the gun barrels go slack as the quadcopters pull up. The *Minnow* speeds away. Over the wave tops, I spot the narrow hulls of the Splinters peeling off and heading back my way as if they're coming to collect me. I really hope they aren't.

"Please!" I yell again. With the left-hand Otachi weighing me down, it's getting harder and harder to tread water. I glance beneath my feet and find a familiar shadow rising fast. Up above, the copters start to sink. They're coming for me.

No going back now.

I yank my left arm out of the sea, throwing the Otachi's beams against the lowering hull of the quadcopter above me and twisting the dial to the aggression setting. I thrash my legs, trying to propel myself out of the way. The water beneath me swells.

I slide clear with inches to spare, caught in a tumult of water as Bao breaches clean out of the NeoPacific, his massive limbs slashing at the quadcopter above. With a crash like a freight train derailing, he bats the copter into one of its fellows, but I plunge back underwater before I can see anything else. I throw my arms up over my head, trying to protect it, trying to make myself as small as possible. In this clash of giants, I'm just a skinny blip, washed to the side by the force of the wave Bao produces when he splashes back down.

I choke on saltwater as I try to surface again. All around me is noise and sea, and somewhere out there, a beast is tearing into metal the way a tsunami hits a coast. My whole body feels bruised, pummeled by the waves that keep crashing over me. I kick and gasp, trying to push myself away from the chaos that's been unleashed.

By the time I'm clear, one of the copters is inside out. Thick smoke clots the air, and tiny fires dot the waves. The second copter is limping back into the air, but Bao's not letting it go that easily. As it spins, trying to compensate for the damage he dealt to one of its rotors, the Reckoner lunges up, his beak snapping shut on the mount of the machine gun chugging bullets into his hide. With one twist of his neck, Bao turns the quadcopter end over end, slamming down into the wreckage of its fellow as he falls on top of it, his claws ripping at its steel-plated hull.

The third copter's a fast-retreating speck on the horizon.

I float on my back, watching it get smaller and smaller, a sinking feeling overtaking my stomach. That bird carries people who saw me alive. Saw me throw myself from the *Minnow*. Saw me turn the Otachi on the copters.

Saw me summon a beast from the depths to crush the people trying to bring me home.

I flash the Otachi at Bao, and the Reckoner's head snaps toward me. His vast, reptilian eyes narrow to slits, his blowholes flaring as he lets a slice of the copter's hull slip from his mouth. I can see the gears in his brain working. He's flushed with rage, filled with the need to savage, but the lights that blaze from my wrist are calling him in a way he can't ignore. I silently plead with him not to reconcile the two impulses on me. If I can attract him, if I can just pull him away from the wreckage, there might be survivors.

I might be able to spare a few of the people I just tried to slaughter.

I never meant for it to go this far. My stomach twists and surges, and before I can swallow it back, I'm emptying my guts in the ocean. I struggle to keep the Otachi level as I retch, but Bao's losing interest in the beams. He lowers his beak back into the water, prowling closer to the quadcopter's ragged hull.

"Get over here, you little shit," I choke, and slash the lights over his eyes.

Bao roars, rearing up again. With two quick strokes of his back legs, he drifts toward me, and as he draws close, I can smell the acrid smoke and gasoline fumes that roll off him. His beak snaps shut impatiently, and I shut off the Otachi.

For a moment we regard each other, one monster to another. The one who took down the quadcopters and the one who made him do it.

Then I twist a knob on my wrist, and the *dive* signal flashes out into the depths, the noise of it ringing in my ears. Bao hauls in a deep breath through his blowholes, then slips silently under the surface, sinking fast, but not fast enough to avoid brushing me with his singed keratin plates as his shoulders rush beneath my feet. I flinch when my toes skim over a scorching-hot bullet hole.

It doesn't seem worth it to go back to the *Minnow*. For a moment, I fantasize about crawling into the wreckage of the quadcopters, about trying to pull out whoever's left alive in there, as if I can undo some of the damage that Bao's—that *I've*—done.

But that doesn't seem worth it either. If there are people

living and breathing in those twisted remains bobbing on the waves, my face is probably the last thing they want to see.

My best option at this point is probably just to follow Bao. Let myself sink. Let the ocean take me, let the water fill my lungs like it's been trying to do. It would be painful, but then it wouldn't, and I would never hurt anyone again.

No, that's not true. That can't ever be true. If I let myself sink, it would kill Swift, and I can't abide that. I wrecked these quadcopters without hesitation, and it saved her life, but now even that doesn't seem like it's enough. Was her life worth the lives I just took? Is she worth that to me?

———————

I'm still stuck on those questions when Varma's Splinter comes to collect me. Chuck leans out of the copilot's seat and scoops me out of the NeoPacific. There's no fight left in me; I let her drop me on the floor like a rag doll. They could easily kill me now, but I don't think they're in the mood for favors.

"Holy shit, girl," she says.

"I've never seen anything like that," Varma agrees. "Is that what your job is always like, huh? Damn, that's some beautiful carnage." He leans back in the pilot's seat, smirking as he gazes out over the sea. Something quick and low escapes his lips. It sounds like a Hindi prayer.

Chuck checks him with her shoulder. "Quit dawdling, *lelemu*. We're running again."

"Right," he says, and guns the engines.

28

The Splinter sidles up to the *Minnow*, and the ship's claws snap around our hull, winching us up to the cradles on the second deck. Our breakneck pace hasn't slowed. This was only the first attack—the SRC will try again, and next time it won't be just quadcopters. But I don't feel ready to think about that. As it is, I'm not even sure if I can walk on my own when the Splinter finally settles into its mounts.

Varma and Chuck clamber out before we're properly docked, and I try my best to crawl after them, but my arms shake as I haul myself over the ship's side. My breath comes in unsteady gasps, and darkness seeps into the corners of my vision. The ocean has a funny way of sapping your strength without you noticing. Once you're out of the water, you're shattered.

But then a pair of hands finds me, and Swift is there, slinging my Otachi-clad arm over her shoulder. "She's dead on her feet, boss," she says, and I wince, knowing Santa Elena is seeing me at the weakest I've ever felt.

"Let her rest," the captain declares, and I could kiss her if I had the strength for it. "She's done well."

And the worst part is, I'm glad to hear her say it. If it had been the other way around, if it had been pirate aircraft attacking an innocent ship, I'd have been ecstatic over how well the fight went. I *deserve* this praise. The pattern was exactly the same as a regular Reckoner fight: An act of aggression was met with a monster. Innocent lives were saved. It was self-defense, through and through.

And I don't know anything about myself anymore if I can justify it like this.

Swift's arm tightens around my waist, guiding me carefully past the gawking crew. My feet don't feel real. I do my best to drag them into something resembling steps, but she has to take most of my weight, and by the time we're down to the hall of bunks, I've given up on trying to contribute. I don't question that she's taking me to Code's old room rather than the closet. Maybe the captain gave her the all clear, or maybe this is just another tiny rebellion, but all that matters to me is that I have a bed to sleep in.

Swift kicks the door open and deposits me haphazardly on the bunk. "I'll get you some blankets," she says, turning away. "Don't go anywhere."

"Hah," I grumble against the vinyl of the bare mattress, but she's gone and I don't think she heard me. I couldn't lift my head if I tried.

That copter must be getting back to its carrier. Must be

connecting to an uplink, must be downloading the data from the fight: videos, heat signatures, statistics. A rescue ship has probably already been dispatched to the wreckage that Bao left in his wake. The families are being notified.

And my family is being notified.

First I failed to protect the *Nereid*. Then I failed to take the pill. And now they're going to see exactly what I just did. They're going to think I've turned, that I want to stay with my captors, that I'm one of them now. The worst failure of all, in their eyes.

E tan e epi tas.

Come back alive and victorious, or don't come back at all.

The message couldn't be clearer. Even if the copters succeeded, even if I'd been plucked from the ocean and dragged back to the California coast, I wouldn't have a place waiting for me in our stables. I don't belong there anymore. I try to picture the look on my parents' faces when they see what I did. I don't know if I'll ever be able to justify it to them.

At least there's *someone* on this big blue Earth who doesn't seem to care how much I fuck up, someone who's spreading her own comforter over my crumpled, beaten body. I didn't notice her sneak back into the room. I guess I was too busy wallowing. Swift pries at the straps around my arm until the Otachi comes loose, and a moment later, I hear a clunk as she sets it on the floor.

"Thanks," I mumble, my eyelids sealed shut.

"I'm sorry," she whispers. For what, I'm not sure. I feel the brush of fingertips on my cheek as she tucks a strand of hair behind my ear, and then her footsteps are moving back toward the door.

"Swift?"

"Yeah?" she croaks.

My next words are whispered through my teeth, something small and secret, something I can barely admit to myself, but she needs to know. "It was worth it," I tell her, and the rest is darkness.

29

I feel like a ghost aboard this ship. When I wander to the mess, nobody pays me any mind. I don't get eye contact or nods. Swift's vanished. Her trainee duties must be keeping her busy. I half expect her to be there when I wake up the morning after sinking the copters, but the only part of her left when my eyes slide open is the warmth of her blanket around me and the scent of her in its fibers.

I haven't returned it.

I go about my usual duties, not knowing what else to do. When the Minnow makes berth at an island to refuel, I check on Bao, making sure that the quadcopters' guns haven't hit him anywhere vital. He's got battle scars now, in the form of bullet holes peppering his plating. A few of them struck true in the cracks between his keratin. I have to probe them with a long metal lance to make sure no bullets made it through his hide and into his muscle. It's exhausting work, climbing over every inch of his monstrous bulk, and when I'm done I end up napping on the trainer deck, leaning against the wall under the counter. The rattle of the engines jolts me awake an hour later as the *Minnow* puts to flight again.

———————

That night, I wake to a knock. If it were another attack, they wouldn't be knocking, so I throw on a hoodie and answer it, half-expecting the sight that greets me when I swing the door open.

Swift stands in the hall, her hair swept back and her hands stuck so deep in her pockets that she looks like she's about to fold in on herself.

"Do you … uh, do you want to talk?" she asks, flashing me a nervous grimace. From the way she glances over her shoulder, I assume this visit isn't captain-sanctioned.

I nod.

"Cool. Got something I think you'd like to see. Come on."

I follow her to the *Minnow*'s main deck, where the hulking shadows of Phobos and Diemos loom against the night. Swift clambers up on the barrel of the aft gun and motions for me to follow. The metal is warm under my palms as I pull myself up after her; the chill of the night hasn't stolen the sun's heat from it yet.

"Look up," Swift says when I settle at her side.

The moonless night is a gift. The Milky Way stretches out above us, a spillage of light in the deep black of the ocean. With the slumbering *Minnow*'s lights off, we can see for millennia.

"That's Cygnus, over there—the swan. And Pisces. Fish. And there's Cetus," Swift says her fingertips brushing up against the sky as she connects the dots between each one. "The whale."

"You know your stuff, huh?" I ask, leaning back against the cannon.

"Mom always told me stories. Y'know, about the goddesses and heroes and monsters. And she taught me where to find them in the sky. Showed me how to navigate with them, told me what they were like. Never quite became one, though," she says, rubbing the back of her neck with one hand.

When her fingers fall away, I spot the little fish inked there. "So I get that everyone on this ship has one of those tattoos," I say, "but why…"

The darkness emboldens me. I reach over and brush the sliver of ink. Swift's spine goes rigid under the pad of my finger, and I jerk my hand back.

She smirks, her gaze fixed on the distant line of the horizon barely distinguishable from the dark of the night. "One of Mom's best stories was about a Greek king and a man named Damocles. One day, Damocles goes to his king and starts sucking up, telling him how great his life must be and how wonderful his power is. So the king offers to switch places with Damocles, to give him a taste of what being king is like. Of course the sucker accepts, so the king lays out a lavish banquet for him, and Damocles is jazzed. Then the king shows him where he'll be sitting. It's a throne, totally tricked out, but suspended above it by a single thread of horsehair is a sword, pointed right at the seat. Damocles gets it now—he understands that with great power comes a shit-ton of danger. So when Santa Elena asked where I wanted my tattoo, I decided to put it where it would remind me of that story. 'Cause you're at the top of the world—you're the most powerful thing on the sea when you're serving under her—but there's a cost. There's always a cost." She trails off, staring out at the dark waves.

"Is it worth it?" I ask.

"Why, you thinking of signing on?"

My lips twist, as does an invisible dagger in my gut. It's an innocent-enough joke, but there's weight behind it. With rescue ships inbound, my days on the *Minnow* are numbered, no matter what happens when they catch up. As much as I hate to admit it—which isn't very much, I'm finding—this ship's become home in the past few months.

Swift snorts, folding her arms against the chill sea winds. "It's never going to end," she groans. "That's the worst bit. I...I dunno, when I signed on to this crew, I thought it'd be over someday, or at least I'd be the one calling the shots in the end. Y'know, I was a kid. I thought I could change, I thought I could get out. I thought I wouldn't end up like..." There's something breaking inside her, something that's pushing her close to tears, but she bites down on them, ducking her head to keep me from seeing. "I'm trapped."

"Yeah, me too," I tell her, and her watery gaze snaps up, her bright blue eyes fixed on mine. "I mean...I used to want more than anything to get off this ship, to go home, to do some good in the world. But after...yesterday, after what I've done—" I break off, trying to collect my thoughts. "I've spent my whole life fighting pirates. It's in my blood. It's what I *do*. And then three months on this boat and I'm just one of them."

"Am I 'just one of them'?" Swift asks, miffed.

"No. You're so much more." The traitorous truth slips from my lips far too quickly for me to rescind it. I can feel a blush building in my cheeks, and from the stunned look on Swift's face, the darkness is doing nothing to conceal it. "I mean—"

"Oh, *shit*."

"If it weren't for … everything … "

She buries her face in her hands, her shoulders shaking with laughter.

"Quit it," I yelp, swatting her on the shoulder. "It's not funny."

"It really isn't," Swift says, but she's giggling still, and I can't help but laugh with her. It's ridiculous. It's outrageous. Bao could tap dance across the NeoPacific right now and it wouldn't seem that out of place, because I'm in way over my head and I'm falling.

I'm falling for her, she's fallen for me, and the whole thing is so desperate and stupid that we're both reduced to fits of laughter that ring out across the *Minnow*'s deck. We're two trapped girls with nothing but each other on a ship of people who'd be better off with us dead, and somehow on top of that we've managed to do the one thing we shouldn't be able to do.

Three months ago, Swift dragged me on this ship and I punched her in the face. And now I'm so tied to her that my heart aches at the thought of having to leave this boat. Home used to be Reckoner pens, Mom's lab, Dad and Tom in the kitchen. But the *Minnow*'s taught me a truth that's been hiding in plain sight my entire life.

Home is what you kill for.

And I killed for Swift.

But even though I want to, even though there's an energy crackling between us right now that's almost impossible to deny, I know we can't do anything about this. I know how that would look. No matter how you swing it, I'm still a prisoner on this ship, and Swift is still one of my jailers. We go this far, no farther.

She catches my eye and grimaces. "Equal footing, huh?" she says, as if she's read my mind.

I nod, knowing it crushes her, knowing it crushes me. We're oceans away from a world where Swift doesn't have power over me, power I can't ignore, power I can't afford to expose myself to. And until we stand on the same level, absolutely nothing can happen between us.

And it sucks, because all I want to do is kiss her. It's infuriating how perfect it would be to kiss her right now, perched on a cannon on a pirate ship under the stars. That sounds like something off the pages of an adventure novel. But my life isn't one of those stories. My story is a hurricane, and here with Swift is just the eye.

And so I stare up at the constellations she outlined and listen to the engines churning below us, the waves sliding off our bow, and somewhere under that, the gentle sound of her breathing, and let that be enough.

30

Santa Elena holds court the next evening.

She puts out an all-call after dinner, and the entire crew packs into her throne room. My newfound invisibility has me pressed up against the back wall, trapped behind a sea of bodies that block my view of the dais where the captain sits. From the glimpses I catch between shoulders, she isn't dressed up like the last time we were in here; instead she's armed to the teeth and decked out in a sleek set of body armor. The pursuit is coming, and our captain is ready for war.

"Cassandra," she barks over the grumble of the crowd, and silence washes over the room. I push off the wall and make my way forward, nudging my way past the crew members that block my path.

Santa Elena steps off the dais to meet me as I approach. She wears a predatory grin, but underneath it I can see the stress that's eating away at her. The whole room aches with tension. My gaze flickers to Swift, who sits on the dais's edge with Chuck and Varma. Lemon's off in the navigation tower, keeping watch over the instruments and the horizon. While Chuck and Varma keep their eyes fixed on the captain, Swift's are locked on me.

I draw my lips tight, trying not to give anything away as Santa Elena circles around me, her hands folded behind her back.

"We have a bit of a situation here," the captain starts. "Which is to say, we have a complete clusterfuck on our hands, and it's centered around you. Your IGEOC friend's got hell raining down on us, and from what I've gathered, we've got ships with Reckoners of their own inbound to bring our merry little adventures to an end."

A discontented mumble rises from the ranks, but Santa Elena quiets it with a wave of her hand as she stalks back around to face me. She lays her hands on my shoulders and I wince as her nails bite against the cotton of my shirt. "Fortunately for us," she says, her gaze unflinching as she stares me down, "you're also our way out of this mess."

I can't blink. Not now. I shift my weight, but Santa Elena's grip stays rooted in me.

"You did a fine job with the quadcopters. I'm genuinely impressed with how far the beast's training has come. But it's become clear to me that our endeavor with him is not sustainable. We're abandoning it."

A roar fills my ears, overwhelming the shouts of the crew. Bao is my life aboard this ship. I've put so much work into making him the monster he is today—what *right* does she have to throw that away?

She must see the defiance, the rejection in my eyes. "Cassandra, there are *children* on this ship. Children I'm trying to do right by, children that I can't have falling to 'Reckoner justice.' My son among them. I never anticipated that the response from shore would be this severe, and my miscalculation has put every soul on this boat at risk. We need the SRC off our case permanently, and that means ridding this ship of both its Reckoner and its trainer. No, I'm not going to kill you," she drawls as she feels me tense under her grip. "Until we're in the clear, you are this ship's best defense. And I know you're going to defend it," she mutters, casting a glance back at Swift. "You'd do anything to protect 'this ship,' right?"

I nod. There's no point in lying.

"That's the spirit!" She claps her hands together and turns back toward her throne. "Here's the plan. You lot!"

The crew roars.

"You wear your loyalty on your skin. Show it to me."

Arms thrust into the air with little black fish sketched across them. Trousers roll up to reveal calves stained with the ship's mark. On the dais, Varma's grin widens, stretching the Minnow on his cheek, and Chuck sweeps her mane of wild hair to the side, revealing the ink that slashes between her shoulder blades. Swift nods her head to expose her neck, but her brow is still set in that resentful furrow.

"I'm not gonna hide it. We're in deep shit. But when has that ever stopped us?"

"Never!" the crew screams back at her. Some of them have slid their weapons out; others brandish their fists.

"When the inbound hits, I want you to hit back with everything you've got. We're gonna show them that trifling with us is the worst mistake they're ever gonna make. But Cassandra, here—" She points to me, and my spine stiffens. "Cassandra will be doing the brunt of the attack. She and our beast are going to make our stand, and those shore-rat bastards are going to fall on her like flies on meat. And when they do, that's when we start running."

Varma frowns, and I feel like I need to pinch myself to make sure I'm seeing it. The whole crew seems flummoxed.

"You heard me right," Santa Elena says, mounting the dais. "This is the plan: Cassandra is going to crush the pursuit until they can't catch us, no matter what. And then she's going to turn herself over to whatever's left."

"How do we know she isn't going to turn on us the second she's got an SRCese fleet at her back?" Hina shouts over the grumbling noise building in the crowd.

Santa Elena flashes a wicked grin as she prowls around behind Swift. "Because we have something she's interested in protecting," the captain says, sinking her nails into Swift's shoulder.

Swift sits up straighter. A bubble of laughter rises from the crew, and a blush starts to work its way into her cheeks.

"You've done well, kid. Exceeded expectations, that's for sure. You kept both Cassandra and the beast alive. And there were…certain bonuses to putting you two together, it seems." Santa Elena pauses to let everyone savor the implication of her words. "But all things end, Swift, and you've reaped the benefits of this opportunity enough."

If she doesn't step away from Swift soon, I'm going to do something drastic. My fingers twitch, itching for Otachi controls, and for a second I forget my place on this ship. I forget that the captain has forty people at her back who would kill me if I went near her. I forget that the only thing protecting me is an inbound fleet that's probably still leagues off. All I care about right here and now is putting myself between Swift and the captain.

I've taken three steps before I realize what's happening, and Santa Elena slips her gun out of her holster, her fingers still crimped in Swift's shoulder. She doesn't seem to notice that she's drawn her weapon until the silence of the room around us sinks in.

The captain snorts. "Cassandra, let me make one thing very, very clear." She lifts the gun and points it at me. "There's going to come a time when I ask you to jump and instead of saying 'how high,' you're going to refuse, even with a gun to your head. I know it has its limits. But *this*," she says, shifting her aim to Swift. "This doesn't."

Swift glares up at me, her eyes shimmering slightly in the low light. Her fists are clenched so tightly that her knuckles flash bone-white. Here, before the entire crew, the crew she's supposed to be in contention to lead someday, Swift is being strung out like bait. And it's all my fault.

I shudder, knowing the worst of it. When I get off this boat, when the pursuit catches up and Santa Elena relinquishes me, there's going to be no one left on the *Minnow* who's really on Swift's side.

"Fail to defend this ship, and I think you know me well enough to guess what happens next," she says, nosing the barrel into the side of Swift's skull.

The crew, surprisingly enough, looks worried. They don't know how to confront this development. Santa Elena's trainees are supposed to be some of the most respected people on this boat. Now one of them is being cast down when she ought to be exalted. With the confirmation that Swift's succeeded in protecting me, her status should inflate. But the reward for her loyalty and service is a gun to her head.

Santa Elena must sense that someone's about to speak up, because she chooses that moment to draw her gun back and stow it at her hip. "I'll admit that was a little dramatic," she says, laughing.

The tension breaks, the crew picking up her cues and chuckling along with her. Santa Elena glances down at Swift and offers a hand.

Swift takes it. Applause joins the laughter as the captain pulls her to her feet. "Well done!" a large man in the back thunders, and Swift cracks a strained smile. But her eyes are fixed on me, and I can see the hollowness. The betrayal. She's had plenty of guns pointed at her in her career, but I'm willing to bet that this was the first time the captain was on the other end of it.

31

When the all-call stutters on the next evening to report that a SRCese fleet is closing in, it feels inevitable. Like just another day on the job. I sprint down to the trainer deck amid the chaos of the pre-battle rush, dodging past the crew members hauling giant ammunition crates out of the ship's stores. It's all or nothing tonight, and everyone seems to know it.

Swift's already waiting when I arrive, and she's saddled with a huge, dark package that she nearly drops when I come skidding onto the deck. "Captain's got a parting gift," she says, foisting it over to me. Her eyes stay fixed on the ground. There's a hint of red creeping in on their edges.

Stringlets? Or just sleeplessness? I wonder as I accept the bundle.

It's body armor. On the top of the pile rests a beetle-black, sculpted chestpiece, woven out of fiber that I'm assuming will stop bullets. There's some sort of flotation device that accompanies it to counteract its weight in the water. I set the heap of armor gingerly on the counter and lift the chestpiece off, sliding it over my shoulders. It's got straps on it, buckles and velcro that I have no idea where to pull tight.

"I don't—" I start, but Swift is already stepping around behind me, her hands twisting the belts around my back as she tugs them into place. For a moment, the armor squeezes too tight against my chest. I grunt, but the pressure lifts a second later.

"This'll go faster if you help. Get the armpieces on. I'll handle the legs." Swift snatches a few components off the counter and tosses them to me.

"Swift."

She ignores me, already working on securing a plated skirt around my waist. My breath hitches when her fingers brush against my wetsuit.

"*Swift.*"

"Please, just … just let me … "

I feel like my bones have been inverted. I've been broken, and everything's been pieced back together wrong. When I step off this boat and onto Bao's back, I'll be completely free. Once the pursuit is disabled, I can go with them. I can expose Fabian Murphy for the traitor he is. I can escape the *Minnow* and Santa Elena and all of the blood and death I was supposed to unleash. I wanted to get away from that.

My fingers fumble over the armpieces, locking them into place around my biceps. I slide the Otachi onto my forearms, cinching my fingers in the controls. With a deep breath, I point them out across the sea and fire the homing signal. The noise of the call rattles the deck, and somewhere off in the deep, Bao's reply thunders in return.

As she finishes up with my legs, Swift takes a step back to admire her handiwork. "You look like a fucking knight," she says, glowing with pride as a smile breaks over her face.

Relief rushes through me. At least here at the end, I get to see her happy one last time.

There's one piece left. Swift lifts the helmet off the counter and hands me my earpiece. I slip the little device in, and she sets the helmet over my head. "Jesus, cheer up. You're going home, just like you want," she grumbles.

But that's not what I want, not at all. Everything I want, everything I have left, is standing right in front of me, and I'm about to leave her behind.

The sea opens up beneath the deck as Bao's head crests out of the water. He lets his jaw hang open, putting the nubby spikes that line his mouth on display. His rank breath washes out over us. I take a hesitant step away from Swift, toward the monster I've raised. I don't know what else I'm supposed to do, so I flash the beacon again, and Bao slides his beak onto the trainer deck. His head is so massive that it barely fits in the rear port, and I think back to the days when he was small enough to swim in the makeshift pool. He's come so far.

I've come even farther.

"Cas?"

I pause, my heart thundering in my chest as I turn to face her, as I meet that red-rimmed gaze that's boring into me.

"There's line-hooks in the belt. They'll anchor you."

Oh.

"And..." She trails off, shrugging, and I feel the pressure of saying goodbye crash down on my shoulders.

There are only two words I need to say. Four syllables. I can feel them in my throat, and I'm terrified of what could happen if I let them loose. But three months on this ship have robbed me of the connection between my fear and my actions, and last chances have a funny way of shaking up your priorities.

"Equal footing?" I breathe, because here and now is as free as I'm ever going to be.

"Equal footing."

I don't know who moves first. We lunge for each other. The feet between us collapse into nothing and my hands wind in that stupid, stupid hair as her arms ensnare my waist and her lips come crashing over mine. I want hours, I want weeks, I want more than these bare seconds to be free like this. She holds me so tightly that my armor warps under her grip, and I kiss her with everything I have left. There's no time for hesitation, no time for uncertainty.

There's just me and her, and the rest of it falls away.

Swift groans, the noise vibrating against my chest as she sinks against me, her lips urging mine open with all of the hunger I've seen inside her, all of the need and impatience that I've watched her battle and been unable to comfort. But now I can. Now I surge up on my tiptoes and grin against the soft curves of her mouth as I let one hand slide down to cradle her jaw, to bring her chasing after me.

When we break apart, she buries her nose in the crook

of my neck and I smooth down her unkempt hair, and together we stay like that: giddy, out of breath, and scared to pieces of what comes next.

It's only when Bao tosses his head impatiently, causing the whole deck to lurch, that we snap out of it. I pull myself out of Swift's grip and move to his eye, running my fingertips over one of the ridges that crests it, and the touch seems to quiet him. When I glance back at Swift, I catch her swiping her hand over her cheek.

"I should probably … " I start.

"Captain'll be looking for me," she says. "And you need to get in the water, stat."

I can feel the void widening between us already, the distance that separates us growing with every passing second, and I want nothing more than to run back to her side. But there's a job to do here, one that both our lives are staked on. I crimp my fingers between Bao's keratin plates and slot one of my boots on top of the spikes that line his jaw.

I'm just about to haul myself up when her hand comes down on my shoulder, twisting me away from my beast and back to face her. Swift presses her forehead against the helmet that shields mine, her eyes squeezed tightly shut as she whispers, "It's not goodbye until you're out of sight."

And then, just like that, she turns and sprints off the trainer deck before I can get a word in.

I push off the ground and scramble onto Bao's head, cursing pirate girls under my breath as he bucks underneath my weight and pulls back out of the rear port. I check the respirator around my neck and slip my goggles up over my eyes.

The piece in my ear crackles on. "So now that *that's* over with…"

Varma.

"You, uh…you heard that, then," I say just before setting the respirator in my teeth.

"Funny thing about these comms—they pick up anything that shakes your bones. You're lucky the captain put me in charge of your line," he says, and I can feel the laughter he's suppressing. I clench my jaw. As we slide away from the ship, Bao rears, lifting his head until we're level with the main deck.

Santa Elena stands there, dressed to the nines in her own elegant, bulletproof armor. Her chin lifts, a vicious grin spreading across her face as she watches her handiwork rise up to meet her. The sunset blazes at her back, casting her long shadow out to touch us, as if marking us as inevitably, unquestionably hers.

And though part of me is certain that after tonight, we'll be free of the *Minnow* at last, another part knows that this boat will last with me to the end of my days.

"Inbound is ten minutes out. Splinters away at my mark," the all-call announces, and here atop Bao's back, I finally have the vantage point I need, the one that lets me see right into the navigation tower where Lemon bends over a microphone.

The white hulls snap off the sides of the *Minnow*, and a swell of nostalgia sings through me. Bao's upper body plunges back down toward the water; my stomach swoops as I crouch, winding my fingertips in his plates. His blowholes heave beneath me, drawing a quick breath before he submerges. The waters churn around us, and I fight to keep my hands rooted when they crash over me.

"Cas, you there?" Varma's voice mutters in my ear. "Captain wants you to keep him submerged until she says otherwise. We'll draw them in, then you do the rest." He says it as if it'll be easy.

"Got it," I reply around the respirator. The comm's smart enough to fill in the consonants where the piece in my mouth has stolen them. I unspool a line-hook from my belt and drive it into Bao's plating, praying that the barbs will hold fast when the time comes. Once I'm secured to his back, I turn the Otachi to the dive command and blaze them out.

Bao sinks lower. Shadows close in around us, the dark of the night settling into the sea long before it touches the world above us. I can barely make out the sleek curve of the *Minnow*'s hull in the murk. We drop lower still. I pinch my nose and blow to pop my ears.

It's so quiet, so calm down here. There's nothing but the rush of water from the churn of Bao's forelegs and the rock-solid sureness of his skull underneath me. I find myself wishing I could stay, wishing we could wait until Bao's breath runs out or until the respirator sputters and quits. But somewhere up there on the *Minnow*'s deck, Santa Elena has Swift in her sights, and that thought keeps me rooted, waiting for the next instruction that comes through the comm.

Light spools through the deep as the *Minnow*'s engines flare, and I know it's almost time. I don't need to direct Bao with the Otachi. His bond with the ship is enough to set him after her as she runs, the Splinters' hulls skimming in her wake.

There are six shadows trailing her, and three of them are swimming.

"Drop back, Cas," Varma hisses in my ear. "They'll be expecting signals to be coming from our ship. The farther Bao is from us, the more confident they'll be. Wait for our signal to strike."

I snap on the Otachi and cast Bao's homing signal back toward his tail, my eyes fixed on the hulking forms of the three Reckoners overhead. Every homing signal is unique, coded to make sure that the beasts can only be controlled by their masters. But sometimes they forget themselves. Sometimes when they're too amped up, they'll go after any flashing light and any siren. But Bao is the only one who heeds my call, and the tightness in my chest unclenches as the pursuit boats and Reckoners pull ahead, still chasing after the *Minnow*'s shadow.

The biggest of the beasts is a cetoid. Its jointed flippers are tipped with vestigial claws that carve through the water as it leads the pack, plunging ahead with powerful strokes of its flukes. A cephalopoid follows close in its wake, tentacles rippling through the darkening waves, and a serpentoid brings up the rear. Its sinuous body dips underneath its companion ship, coiling against it before pushing off again. There's a part of me that cries out at the sight of the other beasts, of the animals that I've spent my whole life raising.

There's another part of me that reaches out to crush it.

Like Varma said, they're focused on the *Minnow*. They're expecting any signal to come from its decks. They won't see me coming. Trainers have conducted battles from decks, from shattered hulls, and in their most desperate moments, from the sea. No one's ever dared to fight from the back of the beast they're directing.

No one has ever needed to.

Heavy pulses ring through the water, and flashes of light up above mark where the opening shells have struck. Santa Elena's drawing them on, triggering the Reckoners' responses. The three beasts lunge ahead, leaving their companion vessels defenseless in their wake.

"Cas," Varma says in my ear. "Now."

32

The lasers blast from my wrists, and Bao's head wrenches up, forcing me flat against the plating. I'm lost against the surge, the line at my waist the only thing keeping me attached to his head. My ears swell and pop viciously—I can't equalize in time. A scream bubbles out of me, and we break the surface like a geyser.

There's no time for hesitation, no time for second thoughts. I point my wrist at the rearmost ship, whose guns are still trained on the *Minnow*'s retreating aft, and twist the setting to *charge*. Bao obeys with a roar, lunging forward so ferociously that I lose my grip and tumble back against his neck.

It's too late for the people on the deck to do anything. They're powerless as Bao comes crashing over them like a hurricane, his claws sinking into the ship's rear as he closes his beak around the aft gun mounts.

Then their eyes shift to me, and they recognize who's

commanding the beast. Me in my mirrored goggles. Me in my respirator and armor. Me with the Otachi on my wrists, tied to the back of the monster raining hell on them, fighting on the wrong side of the war.

There's no point in apologizing. I snap the Otachi to *destroy* and lean out over the side of Bao's head, throwing the beams against the engines that protrude from the boat's sides. Bao chases after them, but this time I keep my grip solid and sure in the plating, and my aim doesn't waver. His claws slash once, and the boat is dead in the water.

The serpentoid peels off the *Minnow*'s tail, its arrow-like snout whipping around to find us, and I know that this boat must be its companion. It lets out a fell shriek and launches itself forward. Its winding body slices through the inky waves like they're nothing.

I crouch against Bao's neck, trying to make myself as small as possible as my monster wheels to meet the other Reckoner head-on. The serpentoid ducks beneath the waves, and Bao heaves toward it—and his beak closes on thin air with a crack that nearly knocks me senseless. My ears ring, but I can't waver now, can't let it get the better of me, because I've trained enough serpentoids to know exactly what the snake beast is about to do.

I flick the Otachi to *charge* and throw the beam out to our right. Bao veers, just as the first of the serpentoid's coils lash up around his midsection. He escapes its grip, but just barely, and the strike sends him rolling onto his back. I cling to his plating so hard that my knuckles creak. The water slams me flat against him, and I reach down and anchor another line-hook to his keratin. He rolls his head forward, fueled by an instinct I can't break him from, and this time the serpentoid's too busy recovering to get out of the way. Bao's jaws cinch around its neck.

The muscles snap taut underneath me as Bao bites down, and a sick, wet crunch rattles my bones. The serpentoid goes limp.

Two down. But in the frenzy of the fight, I've lost track of the other ships, and it takes me a minute to get my wits about me, my thoughts still stuck on the fact that I've just helped kill a Reckoner. The smell of the serpentoid's blood washes over me, thick and pungent, and I drink it in before I can tell myself not to. Bao lets out a roar that shakes the NeoPacific, letting his kill tumble back into the waves.

A spotlight flares from one of the ships, its light nearly blinding me as they aim it at us. Then the other ship's lights blast on, and I can't see the stars above me anymore. Bao roars again, but this time it chokes off in a confused warble as he tries to make sense of the new signals blazing across him. I squint through my goggles, searching for what I know must be coming.

The lasers carve in the wake of the spotlights, their bright beams coming to rest squarely on Bao's head. *Shit.* I throw up his *charge* signal, aiming it right back at the closest boat, but he shakes his snout from side to side, still confused.

"C'mon, c'mon, c'mon," I growl into the respirator. It's no use.

The cetoid is the first to strike, coming up hard against Bao's underbelly with its plated snout. The hit sends me flying into the air as Bao shrieks in pain, and my fingers instinctively wind around the line-hook cables as my feet go sailing over my head. I land hard on my back, the helmet cracking against Bao's plates. A thick tentacle towers out of the sea to our left and lashes down around his neck, inches from my position. I grit my teeth, turn the Otachi to their brightest setting, and plunge them against the cephalopoid's soft flesh.

A scream echoes out from somewhere beneath Bao and the tentacle snaps back, a curl of smoke wafting up from the neat hole I've just burned in it. But before I can congratulate myself, the cephalopoid's limb slams down again, and this time I can't roll out of the way.

The world goes dark. I feel like I'm suffocating, like I'm spinning, like "up" and "down" are figments of my imagination, and then suddenly I'm back. I choke in a breath through the respirator and discover that we're underwater, that the blackness wasn't all imagined. My head throbs so viciously that for a second I think my skull has cracked. I've been tossed around far too much to get away intact at this point. Bao flexes underneath me, his jaws gnawing insistently at something, but everything else seems too still.

Then the cephalopoid's tentacles loom out of the darkness again, lashing down around Bao's body. He rolls his head and catches one in his beak, and thick Reckoner blood flushes into the water around us, blinding me. I flatten myself against Bao's skull. There's nothing I can do in this blackness but feel the power of the monster beneath my feet as he struggles, locked in mortal combat.

The only consolation is that the trainers up above are just

as blind as me. With the fight underwater, they can't afford the refraction throwing off their aim, can't risk setting their beasts on each other. It's all down to the three Reckoners.

And Bao's giving it all he has. As the blood in the water clears, I see that he's managed to rend the cephalopoid nearly in half. The squid beast still flails, but it's mostly trying to get away from Bao's snapping jaws, which slice into its tender flesh like it's nothing. A twinge of pity rattles my bones as I think of all of the pups I've raised, of the sucker scars on my ankle, of how much pain the Reckoner is in.

Then Bao lunges forward and ends it.

But there's no relief, no time to catch a breath as the cetoid rockets out of the murk. Its flukes pump furiously and it slams into Bao, sending me flying to the end of my lines again. There's a horrible, muted scraping noise as somewhere its teeth rake along Bao's keratin plates, and he convulses underneath me, his forelegs flailing as he tries to kick the cetoid away.

I yank myself against his hide, close my eyes, and wait.

This, I imagine, is what a cow that's been sucked up by a tornado feels like. I can't cut myself loose, and even if I could somehow unlatch the line-hooks, it'd only increase my chances of being crushed to a pulp by one of the beasts. The tendons in my hand creak as Bao swings his head from side to side, but I keep my eyes squeezed shut. I don't want to know what he's doing. I don't want to know if the cetoid's made it through his shell, if Bao's gotten his razor-sharp claws into the whale beast's tough hide, if they've managed to tear each other's throats out in the same instant.

No matter what, it's beyond my control. All I can do is pray.

When stillness finally comes, my eyes drift open. I see the pieces. The two-pronged fluke of the cetoid looming out of the shadows above me. The meaty, pulpy mass of the cephalopoid's head to my left. My breath catches in my throat as I watch them sink past us. And beneath me, Bao's as alive as ever.

He did it.

A glow of pride warms through me, and I can't help but grin against the respirator. "Varma, you there? The Reckoners and one of the boats are down."

But the piece in my ear only crackles in reply. The *Minnow*'s out of range.

Which means the boats might be on its tail again.

Which means Santa Elena has a gun to Swift's head.

33

I pull the Otachi triggers, and my stomach lurches as Bao raises his head to follow the projections. A familiar stabbing pain shoots through my ribs. I get my feet underneath me and lash the line-hooks tighter, fingers fumbling over the cables. No matter what, I can't let those boats catch up.

If I'm too late—

I can't afford to—

But I feel the sensation start to curdle somewhere in the back of my throat, the urge to come crashing down, to become the reckoning that I'm owed after so long at Santa Elena's mercy. If she dares take my last good thing, there'll be no saving her. She thought that using Swift as a shield would protect the *Minnow*.

But she underestimated me. I played my cards, I laid in wait, I let myself be beaten and manipulated. If she keeps that promise she made to me, I'll show her the truth I've learned on her boat. I don't just raise monsters.

I am one.

Bao breaks the surface with a growl that shakes me to the bones, and I squint through the spray, searching for the lights of boats on the horizon.

I find them. Three of them. The *Minnow's* retreating shadow barely glows in the distance, but bound right for it are two keels that blaze brightly half a league's length from us. There's still time. I flick the Otachi to *charge*. There's no holding back now.

Bao lunges after his lights with every last ounce of speed he can give. The pursuit is defenseless, their Reckoners dismembered, their guns their only hope against me and my beast. If we can catch them in time, it's all over.

I point Bao under the water and we plunge beneath the waves again. This time I brace against it, keeping my feet firmly planted on his head. The night betrays the Otachi beams too much for us to stay above—it would tell them exactly where to point their guns. But in the shadows of the NeoPacific, their shots are uncertain, their aim thrown off by the refraction of the water. All we'll have to do is kill the engines.

With the water cutting over my face, with Bao's strength beneath my feet, I feel invincible. I nudge him upward, teasing us toward the surface until my head skims out of the sea, just enough to check our position and adjust before we dive again. No lasers sweep over the waters from the pursuit boats. They've long since given up on their beasts after they disappeared into the depths with Bao.

We prowl the night, every bit the ancient horror we were meant to be.

When I next edge my head past the surface, the boats have split off from the *Minnow*'s tail, turning their bows toward us. Our approach is no secret. Their radar tells them exactly where we are every time we brush the surface, but once we take to the depths, we drop out of their sight on all frequencies. The darkness is ours.

And soon we're right underneath them. The harsh cut of their hulls looms above us, outlined by the scant lights they've left on. Bao tenses below me. With the *Minnow* almost out of range, he's growing more and more nervous by the second, the strength of his imprint urging him to fall back on his companion's tail. But he holds true to the Otachi's direction when I give it, and when at last I blaze the *destroy* signal at the hull overhead, he rises from the depths like a freight train.

A blast of heat hits me like the summer sun as we run up against the engines, but Bao's claws are there to mitigate it. The ship bucks upward when he strikes, and the muted shriek of rending metal makes my ears ring.

But before we can call it a job well-done, the clatter of gunfire echoes out to our left, and suddenly the murk is alive with heavy machine gun rounds that punch through the darkness with impunity. Lasers carve through the water, learning us as they trace, and I duck my head to avoid being blinded. A shriek rings out from above, and a small explosion rocks Bao's side.

We have to get deeper. We have to get deeper *now*.

I point the Otachi down, or at least my best guess of

down. The Reckoner underneath me is tossing his head and rolling his shoulders far too much for me to tell which way it is for certain. In the confused tangle of beams, Bao picks out his signal and charges after it.

Then something punches me in the back, and all of the air in my lungs flushes into the respirator with a scream. My head throbs savagely as we sink farther into the depths and I pitch forward, desperately trying to draw in a breath that keeps running away from me. For a moment, I think I've been shot.

Then I realize that I've definitely been shot. I twist my arm around my back, fingertips rushing over the armor, and find a dent right between my shoulder blades. My heart hammers against the plating on my chest as if it realizes just how close it came to being destroyed. I try to look over Bao and see how much damage he took, but in the darkness all I can pick out is the slow curve of his heavily-armored back.

One more run. One more run and it's all over.

I twist the Otachi skyward again, and Bao reorients himself with a roll that sends my stomach swooping and my head spinning. This is it.

I find the hull of the last boat, find the glow of the engines that power it, and point my beams. Bao surges up.

As we rush toward the surface, the fire reignites, the bullets blazing around us, the lasers doing their best to steal my sight, but I hold true with everything in me. I can't lower the Otachi, can't change course. This is the final blow. This is what's going to save her, save all of them.

When he hits the boat, I don't hold him back. Bao's claws rake the hull far past the engine mounts as he rolls onto his back, bringing his massive rear legs up to kick the ship. His beak closes around a twisted piece of metal, and I brace myself as he rips it clean from the ship. I squeeze my eyes closed, lunging forward until I'm pressed flat against his skull and praying that his bulk shields me from the bullets strafing the water.

He keeps going.

It's pure, relentless savagery, the sort I learned aboard the *Minnow*, the sort that's so innate to Bao that it's a crime not to release it. And just like that, the third boat is dead in the water.

I pull the Otachi triggers to force my beast to fall back, and there's a certain amount of reluctance to it. I want to see how good I did. I want to see how far he'll go.

And it brings me around.

It brings me all the way around, and as I sink into the deep, dark waters, leaving the chaos above and descending into the black, I realize that there's no way to explain what I've just done to the people rescuing me. They didn't see a lost girl, a prisoner, a victim. No, they saw me for what I am.

And what I am doesn't belong where I came from. What I am doesn't even deserve to go back there.

A chill sinks into me, or maybe it's just the waters. All I can see is the beam of light dropping endlessly below and the faint outline of Bao's head that the glow catches. The pressure sits uncomfortably on my shoulders.

I could still make an attempt to communicate with the ships I've just disabled, to win them over. To go home.

But that feels like denial. The industry I fought so desperately to save all these months is rotten from the inside, and there's no way I can go back there knowing what I know. I could bring the truth about Fabian Murphy to shore, but all they'd see is the girl who spent three months on a pirate boat, raising a pirate-born monster. The girl who wrecked the quadcopters. The girl who trashed the pursuit boats and shredded their companions. They wouldn't take my word for it.

But out here, maybe I can find a way to show them. I click off the Otachi, and Bao drifts to a halt.

There's something out on the NeoPacific that I'm meant for, that everything in these past months have been aligning me to reach out and take. I glance up at the faint lights and the shadows of the hulls overhead.

They aren't for me.

But out on the horizon somewhere, there's freedom to roam the seas, to be the beast that I've found inside me, to stand up against the imbalance and find a way to make the oceans right again. Somewhere out there, the *Minnow* is finally free of pursuit.

I flash the Otachi on and let Bao's homing signal do the rest.

34

We come up underneath them, paralleling their flight as the ship skims over the waves. Bao's speed has sagged with the hits that he took during the fight, but the presence of his companion vessel invigorates him enough to keep the relentless pace they set. I raise a hand to my earpiece and pray as I speak into the respirator. "Varma, are you there?"

Static. Nothing.

But then a crack snaps through the comm, and a clear peal of laughter follows. "Cas? How the hell are you still in range?"

"Don't look down."

"You can't be that stupid."

"I'm that stupid and more. Pursuit's disabled. That enough to give me an audience with the captain?"

"I'll check." His voice pulls back to a distance as he hollers,

"Hey, captain? Got a bogey underneath us who seems to want a word with you. Says there aren't any more boats on our tail."

There's a thunder of footsteps, and then Santa Elena's harsh, musical voice is right in my ear. "Cassandra, I seem to recall instructing you to surrender to the pursuit ships. Kind of defeats the purpose if you're back here with us."

"I wanted to run an alternate arrangement by you. Can I get a promise that if we surface, you won't riddle us with holes? I had a little trouble from the SRCese on that point, so I'd like a guarantee."

"I'm a pirate queen. I don't make promises."

"Fair enough. We're coming up."

If I act casual, maybe I'll fool myself into being calm about this. So far it isn't working.

When we break the surface, the crew's already mostly assembled on the main deck. Phobos and Diemos are pointed straight at us, and a pair of spotlights snaps on. The acrid smell of smoke washes over me, and I inhale sharply as I get a good look at the damage Bao took in the fight.

His right eye is gone, a charred mass of flesh left in its place. I was so caught up in getting to the boat engines that I completely neglected his protection. I used him as a shield, and this is the price he had to pay. His hide is marked with bullet pocks, and a small chunk of his shell has been blown off where another rocket struck him. My stomach churns at the familiar scent of burnt Reckoner flesh, and for a moment I taste bile. I spit my respirator out and mouth, "I'm sorry."

My focus shifts to the figures on the *Minnow*'s deck. Santa Elena hops off the ladder from the navigation tower, and I spot Swift tailing reluctantly behind her, almost as if she wants to hide behind the captain's shoulders. But she's alive and well and relatively unshaken, and it makes my heart turn backflips at the thought of what I'm about to try.

Santa Elena lifts a radio to her lips, and a second later, her voice snaps into my ear. "Your orders were to dismantle the pursuit and then surrender. The *purpose* of those orders was to get the damn SRC off our tail. You do realize that by coming back here, you ensured that all of that hard work was for nothing, right? I'm just so curious about what possessed you to come chasing after us. It sure as hell isn't Swift, here. You can't possibly be in *that* deep."

I set my jaw and lift my goggles up onto my head. "I upheld my end. Mostly. But in the interest of self-preservation, I didn't turn myself in."

"Because?"

"Because there's no place for me with them anymore," I growl through my teeth. The truth in my mouth tastes like salt and blood, and I hate it. I hate its necessity. "If you want to go back and see exactly what I did to those boats, be my guest."

"I'll take your word for it. But stop dancing around the topic, Cassandra. You came back here for something, didn't you?" The captain folds her arms, daring me to speak.

My eyes fix on Swift, and I can tell instantly that she wants me to do anything but what I'm about to. She's got her hands shoved deep in her pockets, her eyes downcast, and I can't help but think back to what she said that night beneath the stars about choices and snares.

But no matter the snares, it's worth it to have a place that'll let you call it home, and so I lift my chin and say as loudly and clearly as I can, "I want in."

I don't have to see the smirk curling over Santa Elena's lips. I can all but hear it across the fifty yards that separate us. Behind her, Swift deflates.

Before tonight, my safety on the *Minnow* was tied to Bao. My bout in the Slew made it clear enough that I can't defend myself on my own. But if I'm going to make it in this big blue world, I'll have to learn. And if I'm going to learn, I need the best teacher the seas can give me.

"You have an empty trainee slot," I say, fighting to keep my voice even as I think of what happened to Code. "I've gotten used to sleeping in that bunk, and I want everything else that comes with it. Sign me on as Code's replacement."

"Name your terms."

This is the tricky bit. I'm still delirious from that blow to the head, and exhaustion is weighing heavy on my shoulders. I can't flub this negotiation, or it'll all be for naught. With fumbling fingers, I pluck the Otachi from my left wrist. "The people on those boats know exactly who and what came after them. They don't want me back—they want Bao taken out. Me, I'm nothing. I'm just another person from the fringes now. But he's a threat to the NeoPacific's economic ecosystem, an imbalance that needs to be corrected. As long as we have him, they'll be after us." I hold out the device with one hand and unlatch the line-hooks from my belt with the other. "So my first condition is that Bao goes free. I'll set this to call him and then drop it. He'll follow it to the depths until he can't any more, and the *Minnow* takes off. We give him the slip and never go near him again."

"And what's your second condition?" the captain asks.

The smell of Bao's singed flesh is overwhelming as I gather my courage and say, "You never ask me to kill a Reckoner. Give me a place on your ship and I'll do anything you command, except for that."

The captain snorts, throwing her head back as a laugh breaks out of her. "Hate to say it, Cassandra, but if that situation were to arise, I've already got a trainee with a knack for that sort of thing." She claps Swift on the back.

I feel as if my stomach's been tied to a sinking stone. But it takes me a second to fully catch her meaning.

"You—" I stutter. "But *you*—"

"I put the *Nereid*'s beast out of its misery, kid. This clever devil here"—she gives Swift's shoulders a shake—"snuck into your stables and dosed it with enough cull serum to tear it apart from the inside before the bucket left its berth. With man or monster, Swift always knows where to put a killing blow. Why else do you think I keep her worthless ass around?"

Bao shifts underneath me, and I almost lose my footing on his skull. I want Swift to object, to deny it, but she looks about ready to throw herself into the sea, and there's something dark rising in me, urging her to do it. Santa Elena may have been the one to land the final strike on Durga, but because of Swift, Durga's last hours were spent in utter agony.

And of course Santa Elena wouldn't let me onto her ship without making sure I knew that. Not if I'm going to be one of her precious trainees, not when she has a chance to pit us against each other and see who comes out on top. She stands tall, hands on her hips, soaking in this moment, this victory, and I can't help but admire her for it.

"Is there anything else?" she asks.

There used to be. But my conditions about Swift and shipboard politics and guaranteeing Swift's safety fall away until there's only one thing left standing.

Me.

And as the fury within me comes to boil, I know for sure that I'm ready to take on whatever the captain can throw at me.

"That's everything," I declare, and loft the Otachi over my head. "What do you say?"

Santa Elena shrugs. "I say you're untested. I say everything remarkable about you comes from that beast under your feet. But you're the only one with the guts to ask for it," she chuckles, glancing back over her shoulder at the crew. "And there certainly aren't any ships behind us. That tells me that maybe you've got a hint of potential in you. If you don't, it'll be fun to see you fail. Drop the Otachi."

No going back now. I click the device to Bao's homing signal, and it begins to ring in my hands as the lights flare skyward. For a moment, my fingers curl tighter around the device, but I grit my teeth and force them open one by one as I swing my arm out over the side of Bao's head.

The Otachi slips from my grip and plunges into the inky waves.

Bao must be hurting badly—he rolls slowly after it, heaving in a deep breath through his blowholes. I leap to the side, throwing my arms up over my head as I dive into the water and start swimming for the *Minnow*'s hull. The NeoPacific swells beneath me. Bao's massive body slips under the water, and just like that, he's gone.

If he survives his injuries, he'll be a legend. The first free Reckoner, like the monsters of old stories. None of our beasts have ever lived a natural life or died a natural death. Maybe he'll be the first. Until then, he'll roam. He'll do as he pleases and answer to no one. He'll be free.

I find the familiar set of handholds built into the *Minnow*'s side and start the climb up, my legs shaking horribly as I pull them up out of the water. The weight of the armor drags me down, but I push against it, my jaw set, my eyes narrowed. Jeers echo down from above as some of the crew lean out over the railing. I can't fall. Not now.

I haul myself up to the main deck and roll over the railing, doing my best to land on my feet. Everything feels shaky, and my breaths come in ragged gasps as I meet the captain's steely gaze.

"Cassandra," she says, her smile triumphant. "Welcome aboard."

Swift stands behind her, staring at me with eyes begging for forgiveness that I can't give. Here and now—*this* is equal footing, and I won't back down from it.

I haul in a breath and grin, letting every vicious thing inside me loose as I shift my focus back to Santa Elena and say, "Captain. Call me Cas."

The End

Acknowledgments

The process of making a book "happen" takes so many people, but in this case, there's one man who has to be thanked above all others. Thank you so much, Brian Farrey-Latz, for spotting my pitch, for begging the book out of me, for putting this whole thing in motion, for totally upending my senior year of college, and for coming up with that twisted suicide pill thing. Chapter 4 is forever dedicated to you.

Thanks to the whole team at Flux who helped bring this book to life.

To Thao Le, agent extraordinaire, for negotiating contracts, championing me in battle, and loving the way my characters swear.

To the teachers and mentors I've had along the way, especially Austin Bunn, who taught me everything from storytelling to launch party logistics, and Elizabeth Briggs, who kept my head on straight when my publishing career went from zero to sixty in the span of one email.

To my first reader, Marisa Perez-Reyes, who told me without hesitation, and I quote, "Dude, this book is going places."

To my critique partners: Tara Sim, master of crossover AUs and the Stark to my Cap, and Traci Chee, who's a pirate queen in her own right. To the kids on the NW who got me started and the ones who kept me going long after we'd left it behind. To the Sixteeners braving this journey with me and the bloggers who've been cheering us on all the way.

And to Mom and Dad, Sarah, and Ivy, for tolerating me when I moved back home after college with no job and a little book deal. The future is scary and full of monsters. Thanks for making it less so.

About the Author

Emily Skrutskie is six feet tall. She was born in Massachusetts, raised in Virginia, and forged in the mountains above Boulder, Colorado. She holds a BA in Performing and Media Arts from Cornell University, where she studied an outrageous and demanding combination of film, computer science, and game design. *The Abyss Surrounds Us* is her first novel.

She can be found online at @skrutskie on Twitter, or on her website, skrutskie.com.